Karen Woods was born and raised in Manchester, where she still lives. Karen left school without any formal qualifications and obtained her inspiration from attending an adult literacy course. Since then she's written twenty novels as well as adapting some of them for the stage. Karen works in education and is passionate about introducing people of all ages to the power of storytelling.

TRACKS

KAREN WOODS

Harper
North

HarperNorth
111 Piccadilly,
Manchester, M1 2HY

A division of
HarperCollins*Publishers*
1 London Bridge Street
London SE1 9GF

www.harpercollins.co.uk

HarperCollins*Publishers*
1st Floor, Watermarque Building, Ringsend Road
Dublin 4, Ireland

First published by HarperNorth in 2021

1 3 5 7 9 10 8 6 4 2

A catalogue record for this book is
available from the British Library

ISBN: 978-0-00-846169-0

Printed and bound in Great Britain by
CPI Group (UK) Ltd, Croydon

MIX
Paper from
responsible sources
FSC™ C007454

For my brother, Darren Woods (Woody).
You are never far from my thoughts our kid.
Thank you for all the stories you told me.
A legend always Daz xxxxxx

Chapter One

Donny Knight stood in front of the large silver-framed mirror in the bathroom and flexed his muscles. He loved that mirror. He'd picked it up in an antique shop a few months before; he'd always had an eye for a deal.

He was ripped, handsome. Small droplets of clear water dripped down his smooth golden skin, like an ice cube melting on a hot summer's day. His muscles looked like two swans dancing as he twisted his arms right and then left. *What a poser*, he thought. But he didn't stop looking. The corners of his mouth started to rise as he smiled at his reflection. Those gym sessions had paid off – he was hench. All the hours of sweating, pumping iron, running, were worth it. Donny looked mint and he knew it. It hadn't always been like that though. There was no way he would ever let himself become a couch potato again, no way in this world. He'd been down that road before and his lack of motivation on the inside had shown on the outside. He'd hated everything back then and when he pulled himself out of that life, he'd made a promise to himself that there was no going back.

Now looking the part was half the trick. And it started with keeping a close eye on what he stuck in his gob. Clean eating, he called it. Although he knew his mum would have laughed at that: 'It's just fruit and veg, Donny,' she'd have told him. 'Eat your greens and don't pretend it's a new religion.' But it was to Donny. Protein, protein and more protein. Those muscles didn't come from nowhere.

His eyes were sea blue. Come-to-bed eyes he liked to call them. And his hair? That was a masterpiece; every day he'd spend a good ten minutes styling it, making sure it was on point. What with the wax and the setting creams, he spent a bomb on his products. Looking good didn't come cheap.

He heard footsteps heading down the hallway towards him and paused for a second, then carried on admiring himself in the mirror. It'd only be the missus. Donny had started to slip his crisp white shirt over his broad shoulders when she opened the door.

'Oh my God, how much longer are you going to spend in there, Donny? I'm going to be late. Every bleeding morning you hog the bathroom, you're worse than any woman I know.'

Susan stood with one hand placed firmly on her hip and shook her head as she watched him preening. She couldn't see the point – unless he was trying to impress someone? She felt a sudden rush of jealousy. Was he seeing somebody else? Did he have his eye on another woman? After what happened two years back he'd promised her that he'd never go there again, vowed he would never be unfaithful. But the signs were there, right in front of her. If there was no one else surely he'd just have a quick wash like any normal bloke? One thing was for sure, Susan would cut his balls off and make a necklace out of them if he was up to something. Her brothers had wanted to put him in a body bag when they'd got wind of what he was up to before, but she had held them back, begged them to leave him alone. More fool her if he was at it again. She exhaled slowly, let the thought pass. No, he loved her, nobody else.

She checked her watch and sighed. Whatever he was or wasn't up to, one thing he wasn't doing was listening to her. No effort to let her have the bathroom, still staring in the bloody mirror. She'd had enough. She banged her fist on the wooden cabinet.

'Move your arse. Now. I need to get ready. The salon's rammed today and I need to be on time. It's always me who ends up running around like a headless chicken, and that's your fault. Why do you need to doll yourself up every bleeding morning to go to work? You don't see me taking this long do you and I'm in the bloody beauty industry.'

Donny ignored her, fastening the buttons on his shirt and reaching for his aftershave. He wasn't going to rush. Taking his time, he sprayed it on his face and then added a spritz to his chest for the hell of it. It smelt good – he smelt good – fresh and clean, like washing that had been dried outside on a summer's day.

'You should be pleased I like to take care of myself, babe. This here's the body of a Greek god who has risen from the dead, not some fat slob. It takes time and effort. I've had to work hard for it. You'd leave me if I started to pile on the timber. Imagine your kite if I was a big, fat mess,' his eyebrows arched as he continued. 'You're always going on about him next door, that he should take more care of himself. You'd go mad if I looked like him.'

Susan rolled her eyes. 'Yes, I do know how long it bloody takes.' Her voice louder now. 'It takes all the time I should be in here getting ready myself. Every bloody morning. So, do one, pretty boy. And give someone else a chance to take care of themselves.'

Donny chuckled and walked towards his wife, wiggling his hips. He grabbed her round the waist and pulled her close.

As he touched her, the thought of his hands all over another woman came flooding back to Susan, made her stomach churn like a washing machine on a spin cycle.

'We look good though, don't we? You and me.' He held one hand under her chin, turned her face towards the mirror. 'Posh and Becks have nothing on us two. We're the ones who should be on the front of *Hello!* magazine. I might give them a ring and see what they say.'

He poked her in the ribs, made her laugh; the nagging seemed to be over. With a quick peck on the cheek he finally left the bathroom, smirking when he heard her shouting after him, then cringing when the usual refrain pounded his ears like a drill. He mouthed the familiar words in time with her.

'I'll pick the wet towels up then, should I? Sometimes, Donny, I swear you just married me so you had a twenty-four-hour cleaning service on tap.'

He never bothered replying. He knew she was right.

He headed into the front room, black leather brogues in his hand. He felt bad for a minute; Susan fetched and carried for him all day long. But then he shook his head. It was her own fault really, she was the one who let him get away with it.

———————

Susan held her ear to the door to make sure Donny had gone downstairs. She moved quickly, scrambled across the floor to find his dirty boxers. She felt like a police dog searching for drugs. She winced and held them up to the light, then paused and stood thinking for a few seconds before flinging the duds back onto the heap of stuff he'd left on the floor. There was no evidence of another woman on them. Not this time. *Fool me once*, thought Susan…

———————

Donny and Susan's home was top notch, everything neatly in place. It was like a show house. A fifty-inch flatscreen TV dominated the front room; you could see the screen from wherever you sat. Donny loved his gadgets, his surround sound; small speakers here, larger ones over there. He sat down on the white leather corner sofa and started to tie his shoelaces. The couch was still pretty new. You could tell by the smell of the leather – the same smell you get when you've bought a new wallet or handbag, he thought. It smelt like money to him. There was no clutter in this room either. Every wall was painted ice-white and two sparkling silver picture frames hung on either side of the fireplace. In one of them was a woman wearing a red hat, sparkling diamonds on the tall, slender cocktail glass she was holding. The colour made the picture stand out; it drew your eyes right into it. Donny sat back for a moment, thinking of the flames when the fire was lit. If anyone had asked him what his favourite piece was in his home, he always said it was the fire. He was mesmerised by it. There was something pure about it. The flames looked like ribbons of gold silk dancing in the wind, every second that passed, changing in their shape. He would have sat here all day watching the flames if he could. But there were people out there depending on him.

Donny straightened his navy-blue tie with the gold diamonds. Susan had bought it for his birthday and he always smiled when he put it on. She'd told him that every time he wore it, he should imagine it was her arms around him, smothering him with love. She was cute like that, Susan. A hopeless romantic, she loved showing she cared, doing little things to keep the marriage alive. Even now she wrote him love letters, left little gifts under the pillow, booked surprise weekends away. They had it all, what more could they ask for?

This was the same question Susan asked herself every day. They had it all, so why had he felt the need to sleep with another woman? When she'd found out about the affair, two years back now, she'd done everything she could to keep him. Got herself a makeover, haircut, put in the hours at the gym, dug out the sexy underwear, offered him sex whenever he wanted it. He'd sworn blind it was a stupid mistake. Now she wondered if she should have played a different game. There was no way she was ever going to go down that road again, ever. Maybe she should have got her own back? She'd said she'd shag the brains out of the next man who gave her any attention when she first found out what Donny was up to, but it never happened. Her heart had been broken and all she really wanted was her husband back and for things to return to normal as quickly as they could. But it was never going to be that simple; the trust was gone, and now she watched him like a hawk every moment she could. But between her shifts at the salon and him working all hours – as well as hanging out with his mates, playing poker, there was still plenty of time for him to get up to no good. And he was always on his phone. Still, any chance she got, she checked his phone, checked his messages, checked his call log. She was all over everything he did; he was going to have to get up early if he ever thought he was having her over again.

Donny looked at his silver Rolex and rubbed the glass against his trousers. He'd paid a few quid for this watch and wanted to make sure it always looked the way it did the day he got it. He'd told Susan he'd bought it on the cheap; if she'd known what he really paid, she'd have hit the roof. Ask no questions, hear no lies was his motto. But Susan enjoyed the finer things in life too, and if that meant her sometimes looking the other way when he came into some cash, so be it. She knew he liked a flutter, even put a bit of it through the books at work from time to time. But there were some things she was better off not knowing.

He stretched his arms above his head and yawned. He'd never been a good sleeper and last night he'd tossed and turned for hours. He shouted up to her. 'Suse, want a lift or are you driving to work yourself?' His wife appeared at the door clipping in her silver hooped earrings. 'No, I'll drive today. I need to go to the bank, and I've got a few clients booked in this morning. And then I'm going to meet Sadie. I've not seen her for a bit and she's having a hard time again so I said I'd meet her even though we're busy today. It'll help, I reckon, if we can have a bit of a chat.'

Donny picked up his car keys and shook his head. 'Tell me when Sadie isn't having a hard time. Maybe if she kept her legs shut then she wouldn't have all the ball ache she gets. I've said it a hundred times – no man's going to have any respect for a woman who's as easy as she is. She'll sleep with them before they've even bought her a drink. She's had more pricks than a second-hand dartboard.'

Susan snapped back at him, unhappy that he was dissing one of her girls when she never slagged off his mates. And there was plenty she could have said about the riff-raff he'd hung out with over the years. Womanisers, gamblers, pissheads – and the rest. He was bang out of order. She glared at him, nostrils flaring. 'Piss off, Donny. If she was a bloke, you'd be patting her on the back and shaking her hand. Sadie is just looking for love, she's mixed up. She reads the signs wrong, thinks every man she meets is the one she'll end up marrying. It's not her fault if they're just pretending to be into her, is it? Have a bit of sympathy, she's not been herself lately.'

Donny sucked on his gums, trying not to laugh. He knew he should back off but couldn't help himself, he had to carry on adding fuel to the fire. 'Yeah right. Tell her to keep her knickers on and she might find a man who'll stick around longer than the first date.' Donny could see he'd overstepped the mark, she was about to lose it. He edged cautiously towards the door, half expecting a shoe to be chucked at his head. He could sense another lecture coming; time to go. He walked over and pecked her on the cheek, but she pushed him away, still fuming.

Donny changed the subject. 'I'll be home late tonight, I've got a few meetings after school and if you're out with Sadie, then I may as well grab something to eat on the way home because you won't be cooking, will you?'

Susan looked at him, flicked her hair over her shoulders. She'd always had great hair, silky and bouncy like in a shampoo advert. The chestnut colour complemented her skin tone and made her eyes stand out. 'Correct, mouth almighty. It's self-service tonight. Get a ding meal, five minutes in the microwave and there you go. It's not exactly rocket science. Easy-peasy.' She thought about what he'd said about Sadie and changed her tune. 'Or go get something to eat with one of your boys. I'm sure one of them will be up for eating out. It's not like they have anything better to do, is it? Low lives they are, the fucking lot of them, no wonder none of them have ever managed to settle down. Nothing better to do all day than sit in the boozer or pissing money away in a card game.' The claws were out, now she'd started it was hard to stop. These pricks probably knew all about his affair, were patting him on the back for it. Snakes they were, dirty lying scumbags, who didn't have a moral between them.

Donny could see where this was heading and decided to bow out before it went any further. He'd rattled her cage and no good was going to come of it. He was out of there. He avoided her gaze. 'Don't want to be late. Have a good day, babe, see you tonight.' But the urge to wind her up hadn't quite disappeared. 'Oh and tell Sadie I was asking about her, send my love.'

Susan shook her head as she watched him leave, 'You're such a smart arse,' she shouted after him as the corners of her mouth started to rise. How could she be angry with him when he made her laugh the way he did? Bloody men. She walked over to the window and watched him drive away before picking up her mobile. 'Sadie? It's me. I reckon Donny's at it again. You should see how he's acting. Spends hours getting ready in the mornings, why's he making all that effort if it's just for work?' She listened to the voice on the other end of the phone and bit her bottom lip before continuing. 'Something just doesn't sit right with me, it's like a gut feeling. I swear to you that if he's at it again, I'll let our John and Dave beat the living daylights out of him. I won't save him this time, not a fucking earthly. He's hiding something, I know it.'

Susan stood listening to the voice of reason for a few more minutes before ending the call. She walked into the hallway and stared at herself in the mirror, her eyes narrowing. Through gritted teeth she hissed at her reflection. 'I'll catch you, Donny, and when I do, I'll ruin you, honest to God, I'll break you into a thousand pieces if you think you can mess with me.'

Chapter Two

The bass was thumping as Donny arrived at work. He was singing his head off, lost in the moment. The pupil referral school was in Moston, about five miles north-east of Manchester city centre. Down at heel would have been gilding the lily; the area around the school was riven by poverty, dangerous too. The crime rate was through the roof – if it wasn't nailed down, it would go on the missing list. Unemployment levels were high, families living hand-to-mouth to survive, doing anything they could to keep their heads above water. For most people, that meant grafting, helping each other out and going without. But for some folk, there was nowhere left to turn, they'd do anything to survive. And that 'anything' included benefit fraud, shop-lifting, robbery. For other people, desperation meant an opportunity to trade off other people's misery. Turn down one wrong street and you'd reach a place most people avoided at all costs, unless they wanted trouble. Sure, there were some parts that felt like they were on the up – but like any city, there was a fine line between the haves and the have-nots.

Next to the streets of houses where people just wanted a quiet life lay the homes and flats and alleys where people wanted the exact opposite. Here, the air stank of doom and gloom; it was a world a passerby would likely turn a blind eye to, pretend it never existed. A concrete jungle with more than its fair share of addicts off their heads, drunks staggering about or bent over the gutters. There was a new class A craze that had just reached the area too; plenty of spice-heads off their faces, walking about like zombies, not a clue what day it was. They seemed to go from normal to drooling idiots in no time, unable to put a sentence together, talking gibberish. Why would you take something that made you act like that, thought Donny. Still, he had no problems working here though, he was a tough cookie, his background had prepared him for this and worse. He'd been brought up on a council estate and wasn't wet behind the ears; he knew the crack on the streets, understood what was what. Streetwise, he was. Knew more about this world than he would ever let on. He was fairly young for a headmaster, only in his thirties, but he'd packed a lot in. And anyway, Donny still reckoned he had it, though he hated that he was getting older. They say life begins at forty, and he told everyone he would welcome it with open arms, embrace it, but in truth he dreaded it. He had things he wanted to have achieved by forty. He had goals – and he knew you didn't make it by playing everything by the book. Still, he wasn't there yet and he could be as down with the kids as the next man. He loved music, kept up to date with all the up-and-coming artists, knew the scene. He would sit for hours listening to his favourite tracks whenever he got the chance. They chilled him out, made him feel relaxed and helped him drift away to a place where he felt safe, secure.

Stormzy's 'Blinded By Your Grace' was the song the kids in his school started their day with. They loved it too, sang their hearts out to the tune. No old fashioned hymns sung here, no thanking the Lord for the gifts he had given them. This was a school of hard knocks and the methods of teaching nothing like what you'd find in the mainstream. That's probably why it worked. The kids sounded great too when they sang, the words meant something to each and every one of them. And to Donny too. He'd been broken in the past and he'd been fixed just like the lyrics said. Susan had saved him back then and for that he would always be thankful. But he wanted to forget about those days: he was strong now, no room for even the memory of weakness.

Second Chance had been running for over four years, with Donny the headteacher from the start; he'd worked his balls off to get to where he was today. A diamond in the rough he branded himself. But three years at university, endless training courses, and jobs in schools trying to work his way up the ladder had finally paid off. He knew he was great with the students no one else could handle, and always dealt with them fairly. His methods of running the school were not always orthodox and provoked regular mutterings in the education department, but he got the job done and had a real connection with the kids. All the staff did; it was more than a job, more like one big family. At least most of the time. It wasn't just about ticking all the boxes and reaching targets.

For Donny it was about caring for these students – listening to them when nobody else would and giving them a voice of their own and someone they could always count on. Most of the kids at Second Chance had nothing positive in their lives; no family support, no money, no motivation. Lost causes in the eyes of everyone else. Kids that society would rather hide away than admit the education system had failed them. His job was about building them up, making them part of the school family – the 'Chance' family he called it.

The kids who came here were all different, each one of them unique. They'd all had problems somewhere along the line, some more serious than others. If you'd read their care plans you'd have been tempted to get your coat on, never step through the front door again. Arson, violence, knife crime, drug abuse; you name it, these kids had done it. But Donny was the backbone of the school and he was always there when the shit hit the fan.

His parents had been amazed when he told them he was going to university – he'd never shown much interest in school, never even wanted to go most of the time. He'd been a nightmare, even at primary school: a real mard arse, moaning constantly, telling his parents that he didn't fit in and that he hated it. Then the bed-wetting started, though that wasn't his fault; it was down to Trevor Beats. A little bastard he was. All the other parents complained about him too, but nothing ever got done. Everyone just seemed to just turn a blind eye to his reign of terror, let him carry on bullying the other kids day in day out. He'd made Donny's life a misery from the moment he met him. Donny looked back now and realised the system had failed back then. Donny's parents had been to the school many times to complain but the story was always the same. 'It's just kids, being kids, and maybe Donny should toughen up,' the headmaster would say – and that was that. Trevor bullied Donny every single day of his primary school life, punching him, kicking him when nobody was looking, nicking his lunch money. And when they finally hit high school, it got worse; the punches got harder, the bruises got darker and Donny hated school more than ever. Most of all he hated that he'd never stood up for himself. He had even thought about running away, never coming back. The stress was too much. He should have been out with his mates, enjoying his teens, but he spent most of those years on the sofa, comfort eating to forget what went on at school. He was nearly sixteen by the time he finally managed to put a lid on it and that was the turning point in his life.

He'd had enough of being the victim. He just wanted to feel normal again and if Trevor was in his life that was never going to happen. He had to sort it out – one way or another.

That day at Morton High School had started out the same as any other, Trevor doing his rounds, picking on all the vulnerable kids, pushing them, spitting at them, making them feel worthless. He was a total gobshite but thought he was the dog's bollocks. He must have been earning a few quid too, even back then, taking money from every student he bullied.

It was survival of the fittest at that school. Every day was a popularity contest – one Donny felt like he was always losing. But it didn't stop him watching the kids who knew how to play the game. Bethany Greggs was one of the hottest girls in the school and every boy there wanted to have her on their arm, including Trevor. She was fit, everyone said so; long, dark hair to her waist and beautiful deep brown eyes. Donny had admired her from afar for years – he'd fancied her along with the rest of the lads, but he never told anyone that. She was way out of his league and what would she see in him, anyway? He was a nobody – a greasy, spotty teenager who would barely even make eye contact. But on the day that everything changed, one of the main reasons that he finally stood up for himself was Bethany. He was sick of feeling helpless, sick of looking like a failure, sick of people talking about him behind his back. He'd heard the names they called him; coward, yellow-belly, waste of space. He'd had enough.

Trevor and a few of his boys walked into the canteen and stood behind Donny. Just his presence in the room changed the atmosphere. Donny could feel Trevor's breath on the back of his neck, could almost feel him nudging his mate and smirking before he flicked Donny's ears and yanked at the hood of his coat, the usual kind of thing. Bethany was also in the queue and when she saw what was going on she turned to face Donny, bent her head forward and whispered at him.

'Why do you let these idiots treat you like this? Do something about it or you'll always be a victim. Go on, knock his block off and put him on his arse. Whatever. Just do something.'

Her words pierced Donny's heart. All the rage that had been bottled up for as long as he could remember came roaring to the surface, bubbling like a volcano, waiting to explode. Everyone was gathered around, but for the first time ever Donny stood tall and answered Trevor back. At first he trembled, stuttered. Maybe he'd not thought this through – but it was too late now, he'd opened his big mouth. He reminded himself that he'd been going to kickboxing for the last two years – and if he couldn't defend himself now, then when would he ever be able to use what he'd learned? What would have been the point? Trevor stood nose to nose with Donny, his eyes burning into his, unflinching. But Donny held his own.

'Oi, muppet, give us your money,' Trevor repeated, snarling, but still Donny didn't reply. He could feel Trevor's pent-up anger making the hairs on the back of his neck stand on end. He swallowed hard and shot a look at Bethany. She was watching intently, and slowly shook her head at him. He'd let her down, the shame was there for everyone to see. He was a coward just like she'd said. But then the adrenaline kicked in. The large vein at the side of his neck started pumping like a beating heart. Was he really going to do this? You could have heard a pin drop. The colour drained from his face. His mouth was dry, and the words seemed trapped behind his lips. He swallowed hard.

'You're not getting any money from me so leave me alone,' he stuttered. The words came out quieter than he'd intended, but in the silence, everybody was listening. Even the geek squad – who never got involved in anything – were hanging on his every word. Had the quiet Donny, who'd never say boo to a goose, really stood up for himself or what?

Trevor's eyes were wide with surprise. He laughed out loud. 'A challenge, eh? This is going to be fun. Did you really just say I'm not getting anything? Think about it, dickhead, before I do something you'll regret, here, in front of everyone. You'll be begging me to stop. Hand over the money, wanker, or I'll flatten you.'

Everyone's eyes were on Donny; was he mad? They'd all seen what Trevor could do. He was a total headcase. The light was on, but nobody was in. Donny licked his dry, cracked lips. Small beads of sweat started to form on his forehead. He swallowed again as his fists began to curl into two tight balls, his knuckles turning white. He couldn't back down now; it was too late.

Donny watched his opponent carefully as the seconds ticked by. When was the right time to make a move? Should he cast the first blow? In the end it all happened so fast no one was quite sure how Donny did it; his arm flung back and the punch connected with Trevor's nose. Bright red blood sprayed around the room. But he didn't stop there. The years of frustration, sadness, humiliation that this prick had caused him were there for everyone to see. He wasn't going to stop, not now, not ever. Every blow dug deep into Trevor's flesh; every kick made sure he wouldn't get back up in a hurry. Donny was in the zone, could hear nothing but his heart thumping, thumping, like the beat of a drum.

'I'm not a coward, I'm not a pissing coward,' he ranted through gritted teeth. Trevor lay still, his arms shielding his face.

One of the other students stepped in, called out. 'He's had enough, leave him now before you do him in. Donny, I said leave it. You've proved your point, let him go.'

Donny stepped back, almost in a trance, though his legs buckled as he stopped and looked at the eyes staring back at him. There was blood on his hands, his shirt was ripped, but he was alive, still breathing. There was an eerie silence, like someone had turned the volume down, but slowly, slowly, the noise started to get louder and louder. He was back in the moment. Had this really happened? Had he just kicked ten tons of shit out of the school bully? It was Bethany who gripped Donny by the arm of his coat and dragged him away. The teachers were on the prowl and there was no way she wanted him getting his collar felt for this. Trevor got what was coming to him, it was long overdue. Every dog had its day and today it was Donny's day. He was a gladiator, the hero of the hour. David and Goliath rolled into one.

It was clearly not what Bethany had expected. She seemed impressed that an average Joe had stood up for himself and chuckled as she twisted her head back to him. 'Oh my God, you done it. I never knew you had it in you, I'm shocked.'

Donny didn't reply. It felt like his windpipe was closing up, like he was going to pass out. He was still white as a sheet and a large salty ball of sweat ran slowly down the side of his forehead. Bethany led him away from the crowds and took him to an empty classroom near the main hall. She sat him down and reached for a box of tissues from the teacher's desk. Her eyes never left him as she wiped the blood away. When she'd cleaned him up, she passed him a bottle of water out of her school bag. His hands trembled as he took small sips. His breathing was returning to normal and reality was setting in. He dropped his head between his legs trying to get rid of the sickly feeling rooted in the pit of his stomach. Bethany just sat staring at him, with a big soppy grin on her face. She reached over and kissed him on his cheek – seemingly oblivious to the sheen of sweat. She was so confident, knew exactly what she wanted. Donny barely registered what was happening as she slowly moved her warm full lips to his, parted them and went for the full wet, tongue-in-mouth kind of kiss – something teenage-Donny had never experienced before. He'd never had a girlfriend, had only ever seen this kind of kissing on TV. Bethany chuckled, grinned at him as she picked up her red schoolbag and threw it over her shoulder.

'Bye, see you later,' she said as she left the room.

Donny was bewildered, not sure what to do next. He shook his head and sighed, then sat there alone gathering his thoughts.

By the end of the day everybody knew Donny's name – his street cred had gone through the roof. Suddenly everyone wanted to be his mate, to talk to him, hang out with him – including Bethany. But what mattered most to him was the fact he'd finally found his voice, stood up for himself. Nobody would ever make him feel like that again, ever. Trevor Beats' mother picked him up, took him home. He never came back – which suited everyone else just fine. Let a new school deal with his crap.

There was an investigation – of course – but a pretty half-hearted one. The teachers seemed to be as pleased as the kids that Beats was off their books. And besides, no one was saying a word. It was impossible to get to the bottom of what had actually happened, and while they had their suspicions, they let the whole thing drop pretty sharpish.

Overnight Donny seemed to go from zero to hero and Bethany – never backwards in coming forwards – was at the front of the queue when it came to joining the Donny fan club. He carried on seeing her for a while – who wouldn't? – at one point he even thought it might be love, but that faded soon enough. She was hard work – always blowing hot and cold. She kept comparing him to her old boyfriends, nagged him to do things he didn't want to, like drinking and smoking. He ended it a few months later, he'd had enough. Bethany went ballistic when he told her it was over, cried her eyes out telling him she loved him, but she didn't mean it, he was able to see through her power games by then. She just didn't want to be the one being dumped.

It was lucky for Donny that his dad got a new job in Manchester and the whole family had to up sticks and leave Derbyshire behind. That was the last he heard of her or Trevor. He wanted no memories from the days when he was a victim. He was going start afresh, happy to leave his old life behind. Maybe that was why he understood the kids at Second Chance. Everyone deserved to be able to start over.

Second Chance was modern, had most of what you would expect to see in any mainstream school, with a few things you wouldn't usually find too. Security was tighter and the kids needed places for time-outs, places to cool off when tempers frayed. Every student there was hard work in their own way, each carrying their own issues. It meant no two days were ever the same and Donny had to have his eye on the ball every second.

The students were aged between eleven and eighteen, old enough to know better, young enough not to care or to respect their elders. Small wonder they'd been chucked out of their previous schools, with the swearing, fighting, drugs and all the rest.

Donny pulled up at the main gates, muttering under his breath as he spotted an old bloke stood to the side of the entrance. Whenever Alf was here at this time of the morning it meant trouble; he was here to complain. Donny opened the gates as quickly as he could and jumped back into his car to go and park up.

'One minute, Alf, and I'll be with you.' The old man stood tall, a sour expression on his face. You could see he was agitated by the way he was fidgeting about. Donny's mobile started ringing, Susan's name flashing across the screen.

'Hey, babe, gotta be quick because I've got some old geezer waiting to speak to me.' He listened to his wife, confused. 'Babe, I've just pulled up at school, the traffic was bad, bleeding hell, where do you think I've been?' He held the phone away from his ear and shook his head before he interrupted her. 'Babe, I've got to go. I'll speak to you later. Bye.' He ended the call, sat scratching his head. 'Women,' he sighed as he turned off the engine and grabbed the keys from the ignition.

He loved his Merc as much as he loved his Rolex, so had to double check and make sure it was secure before he left it. Given the chance the students would have had it away for a spot of joyriding. They'd done it before with one of the other teacher's cars and they would do it again. They'd waited until she wasn't looking, dipped their hands into her handbag and had the keys out as fast as any professional pickpocket. Four hours the car was missing, the teacher was distraught. And then when the police found it, it had been smashed into a fence; a total write-off. You had to keep everything here under lock and key. Even the windows had silver bars over them making the place look a bit like a small prison.

Donny walked over to Alf, fishing in his bag for a cigarette on the way. If he was going to listen to him moaning, then a ciggy would help. Susan thought he'd given up months ago so he was doing his best to hide it from her, but he was struggling to kick the habit. He was still getting through at least ten fags a day – but what she didn't know wouldn't hurt her. He flicked his lighter, sparked up, sucked hard to release the first hit of nicotine of the day. He exhaled, blowing out a cloud of thick grey smoke.

'Morning Alf, it's a nice fresh one, isn't it? Bit nippy though. You can tell winter's on the way.'

Alf had no interest in small talk, wasted no time in getting to the point. He jabbed his tobacco-stained finger at Donny, almost knocking the fag out of his mouth. 'Those sodding kids have been at it again. Rubbish all over my bloody garden – you should see it. Took me over an hour to pick it up, me with my back and all. I've had enough. Tried having a word with them when they were walking past later on, and you should have heard the way they spoke to me. A right mouthful I got. They need a proper smacked arse they do. In my day kids were seen and not heard, not like these cheeky bastards. If I was a bit younger, I'd do it myself. I'd have had 'em once upon a time, did a bit of boxing in the army.' Alf made a fist and jabbed first left then right to make his point before grimacing and putting the flat of his palm on his lower back. 'Bit rusty though, not as fit as I used to be.'

Donny sighed. 'I'll have a word with them. Did you get their names because I'll send them round as soon as they get in to do some litter-picking?'

Alf's grip on his walking stick tightened. 'They need more than that, a good kick up the backside wouldn't go amiss. Over twenty years I've lived here and since this school opened, I've had nothing but trouble. This needs sorting or I'll have to go to the council. I'll have this place closed down before you know what's hit you. We're decent folk round here and there's enough going on without your lot adding to it.'

Donny patted Alf's shoulder. 'I'll have a word, mate. Just leave it with me. There's a few new kids just started and they like to take the piss. Don't be doing anything hasty. I'll sort it.'

Alf shook his head. He liked Donny; they had great banter discussing the horse-racing and football. Got on well when they ran into one another, usually a bit later, when Tony the postman was around too. The three of them would share tips, pick out a Yankee in the hope that they would win their fortunes.

Donny knew it was in his interests to keep on the right side of them both; knew everyone round here, they did, could cause big problems for the school if they had a mind to. He tried to change the subject. 'You having a flutter today, Alf? I've not had chance to look at the form, but I'll do it as soon as things are a bit quieter. And we should check with Tony – he might have a few tips from his mate down the stables. Top lad.' It was working – Alf seemed to be calming down, his cheeks less red.

'On the flat anything can win. I've been having no luck though, been betting on donkeys lately; not won a carrot.'

'No worries, let's put our heads together later and see if we can win a placepot or something. And, don't you worry about this lot in here, I'll make sure you don't have any more problems from them.'

And there it was, Alf was back on track. No doubt he'd be back again in future, but for now he was happy. Donny turned and crunched along the gravel path heading back into the school as Alf shouted after him, 'Oh yes, and you can make sure they keep the noise down too. Every morning I have to listen to them shouting and screaming – tell them to put a sock in it.'

'Will do, Alf, see you later, mate.' Donny's mind was on other things now. He was first in as usual; the rest of the staff wouldn't be far behind but he liked to check things over, make sure everything was just so before the kids started to arrive. His phone started ringing again, but this time he ignored it.

Donny sat in front of his computer nursing a hot cup of coffee. He'd never been big on breakfast. A banana was enough. He peeled away the bruised yellow skin and took a big bite, concentrating as he started to read through his emails. The door opened and Tina Davies, the deputy head, walked into the office and flung her coat onto the back of her chair. She patted her hair down. 'Bloody freezing out there, isn't it?'

Donny rubbed at his body with his hands. 'Tell me about it. I found a polar bear in my car this morning it was that cold.' He grinned.

Tina smiled back; he was just what she needed every morning to take her mind off things. She had a lot going on, had had to take time off. To say she'd been depressed would be an understatement; she'd been to hell and back if she was being honest. And you could see, just by looking at her. She had dark circles under her eyes and her skin was blotchy and pale. Tina pulled the blinds back, peered out of the window. 'Oh my God, the traffic was horrible this morning. I left early to try and avoid the worst of it, but it didn't make any difference. I might get a bike and see if that helps. Oh, by the way, I'm sure I saw your Susan parked up near here on my way in, is she coming in today?'

Donny shook his head and looked confused. 'No, Sue's in work. Must have been somebody who looked like her.'

Tina sighed, 'Yeah, you're probably right, I should get my eyes checked. Another thing to add to the list.'

Donny carried on looking at his screen, while he listened to her going on. 'Kettle's just boiled, go and grab a coffee and warm yourself up,' he stretched, arms high above his head, 'unless you want me to warm you up.'

Tina rolled her eyes and groaned. 'I'm fed up, not hard up, Donny, keep your hands to yourself. I'll get a drink in a bit. I just need to sit down for five minutes before the kids start coming in. Look at the state of me, I've hardly slept a wink all night.'

Donny shot her a glance. She did look knackered. Things were obviously still bad. He cared about his staff and Tina

26

had really been through the mill lately. She was a shadow of her former self. All she'd ever wanted was a baby and now she'd had to have a hysterectomy and it was never going to happen – her world had collapsed around her.

It was no wonder she'd hit the bottle. Donny had tried talking to her about it just before she went on sick leave and he hoped, now that she was back in work, that it would have settled down a bit. But he knew things still weren't great at home. She did everything for her two stepchildren but they gave nothing back by the sound of things. Typical stroppy teenagers, untidy, moody and ungrateful. Tina had tried her best, by all accounts, but it never really made a difference. She definitely had her work cut out there.

Most of the teaching staff were in now and Donny walked round the building doing the rest of his morning checks. He glanced at his watch: as well as a tutor coming in from the local college, there was a new teacher starting today and he wanted to be around to welcome her personally.

He popped his head into the kitchen; he could smell the school cook before he could see her. You couldn't really describe the combination of grease, tobacco and vinegar, but it wasn't a good one. Donny tried breathing through his mouth but that just made him cough.

'Morning, Rita. What's on the menu today?'

Rita was more interested in the scratchcard in her hand as the small silver coin uncovered the last couple of numbers. 'Fuck's sake,' she muttered under her breath, ignoring Donny and dipping her head inside the fridge. Donny repeated his question, louder this time. 'What's on the menu today?' She looked up.

'Jacket potatoes, pasta bake and toasties.'

'Lovely. And how are we, Rita, this morning? Are we in a good mood? I can see you've not won your fortune, but you're rich in love, eh?'

She shrugged, scraped her hair back from her face. 'I'm always in a good mood, me. It's these kids that do my head in. Lazy they are, don't do a tap. I only asked Frankie to pass me a few plates through yesterday and you should have heard the way he went off on one. God knows how they live at home because if it's anything like they are here they must live in shit-tips.'

Donny leant back against the wall, his eyebrows arched. 'It's hard enough getting them in school each day, never mind getting them to clean up after themselves, so we have to count ourselves lucky. Don't we?'

'You're a right soft arse, Donny. They are lucky they don't get a clip round the ear. If it was one of mine they wouldn't know what'd hit them. Dirty bleeders.' Rita had worked here for two years and the job suited her, despite what she said. She liked her food, did Rita. Almost every time Donny saw her she was ramming something into her gob. She said it was quality control, but Donny had nicknamed her Mrs Kipling, though he made sure she never knew it. Rita riled was not something he wanted to have to face. She was a battleaxe, rough as a bear's arse someone had once said, he'd forgotten who. And she was gobby, always spoke her mind – maybe that was why she fit in here. But she was not someone to mess with. Wallflowers didn't last long at Second Chance.

Donny looked out of the window. 'You seen Frankie yet, Rita?'

'No, but he usually gets in early, he should be here soon. Going to have a word with him about not helping me?'

Donny started to walk away. 'Yeah, yeah, if you see him can you tell him to bob upstairs and I'll have a quick word with him.' He turned back to face her. 'Oh and, Rita, before I forget, we have two new starters today, a staff member and a new kid, Nancy Parker. Can you keep an eye on her at lunchtime and make sure she's eating something? You know what the new kids are like, they just stand on their own, don't mix with the others.'

Rita closed the fridge door and plonked a massive piece of cheese on the side. 'It's a wonder any new kids stay here longer than a day with this lot. Nutters they are. I don't know how their parents put up with them.'

'So, that's a yes then?' Donny chuckled.

Rita wiped the sweat from her brow with her sleeve. 'I always look out for the new ones. I just hope this one's not as lazy as the others.' As Donny left the room she carried on getting stuff out of cupboards, banging the doors shut and stomping about. The students would be here soon, and they'd be wanting breakfast; there was no time to stand around. It was one of the things Donny had insisted on; that each child started the day with something proper in their stomachs. So every morning she would prepare toast, cereal – even open a packet of biscuits if they wouldn't eat anything else. Rita enjoyed the peace while it lasted; ten more minutes and the place would be alive with the usual screaming and shouting. Every day brought a new drama – but no one ever joined Second Chance for a quiet life.

Chapter Three

G ed Grey lay in his double bed snoring his head off. His red hair was all over the place; he looked like he'd been dragged through a hedge backwards. He hated being ginger, always told his mother he was going to dye his hair once he was old enough. The bedroom door creaked open and his mother walked in. You could see that in her day, Clare might have been a good-looking woman. But now she was scrawny, underweight, her once raven hair streaked with grey. She stood looking at her son for a moment in the hope that he might be awake, but the noise was a giveaway. No such luck. She'd have to wake him, which never ended well. He was a nightmare in the morning, a total stress-head. No hope of getting a conversation out of him. She took a deep breath, braced herself.

'Ged, time to get up. The minibus will be here in half an hour. You need to be up and ready or you'll miss your lift. Mr Knight has already told you they won't wait and I've not got money for bus fares, so move it.' She hovered over him, hands ragging through her hair, dreading another day of arguing. Ged stirred, dragged the duvet over his head and groaned.

'Nah, I'm not going in today. I don't feel well. Just ring them and tell them not to bother coming for me.'

Here they were again, another day in paradise. Clare stormed across the room and yanked the curtains open; a bright yellow light filled the room. She pushed the window open too, letting in the bitter cold from outside. She'd freeze him out of bed if he thought he was lying in his pit all day long.

'Not a chance, Ged. This is the last chance saloon for you and if you lose your place at this school nobody else will have you. You're sixteen – time to stop mucking about. No wonder you're tired when you're playing on that daft bleeding game all night long. I swear, if you're not out of that bed in five minutes I'll throw that sodding Xbox right out the window. Don't test me, Ged, because I mean it. Right out the window and then I'll stamp on it.' This was a code red, his Xbox was his world. He flung the duvet onto the floor and bolted up from the bed with a face on him. Always angry. But then Clare was a hothead too and when she said she was going to do something, she meant it. She would have smashed it into a thousand pieces without a shadow of doubt, just to prove a point.

He raised his arms, protesting. 'Mam, I hate this school. I don't learn nothing anyway. What's the point, it's shit?'

Clare ignored him, marched across the bedroom picking up dirty clothes from the floor. Typical teenager. The room was a tip, stank of sweaty feet. 'It's your own fault you have to go there. What did you expect when you hit a teacher? Did

31

you think they'd say, "Oh, Ged, it doesn't matter that you assaulted one of our staff, come back tomorrow and we can start again"?'

Ged hated it when his mother used that sarky tone. He made a face and dug his hands down the front of his boxers. 'The man was a dickhead. Anyway, he started it when he pushed me up against the wall, what did you want me to do? He had it coming.'

Clare had had enough. 'What I wanted,' she told him, 'was for you to have a bit of respect and stop causing bloody trouble. How many times do I need to tell you how much stress I'm under? I'm a single parent; if I don't go to work then who's going to pay the bastard bills? Just do me a favour, Ged. Keep your head down and do your schoolwork. I can't afford to be taking time off every week to go and see the teachers about your behaviour. This is your last year in school. Just do your exams and get a decent bloody job. It's not a big ask, is it?'

Ged stretched his arms over his head and sighed. He was all skin and bones. You could see more fat on a chip. If he turned sideways you'd have had to report him missing. He'd heard enough of her whining and raised his voice – always a sign that he was getting ready to kick off.

'I get it. Fuck's sake, just stop going on and leave me to wake up. Like I need to hear your voice going on every bloody morning. Turn it in, will you?'

Clare sighed. 'You can stop swearing too. It does my head in. Where is your respect? You was never brought up to be this way, so fucking turn it in before my foot ends up stuck up your arse.'

Ged didn't flinch, just looked at her defiantly. 'You still here? Just close the fucking door and let me get fucking ready. If you carry on moaning, I'm going to get back in bed, end of. Do one.'

Clare edged out of the room, forcing herself to bite her tongue before she said something she would regret. His abusive language was the least of her troubles. The house shook as she slammed the bedroom door shut behind her. She stood with her back to the wall biting her knuckles, her body shaking from head to toe. Deep breaths, long deep breaths.

Ged could hear his mother huffing and puffing outside his room and figured he'd better do as he was told for once. It was such an effort to get dressed. Maybe he should have gone to sleep earlier, not that he'd ever have admitted it. But he wasn't going to miss out on all the action and the banter with his mates online. His legs wobbled as he put his trousers on and he fell back onto the bed. He started to pick at the bits of fluff from the top of the trousers. Maybe he needed some new ones; his mother had already let the hem down, put some of that Wundaweb stuff on them until she could afford some new ones. To be fair, you could hardly see the lines at the bottom, but he knew they were there – a constant reminder that his family were skint, potless. He flicked the fuzz ball across the room and lay back on the bed staring at the ceiling. There was no way he was rushing about. His mother could take a running jump if she thought he was ever going to be a star pupil; that would never happen, not now, not ever. Education was not his thing, none of that studying and revising for exams crap. Ged stared back up at the damp ceiling, black fungus crawling across it like a disease spreading through a body. His eyes pricked with tears – he had no idea why – he had to lift his head up to control his emotions. He was always filling up like this, it just happened. Maybe it was his hormones. His hand rummaged under the thin lumpy pillow and he pulled out a photograph of a middle-aged man. His touch was gentle, holding the picture like he didn't want to spoil it in any shape or form. He studied it for a few seconds, stared at the image. His eyes closed and his mind was away with the fairies until he heard more noises outside his room. He rammed the snap back under his pillow; this was his treasure, the one thing that meant something to him, well, apart from his Xbox. He looked over to the window where he could see the grey clouds hanging low in the sky. It was like a grey blanket of despair creeping slowly over the top of the houses.

Finally, Ged grabbed his navy-blue parka from the back of the chair. His mother was still in a mood and he knew it, could see her chewing on the inside of her lip to keep the words in. His hair was still stuck up all over the place and he made no attempt to do anything with it. When he was a kid, his mum had always said this was a sure sign that he was in a mood, maybe she was right. He didn't break a smile either. Their eyes met from across the room, like two gunslingers meeting at dawn for a duel. 'I need some money for school. I'm not having none again and looking like a scruff. So, don't bother trying to fob me off saying you're skint.'

Clare rolled her eyes but there was no way was she getting involved in any more beef. Anything for a quiet life. She reached over and grabbed her tattered handbag. She'd had it for years. In its day it was probably an eyecatcher, but not anymore; it was worn and torn, just like her. She opened her purse and fumbled about inside. She didn't have to look to know there was hardly anything in it, but what could she do? She exhaled loudly, looked down at the floor. 'Here, I've got a quid. Don't start moaning because that's all I've got.'

Ged's nostrils flared and he started pacing the room like an anxious father waiting for his baby to be born. 'Nah, sack that. I'm not going to fucking school then. What can I buy with a poxy quid? Nothing? Do you know how embarrassing it is when we all go to the shop and I'm stood there like a tramp who can't buy anything? You can do one. Stick your money up your arse. You can fuck off, I'm not going to school, I'm going back to bed.'

Clare banged her fist on the side of the sofa, dust flying up in the air. She'd had enough. Every morning it was the same script, drama, drama. She spoke through gritted teeth. 'I can't make bleeding money out of thin air, Ged. If I had it, you could have it. There's no magic money tree growing in the back garden. It's all I've got, you ungrateful brat. But, one thing is for sure, you are going in to school today, so shut up and just take the money or leave it.'

He stood thinking for a few seconds. It wasn't his mother's fault they were skint – he knew that deep down – but still, he hated being part of a family where they lived from hand to mouth every day. Why did they have to be poor? Clare worked two jobs and some nights she could barely stay awake. She was a grafter, always did her best to put bread on the table, but he was still sick of the whole thing. Ged stormed over to his mother with thunderous expression. 'Just give me the money. I'll have to have it then, won't I?'

He snatched the coin from his mother's hand and stomped out, her calling behind him, 'No kiss then, no goodbye? Yeah it's all my fault again. Tell me something that I don't already know, Ged. Make me feel like shit, why don't you?' There was no reply. Clare flinched as the front door slammed shut. She rolled her eyes while muttering under her breath. A single fat salty tear ran down her cheek and landed on her upper lip and suddenly she was sobbing her heart out. She worked so hard, tried her best, so why was her life so bloody difficult all the time? She blamed Ged's dad, him and his dodgy dealings. All she'd ever wanted was a normal life, but he just wanted more and more, could never be happy with what they had. Tosser. Kevin Grey had been banged up for an endless list of crimes and she'd been left to pick up the pieces. He was due out in a few months' time, had written her endless letters about how he was going to make it up to her, but they all went straight in the bin. It was all bullshit, his words meant nothing to her anymore, they were just lies, lies and more lies.

Chapter Four

G ed was one of the first students to be picked up by the school minibus. He slumped in his seat, his earphones and his scowl a warning to anyone who might think of trying to make conversation. He never talked about the kind of music he listened to either. UB40 was his dad's favourite band and he listened to the same tracks day in, day out to keep the memories of his father alive. He wanted to remember – even if his mother didn't. Kevin was his dad and that wasn't going to change, not ever. His mum was always slagging him off, never had a good word to say about him. She'd have everyone believe he was a no-good bastard, that he'd never change his ways, but Ged just wished he was still around. Maybe that's why he was always getting grief about his behaviour. If his dad was there, he would have understood, shown him a bit of support when he needed it. And there was only so much a lad could talk to his mother about, wasn't there? It wasn't just sex, girls, *lad's* stuff. She didn't even know the basics about playing FIFA, football, any of that – they had nothing in common. And anyway, she was always knackered or talking about work. Ged pulled his hood down over his face. Today more than ever he wanted to be invisible, to be left alone, and the hood helped. He was already in a foul mood and if any of the idiots wound him up today, he was going to lose it. It didn't take much, he was pretty much always on a short fuse.

The driver ignored all the signs, shouted behind him as he headed towards the next stop. 'Morning Ged, ready for a good day of learning?'

Ged eyeballed him from under the hood via the rearview mirror and didn't reply. Since when had he ever had a good day of learning? Was he having a laugh or what? He stayed slumped in his seat and ignored the kids who got on at the next couple of pick-ups.

But then the minibus pulled up outside a house in Harpurhey – another place that was always on the news for all the wrong reasons. Ged lived in Blackley, about a twenty-minute walk away, and didn't really know the area, though he'd heard endless stories about the goings-on here. This was not a place he wanted to be on his own. He stretched his arms, cracked his knuckles as he spotted Chelsea walking down the garden path towards the bus. She had bright-pink hair with blue strands sprinkled through it. She'd clearly been at it with the self-tanning lotion as well; she looked orange, like a satsuma. And God only knew what she'd done to her eyebrows, which now looked like two brown boomerangs. As she got closer, Ged tried to spread across the double seat. She'd be trying to talk to him from the moment she got on the bus to the moment they reached school; she never bloody shut up. A natural-born gobshite she was. The side door slid open and Chelsea jumped inside. Her Lycra skirt looked more like a belt; bend over and there'd be nothing left to the imagination.

'Morning, Gary,' she said in a loud voice as she slammed the door shut behind her.

'Morning, Chelsea, how are you today?'

Despite himself, Ged smiled. Chelsea was no class act – every other word out of her mouth was fuck, bastard, cunt; it was like she had Tourette's. Once she put her mouth into gear she never stopped talking. A right gasbag. Ged waited as Chelsea exhaled and there it was, she was back on track.

'I'm feeling like shit, Gary. That daft bastard of a mother of mine never washed my polo shirt for school, look at it, it's full of marks. And she has the fucking cheek to tell me to put it in the washer myself. Do I look like the kind of girl who knows how to work a washing machine? Fuck me, Gary, I can barely read and write, never mind anything else.'

Gary's eyes opened wide, he'd never quite got used to Chelsea's expletives. He tried to calm her down; if she was in this frame of mind before the school day had even started, she'd be a nightmare when she got there.

'Whoa, language, lady. Don't be talking like that. You're a young lady, don't let yourself down by swearing.'

She moved down the bus and sat opposite Ged as she replied. 'Gary, I think we both know that I'm no lady? Come on, even I know that. So don't try and change me. I am who I am.' There was just something about Chelsea that made you smile. She reached over and nudged Ged. 'That's right, isn't it, you ginger ferret?'

Ged shook his head. She had a way with words for sure. No airs and graces, she just said it how it was.

The engine started again, and Chelsea was eager as ever to chat. 'Was you out last night, Ged? It kicked off outside our house, you should have seen the dibble there too, they were team-handed when they come to arrest him next door. Four cars come for him with loads of officers inside them. I saw the whole thing, it was mint. Stiggy put up a good fight too. He took one down before they got the cuffs on him. Mary, his girlfriend, was up in arms too, you should have seen her; mental she was.'

Ged marvelled at how Chelsea never seemed to stop for breath; the words just rolled off her tongue, kept on coming. She was the opposite of him – he'd never been a big talker, found it hard to hold down a conversation. Maybe because under the tough exterior he was shy, hated making any eye contact with people. But it didn't matter with Chelsea, she never stopped. You just needed to nod your head and listen as she went on and on. Drama, every day, always something that had gone on. Maybe she was making it up? Surely nobody could have that much going on at home? Ged had nothing going on at his – his highlight was two cats fighting outside in the early hours of the morning. The journey continued as Chelsea carried on sharing the ins and outs of the latest drama. When they stopped at a red light, Gary did his best to quieten the kids down.

'Guys, guys, just give me a minute. We're picking up a new girl up in a minute and then the rest of the mob. So be nice to her. You all know what it's like to be the new kid in school so try your best to make her feel welcome.'

Chelsea flicked her hair over her shoulder, annoyed at the interruption to her monologue. 'She'd better not be a cocky bitch, one of those new girls full of attitude,' she hissed.

Gary raised his eyebrows. 'You mean just like you were?' He ignored her, all of them then, and carried on driving. He only had to put up with this lot for a couple of hours each day and that was more than enough. Every day a kid with drama, a parent screaming at her child to get on the bus to school, always something. Gary could tell a few stories about this lot. He had his work cut out for sure.

The bus went quiet when the new kid, Nancy, got on. Shouts and laughter turning to whispers, eyes all over her. The girl's mother was stood watching on the pavement, a worried look on her face. She stepped closer to the window. 'I'll see you later, princess, have a great day at school. I love you.'

Oh my God, what the hell was she thinking? Nancy turned towards her mother and hissed at her, cheeks beetroot, gritted teeth. 'Will you get back in the house. Stop showing me up, you weirdo.'

Chelsea burst out laughing and she couldn't help herself. 'Come on new girl, or shall we call you princess?'

Nancy rammed two fingers in the air towards her mother. That seemed to be her induction over with as far as the kids were concerned. Cheeky? Tick. Attitude? Tick. Didn't care what she said? Tick. She'd have no problems fitting in. There was still the seat left next to him and Ged felt his cheeks burning as Nancy walked down the bus towards him. He pressed his earphones deeper in his ears and pushed his head against the window, the cold glass squashed against his cheek. Nancy was nothing much to look at though she did have piercing sea-blue eyes. She carried a fair few extra pounds, but who cared if she liked her food. Chelsea was the first to introduce herself; mouth almighty was never shy at coming forward.

'Yo, I'm Chelsea. You can chill with me if you want. This lot will corrupt you given half the chance. Whereas me,' she smirked and licked her front teeth, 'I'm a pillar of the community and I will mentor you to a brighter future.'

Ripples of laughter broke out. Liam Beechill piped up. 'Don't even listen to her, she's had more nob ends than weekends. I'd stay well away from her if I was you, if you don't want to get a name for yourself.'

Chelsea was gobsmacked but, being Chelsea, was back on the ball and ready to defend her honour sharpish. 'Oi, nipper knob. Just because I haven't slept with you, stop getting jealous. If you fancy me and want a date, then make an orderly line with the others and I will think about it.' The girls were all behind Chelsea. Liam was a joker and loved the banter. But he had nothing to come back with, she'd well and truly shot him down. All the kids were picked up now and Gary could start to relax. The teachers always said getting the kids into the building was half the battle.

Gary drove through the main gates to where Donny was standing in the car park waiting for the bus to arrive. He checked his watch, yep, bang on time. School started at ten and finished at two – not a full day's learning, but enough to keep these kids in the education system. As the students jumped out, the noise was deafening; no wonder the residents complained.

'Good morning, campers.' Donny had a big smile spread across his face and was almost as loud as the kids. 'Where's the smiley faces? You should be happy to see my beautiful face at this time of the morning. Liam, with a bit of effort, when you're older you might even look this good if you're lucky.' And there it was, the start of the school day. Nancy was the last person to emerge from the bus and Donny walked to her side and spoke in a soft voice. 'So, you've met some of the kids then? I told you it would be fine. They're an alright bunch when you get to know them.'

Nancy plodded to the entrance, in no rush to get inside. You could see she was a bit apprehensive at the thought of staying here all day; Donny knew her file, she was well-known for running away. Last time it'd been five days before the police finally found her in Liverpool. Reading up on her record, no one seemed to have got to the bottom of why she was always on her toes She'd never say, not at first, Donny knew that much. But given enough time, the kids often opened up to him. They'd come to realise he was different to all the other case workers and social services teams they'd usually met by the time children got to Second Chance.

'Coats off, phones need to be put away or hand them in. Anyone found on their phones during lesson time will have them removed and they won't get them back until the end of the day. We all know the rules.' Donny shouted at the top of his voice to make himself heard.

Chelsea was stood with a few other girls, having none of it. 'Like he's going to take my phone from me. I'd like to see him try it. I'll smash his face in,' she whispered.

Everyone was gathered in the main hall and around twenty students sat facing Donny and his staff. Every day started this way and any problems were brought to the table at this time. But before the morning could start properly, the hall doors banged and everyone's eyes turned.

Frankie Owen came in late, swaggered over and sat on a chair at the end of the row. Frankie was the top boy at Second Chance, and he knew it. He oozed confidence. He had the looks, the clothes; everything about him was smooth. He met the eyes of the headteacher and nodded his head slightly. Frankie had been coming here since he was thirteen years old. He lived in Collyhurst with his mother Mary and her husband, Gary. His stepdad was a control freak and he hated the sight of him. Donny had been to see Frankie's stepfather once and whatever they'd discussed seemed to stop the hostilities, but even though things at home had cooled down a bit over the years, Frankie still never gave Gary the time of the day. He wasn't his dad and he owed him nothing.

Frankie had been a lost cause when he first set foot through the doors of the school – always angry, always disrespectful, a total pain in the arse. He'd throw chairs at teachers, spit at them, was forever hurling abuse. Donny was at his wits' end with the kid, but somewhere along the line he sorted him out. Nobody knew quite what went on, but Frankie was a changed lad – still a handful, but nowhere near as bad as he used to be.

As Stormzy's lyrics faded away, Donny addressed his students, coughing to clear his throat before he spoke. 'Right, everybody, can I have your attention please...' Hardly

44

anyone took any notice. The time for niceties was over. 'Just shut up talking and listen!' he roared in a tone which brooked no argument. The students zipped their mouths and looked straight towards him. 'Alf is on the warpath again. He's complained about some kids from this school throwing crap in his garden. How many times do I have to tell you lot about respecting the residents round here? How would you like it if somebody was throwing rubbish in your garden?'

Liam cupped his hands around his mouth and shouted out. 'That wouldn't happen, because I would snap their jaw.'

Donny raised his eyebrows. 'Liam, are you on steroids or something because the last time I looked at you, you were only five foot nothing, so stop gassing and listen to what I have to say.' All the kids started laughing. Donny had a great sense of humour and he got the laughs he was searching for.

'Knob head,' Liam hissed back at him.

Donny continued. 'So, if anyone is found dumping rubbish then they'll have me to answer to. Also, let me tell you now, smoking weed at breaktime will not be tolerated in this school. If needs be, I will get every single one of you drug tested to find out who the blazers are. If the test proves positive, then I will ring the police and your parents. The staff here were not born yesterday, and they know when someone is stoned, so, you have been warned. Now, moving forward, we have some great new lessons for you lucky lot. You can start MMA or gym classes this week or if that's not your scene you've got dance or our brand-new health and beauty sessions. The tutor, Alison, has come in from Parkside College and she can help you achieve a level two qualification. Is Alison here, Mrs Davies?'

Tina put her head round the door into the other room and asked the tutor to come and meet the students. They should have dressed her in body armour and given her a baseball bat. Did she even know what she was letting herself in for? Alison had short brown hair with copper highlights and sharp style. Black shoes with five silver buckles on each side of them, and a chain hung from the pocket of her black jeans. Her makeup was dark too, deep shades of eye shadow smudged on her lower eyelids. The lads looked at each other and you could hear them whispering – probably something sexual because they were sniggering behind their hands when they looked over at her.

'Sir, what's MMA?'

'Mixed martial arts, Chelsea. It might be a bit rough for the girls, so maybe stick with the dancing for now.' He'd picked the wrong person to try that on – Chelsea loved a debate.

'That's sexist, sir. We should have the same rights as these halfwits in here. What do you say girls, do you think we should be able to go to MMA too?'

A few of her supporters joined in. 'Yeah, you're always going on about equal rights, sir, and how everyone should be treated the same, so sort it out!' shouted Jennifer Williams.

Frankie leant back, his chair balanced on its two back legs. He was the spokesman for the male students. He nudged Liam, tipped him the nod. 'If you girls want touching up then just say the word. You don't have to come to MMA just to get a roll with me.' The lads roared laughing. Liam carried on. 'You'd love being touched up, wouldn't you, Chelsea? They'd have to tie a plank to my arse, so I didn't fall in your fanny if we were fighting.' A low blow. Anywhere else he'd have been escorted out of the room and put in exclusion for that last comment. But this was Second Chance, and it was nothing new.

Donny had to keep a straight face, restore order. 'Liam, that's your first warning. Turn it in. And, if the girls want to try MMA, so be it. Come and see me after lessons this morning and I'll sort it out. Anyway, learning time. Listen out for your name and make your way to your lesson as quickly as possible. Remember, no eating in the classroom as well as no phones. Oh, just before you go. We have a new girl called Nancy that I want everyone to meet.'

Motormouth was at it again. 'Sir, we've already met her on the minibus. I've told her she can chill with me if she wants so wind your neck in and let her get to class.' Chelsea stood up, a cocky look on her face. Nothing changed. God help whoever was teaching her this morning, they would have their work cut out for them for sure.

The teachers led the students to their various lessons. Even getting them to the classroom was a job in itself. Maths teacher Robert Sinclair had been teaching here for over a year and knew he had to be firm with his class. When he first started working here, he didn't think he'd last the term. The kids were either bored or abusive – even the capable ones were hard to teach. Sometimes he yearned for the days when corporal punishment was acceptable.

Sinclair waited until the students sat down; there were only four, but that was more than enough. He looked at them. Frankie was as cool as a cucumber; he knew how to keep his nose clean. It wasn't worth the hassle anymore. Parents being dragged to school for meeting after meeting about your behaviour just wasn't cool. Who else had bothered to turn up today? He scanned the class. Ged never really spoke to any of his classmates and most of the time he just put his head on the desk and fell asleep. Paul Tiebury was a bully, a loud-mouth from the Harpurhey estate who intimidated a lot of the lads and tried to make them feel stupid. Paul kept flick-ing Ged's ear from behind, stretching so he could curl his index finger up tightly ready to strike again. You could hear the flick land like an elastic band snapping. 'Fuck off, you prick,' Ged hissed as he felt the back of his ear start to burn.

'Ged, you carry on using language like that and you'll be out of here.' Sinclair was off on one, already hating his job more than ever. Ged lifted his head, his cheeks on fire, his temper boiling, ready to snap. Frankie sat back and started to watch events unfold. This kid rarely said a word and here he was defending himself for a change. A right turn up for the books.

Paul nudged his sidekick, Wayne Johnson. 'Who's this muppet telling to fuck off? I'll twist him up in a minute. I'll batter him and his dad both together.' Ged put his head back down and didn't reply. Paul bent his finger back and waited for a few more seconds to pass, Wayne egging him on.

Sinclair had his back to the class, writing something on the whiteboard. Paul positioned his finger near Ged's ear and flicked the skin with all his might. Ged bolted up from his chair, knocking the table over, screaming at the top of his voice. 'Come on then, you prick, let's have it.'

Wayne needed no encouragement to join the fray. He jumped out of his seat as Paul and Frankie stood up too.

Frankie gripped Wayne by the throat, pulled him forward until they were nose to nose. 'Nothing to do with you, let them sort it out themselves. You get involved, that means I do too. What's it going to be?' Wayne held his hands up and backed off. Frankie continued to eyeball him every now and then to make sure he didn't move a muscle, just stayed stood against the wall. Ged was losing the plot, throwing books about, kicking chairs over. That was enough.

'Out!' Sinclair screamed at the top of his voice. 'All of you, out!' Within seconds the code red team were on the scene.

Tommy Jones was thick-set and used to stuff like this and worse. Used to working as a bouncer on the doors in Manchester's city centre nightclubs, this was child's play to him. If the kid wanted a fight, he was out of luck; he'd have him restrained in seconds. Tommy edged into the room, which looked more like a war zone than a maths lesson. He stood facing Ged. 'Calm it down, lad, deep breaths. Just take your time, deep breaths. Don't be doing anything daft.'

Ged was breathing like a racehorse who'd just run the Grand National, sweat pouring down his face, hair wet at the front. 'I told him to leave me alone, but he kept on doing it. I warned him. I told the prick, but he never listened, and he was disrespecting my dad. Nobody disrespects my dad, fucking nobody.'

Donny was here now. He clocked the state of the room, the broken furniture. 'Ged, come on, son, come into my office and get a cold drink. We can talk about this after you've calmed down.' But Ged was still in the zone, his nostrils flaring as his feet bounced about the room. He rammed a single finger towards Donny. 'Don't call me your fucking son. I have my own dad. He might be in the nick, but I still have one. Fuck off and leave me alone.'

Donny looked over at Tommy and shrugged. He knew all the problems the kid was facing, had been through the risk assessment sheets enough times, knew his story. He took a deep breath and walked a little further into the room. 'Tommy, go on, you go and help Mr Sinclair get the others back into the lesson. They can use another room. I'll stay with Ged for a bit and sort him out. He's calm now, aren't you, mate?'

Ged's legs buckled as he walked towards the open window. The icy breeze was just what he needed to help slow his heartbeat down. He closed his eyes and pressed his head on the cold metal bars across the window. Why couldn't he control his temper, why did he just flip out like that, was he ill? Did he need medication?

Donny waited until Ged slumped down onto the floor then sat down next to him. He'd been through this scenario so many times, watched even the biggest lads in the school break down at one time or another. He reached over and patted the top of Ged's knee. 'It's alright to lose it sometimes, pal. It's hard not having your dad about, especially at your age.'

Ged lifted his head up slowly, clearly upset. 'My mam won't even speak about him, it's like he never existed. But, he does. I want to see him. Why's nobody listening to me? It's my choice not hers.'

This was progress, at least he was talking. Some of them never spoke about what was going on in their heads and it took months, even years to get to the bottom of it. 'Have you told your mam how you feel? Maybe, if you sit down with her, stay calm and tell her how hurt you are it might help.'

Ged sniffed and twisted his knuckle into the corner of his eye to try and get rid of the tears. He sucked on the side of his cheek, looking anywhere except at Donny. 'It's pointless. She won't talk to me about him. She said he's a dirty no-good bastard and we are better off without him. What can I say to that?'

Donny felt for him. 'I can have a word with her if you want? Us grown-ups are stubborn sometimes and we can be dickheads. When the advice comes from somebody else who's not involved, we seem to listen better.'

Ged shook his head. 'Nah, don't be giving my mam any more stress. She'll go sick if she knows I've been discussing our private stuff. Keep it to yourself. I'm OK now. It just gets to me sometimes and that wanker flicking at my ear when I'm tired doesn't help.'

'Did you not sleep properly, Ged?'

'I did, but I was playing on the Xbox til late. It's all I have to do when I get home from school. I just lose track of time sometimes.'

Donny scratched the end of his chin and carried on talking. 'Do you have any mates that you hang out with?'

Ged sat thinking. 'Not really, I talk to a few local kids when I'm online playing the game, but I don't really go out that much. You see my mam's working all the time and she's not home until late. Her new bar job is a late finish and she doesn't get in sometimes until after midnight.' Donny rubbed at his eyes with the heels of his hands. The kid was a minor and his mother shouldn't be leaving him to fend for himself.

He made a mental note and carried on talking. 'That's crap, isn't it? We run a youth club here three times a week, why don't you start coming here, find some friends?'

Ged screwed his face up. 'No way, the kids who come here are special needs. I can find my own mates thanks.'

That was the thing about Donny. Even though Ged had just had a complete meltdown, he was still sat here with him, no screaming, no shouting, just calm. Donny sat in silence for a few seconds. There was no rush to get Ged out of here, he was no danger to anyone anymore. 'You can come and sit in my office if you want or stay here for a bit to clear your head. In fact, you need to clean this room up, first don't you?'

Ged looked at him. 'Yeah, no worries. I'll clean it up. Sorry for losing it too.'

Donny reached his hand out. 'Here's my hand, here's my heart. Let's move on and put this behind us.' They shook hands and Donny stood up. 'You do know that you will go on report for this, don't you?' Ged nodded and exhaled loudly before he got back on his feet. 'I'll start cleaning it now, sir.'

Donny headed back to his office. He ran his fingers through his hair and let out a laboured sigh. Frankie was in the corridor and called to him as Donny got closer. 'That Ged kid is alright, sir, it was Paul winding him up. The guy's a prick, I'll knock him out if he carries on.'

Donny had no time to talk, he was due at a meeting. 'Just look out for him, Frankie, take him under your wing. And, don't you be knocking anybody about, keep your nose clean. Do you hear me, don't get involved?' Donny rushed down the corridor and disappeared into his office.

Chapter Five

The end of the school day. Ged was one of the first to get on the minibus and park his arse. He just wanted to get away from this place, go home. Frankie came and sat in front of him before the rest of the rabble boarded. He twisted round to look at Ged.

'Never thought you had it in you. Paul shit himself today, he's not so loud now is he, now you put him in his place? And quite right too, you shouldn't let no muppet bully you in this place. You have to stand up for yourself, show the fuckers.' Ged was taken aback; Frankie was the main man in this school and since he'd been there, in the last two months, he'd never said a single word to him, nothing. Frankie was like the alpha male of Second Chance, sitting on the top of the hill watching his tribe and making sure there was no messing. If any of these lads wanted to challenge his reign, then he'd soon rip their heads off and sort them out. Ged wasn't going to ignore the guy; he'd seen his chance to make a friend and replied without hesitation. 'He's a dickhead, Frankie.

I've watched him for weeks now harassing some of the others, the guy is a windup.' Frankie looked around the bus. He pulled his iPhone out of his jacket pocket and looked at the screen. 'Here, get my digits typed in your phone. You can one ring me, and I'll save your number. You're an OK kid, Ged, and I'm gonna look after you.'

Ged's hands were shaking as he pressed his number into his phone as quickly as he could. Here he was, a nobody, chatting, swapping numbers with the top boy. Maybe now Ged had a someone, someone who would have his back if he was ever in trouble.

Frankie rammed his phone back in his pocket and patted it down. 'I'll give you a bell later, mate, if you're not doing owt. You can come on the estate with me and meet the crew.' Ged's eyes were wide open, and his mouth was dry. Was this a windup or what? He'd never had a friend like this – nobody had ever really taken the time to get to know him. Frankie sat back in his seat now, watched the rest of the pupils board the bus. Nancy made her way towards Ged and plonked herself down next to him. She smiled softly. 'It's not that bad here, is it?'

Ged swallowed hard, two proper conversations in one day – what was going on? He chewed his lips and tried to remain cool. He was one of Frankie's boys now and if he wanted to impress him, he needed to be confident, show he was game for anything, even talking to girls. He could always fall back on his acting skills. The drama teacher had always told him that from the minute he stepped onto the stage he was no longer Ged Grey, he could be whoever he wanted to be – confident, gobby and fearless, whatever. Ged took a deep breath. 'Is what it is, Nancy. I just keep my head down and I do my rip here.' He had his words on point, no longer the shy kid, he was Ged, mate of Frankie.

'Do you want to hook up tonight? We can go for something to eat if you want, some KFC?'

Not what Ged had been expecting. He went bright red – not so cool now. Nancy was hitting on him; what was going on? No one had ever given him the time of the day before. Ged fidgeted, nervously cracking his knuckles. 'I can't tonight, but give me your number and I'll text you when I can?' There, Ged had asked a girl for her number, whoop, whoop, go on lad, get in there, he told himself.

Chelsea and her mob were on board now and she was eager to make an announcement. 'I'm having a party at the weekend, you lot can come if you want but you need to bring booze. Jack Daniels is my favourite so make sure you bring some. A few glasses of that down your hole and you'll be steaming. What do you say, Frankie, you having it or what?'

Frankie nodded, no words. If he turned up, then he turned up, if he didn't then so what?

Nancy was staring at Ged; he could feel her eyes burning into him. Speak lad, start a conversation, anything, but just don't sit there like a big numpty.

'So, what's your story, why did you get chucked out of normal school?' See, that wasn't so bad, was it? He started to relax. Somehow he was starting to feel comfortable with this girl; even though they'd just met, he didn't know her, he could feel a connection.

Nancy hunched her shoulders, pulled her jacket tighter around herself. There was a sadness in her eyes, an emptiness. 'I'm "not engaging", they said. I keep running away too. My mam is at her wits' end with me. This place is my last chance. God knows what will happen if I mess up here.'

Ged nodded. 'Yep, we're all in the same boat. Everyone's story ends with that line. It's do or die time, isn't it?'

Nancy edged closer, which put Ged on the back foot. It was too soon for all this, he should back off, play it cool. She laid her head on Ged's shoulder and he panicked, embarrassed, as he caught Chelsea's eye. She'd clocked it, she was nudging the girl to the left of her. She was going to make sure everyone else noticed too. Bloody motormouth at it again. 'So what's going on with you two? Ged, first day and you're putting your mark on her. Never had you down as a player.'

That was too much for Nancy, who bolted upright. 'It's not like that,' she hissed. 'We're just friends, so piss off.' On any other day Chelsea would have scratched her eyes out for speaking to her like that; in fact she was lucky she wasn't lying on the floor having ten tons of shit kicked out of her. Chelsea noted that Nancy could stand up for herself and let the comment pass – the new girl was very lucky, very lucky indeed.

Ged walked into his front room and read the message scribbled on the piece of paper on the table. His mother always left him a note before she left for work. He screwed his eyes together slightly as he tried to decipher her handwriting.

Ged, there's a microwave meal in the
fridge. Just put it in for three minutes
and let it stand for one minute.

See you later,

Love Mam X

Nothing new. He tossed the note back onto the table and whipped off his coat. Bloody hell, it was cold in here today. His mam was always turning the central heating off trying to save money, tight arse she was. Ged walked over to the thermostat on the wall and turned it back on. The house would be warm soon, boiling hot, just like he liked it. Tonight, he had planned a Xbox night with his online mates. He wasn't holding his breath that Frankie would be in touch and he settled down on the sofa ready for hours of non-stop FIFA.

The living room was neat and tidy, brown leather sofa, cream walls, basic really. Switching on the telly he suddenly thought that there'd been post on the mat. He should have a look in case there was anything he didn't want his mam to see. He walked slowly into the hallway. As he got closer he could see that among the pizza and takeaway flyers was just one letter. A plain white envelope with his name on the front. He picked it up and slowly made his way back to the front room, unsure yet whether he wanted to open it or not. Maybe later.

Ged started to set the game up instead, every now and then shooting a look over at the letter beside him on the sofa. But as he got into his game he forgot all about it, shouting at the TV screen and focussing on his every move. So it was almost a surprise to see the envelope still sitting there. He reached over for it, closed his eyes for a few seconds and held it, smelt it. Then he slid his fingers inside the envelope and pulled out a standard prison letter, thick blue lines on it, the jail stamp at the top. Ged sat back as he started to read the words from his father. He struggled to decipher the hand-writing, had to take his time to sound some of the words out and it took a while to get through all three pages. Ged held the paper to his chest briefly before shoving it back in the envelope and ramming it in his trouser pocket. If his mother saw this, she would go ape. She usually hid any letters from him. Ged had once found a stack of them in the bottom of her wardrobe and all hell had broken loose. She had no right to hide his mail, Kevin was his dad and Ged had every right to see him and get letters from him.

Not for the first time, Kevin had enclosed a visiting order with his letter. Lucky the post had been late today then, and he'd seen it before his mam, before it was too late. This was it, a chance to see his dad, a chance for his father to sit facing him, look him in the eye and tell him how sorry he was that he hadn't been around for him.

Ged missed his dad, he'd been his hero when he was a kid. They'd gone to the park to play football together, wres-tled, watched wildlife programmes together. His old man had been his best friend.

Ged's thoughts were interrupted by his phone ringing. Bloody hell, Frankie hadn't just been winding him up. Ged's swiped the button and held the phone to his ear.

'Yo, what gwarn,' drawled Frankie.

'Not much, just chilling, what you up to?'

'I'm down the estate just sorting a few things out. Come to Collyhurst, Eastford Square and we can hang for a bit. I'll buy you your tea so don't bother eating first.'

Ged was lost for words, eventually managing to stutter, 'Yeah, alright, let me get changed and I'll ring you when I'm on my way.'

'Sorted.' Frankie ended the call.

Ged sat thinking for a few minutes. He liked his games, never really socialised. What if he didn't fit in, what if nobody liked him? He rushed to his room and pulled out his best Nike tracksuit. He kept it for special occasions – it was his pride and joy. He styled his hair, which didn't look as red once he'd put some wax in it, he reckoned, then looked into the full-length mirror, turning to look first at one side, then the other. Pretty dapper. He quickly checked around the room to make sure everything was alright before he left. His mother would go ballistic if she came home early, she'd know he'd had the heating on. She was a right penny pincher, but she should be glad he'd gone out, saved her the cost of a hot meal. He'd probably get it in the ear later for not letting her know where he'd gone. But Ged had a friend now, a real friend and nothing else seemed to matter.

Chapter Six

It had been quite a day – one all the teachers were glad to see the back of. Three incidents in all, though nothing else as big as Ged's meltdown. The teachers were in the staff room chatting and drinking coffee. Tina was sat with them listening to today's stories.

'That new girl, Nancy, doesn't say much, does she?' Sinclair said. 'It's a shame Chelsea's not more like her – my job would be a lot easier. On my life, that girl has a mouth like a sewer; you should hear how she talks to the boys. She might be underage but you'd never know it, going on about blow jobs and more all the time. Every second word out of her mouth is fuck. Surely, someone should have a look at what's going on?'

Tina sat back in her chair, crossed her legs. 'She's been reported to the safeguarding team. There's definitely something going on with her lately. Her mum said she's out until all hours and she's smoking weed too. Not good news for any family, is it? I'd be worried out of my mind if it was my daughter.'

Robert Sinclair looked up and nodded. 'Yes, I know I could smell it on her the other day. Mind you, I thought weed was supposed to calm you down. It mustn't be working on her though because she's just louder than ever.'

Tina agreed. 'Did any of you see that love bite on her neck last week? She told me it was a rash, but you could tell that was nonsense, it was black and blue. It's a sad state of affairs when the teenagers here are getting more action than the teaching staff,' she gave a wry grin.

Sinclair burst out laughing in surprise. Sure they were a tight-knit team, but this was more than Tina usually let on. 'Don't tell me you're not getting any, Tina, what's to do with that husband of yours?'

Tina looked downcast. 'It's not him, it's me. If I can't have babies, what's the point?' She stopped herself. She wasn't thinking straight. Why on earth was she telling everyone at work about her personal problems?

The other members of staff looked at each other furtively; they knew this was a touchy subject. One by one they made their excuses, started to leave. None of them wanted to get into another long talk about Tina's problems or her health. Tina herself sat staring into space, her hand placed on her stomach, wishing that she didn't feel so empty inside. She seemed oblivious to the fact that everyone else had gone. Her eyes started to well up. 'All I ever wanted was a baby,' she choked. 'All I want is my own child.'

Over at the salon, Susan sat in her office looking stressed. Her brother John was with her, sipping at a cup of coffee. He had a look of Susan – you could tell that they were related – but he could give Donny a run for his money in the poser stakes. He obsessed about his appearance. He looked good though, with his ripped muscles and toned physique. He put the cup down on the white desk and nodded his head slowly over at her. 'So, run it by me again, why do you think he's cheating on you this time?'

Susan sat picking at the skin round her fingernails. 'I just know, don't ask me how, but I do. Something's just not right.'

'So, why are you still with him? Let me and our Dave kick him out and be done with him.'

Susan panicked – this was going too far too fast. 'No, I need to catch him at it first. If I go in now all guns blazing, he will just laugh at me and say I'm being paranoid. But, John, he takes hours getting ready in the morning and in the bedroom he's been throwing some new moves in. Putting legs in places they have never been. Come on, where's he getting that from all of a sudden unless someone's showing him it?'

John scratched the end of his chin and looked at his sister in more detail. 'TMI, sister, TMI. Anyhow, I don't know why you had him back after last time. Our Dave wanted to chop him up and feed him to the pigs. You should have binned the dirty fucker.'

Her voice was quiet, timid. 'He's my husband, John. Everyone deserves a second chance. I mean how many chances have you had from Paige? You've been caught out that many times so don't judge me when your wife has given you chance after chance. I don't know how she does it, honest, I'd have you six foot under by now.'

John smirked and sat back in his chair, folding his arms behind his head. 'I just love the women, don't I? And they love me. I can't help myself. But Donny is another story. You're my sister and I won't have no prick taking the piss out of you. I told you when you first met him that I wasn't sure about him, didn't I?'

Susan was quick to jump in. 'You said that about every man that I dated, John. But now … I just need to put my mind at rest and find out for sure. It's making me ill. Night after night I lie awake and any chance I get, I go through his phone. Can't you get some of your boys to watch him for me? If I could do it myself I would, but I daren't do much more than drive by the school gates.'

'I suppose, but are you sure you want me to? Imagine if he *is* cheating, what then?'

Susan sat cracking her knuckles and her expression changed. The softness and uncertainty vanished; she looked hard, unforgiving. Her voice was slow, deep as she replied. 'Then I'll ruin him. There will be none of what happened last time. I'll make sure I leave the bastard with nothing. I'll take him to the fucking cleaners.'

John chuckled and threw his head back laughing. 'That's my sister sat right there. I knew you were in there some-where. That's it, girl, break him, take him for everything and leave the fucker with nothing but the clothes he's standing in.'

Susan grinned, reached over and patted her brother's knee. 'Let's get this plan into action then. If he's fucking about then God help him. I'm ready this time, ready to destroy him and everything that he loves.'

John nodded his head slowly and sat staring out of the window. 'Consider it done.'

Chapter Seven
___

D onny made his way into the boozer on the way home from work. A pint or two was just what the doctor ordered after today, his head was done in with all the stress. And if Susan wasn't at home, he could grab a few cheeky drinks to help him settle down before he watched the match and she'd never know.

Melanie Peters, the new English teacher, was by his side. She was twenty-eight years old and she oozed confidence – as well she might with her heart-shaped lips, a great figure and legs that seemed to go on forever. Massive rack too, and she didn't exactly hide them away; she seemed to be aware of the effect of low-cut tops on her figure. Maybe that was the reason he'd employed her in the first place, because her CV wasn't that good if he was being honest. Still, it was more about attitude than qualifications in this school. And she had something about her. Donny always had an end-of-day meeting with new staff to see if they'd survived their first day. Some teachers never came back, but Melanie looked like she could handle herself. Donny had offered to drop her off on his way home and when he mentioned he was going for a few drinks in the pub she invited herself along. That was his story anyway. What could he say? Nothing really, he hadn't done anything wrong. Still, if Susan got wind of it, she'd go ape. Drinks with a female member of staff, just the two of them.

'What do you want to drink, Mel?'

'A large white wine thanks, Donny.'

Melanie found some seats in a quiet corner of the pub while he went to the bar, taking it for granted that he was paying. Donny smiled over at her as he waited to be served. He was a happily married man, but he still couldn't help flirting with her. It was in his nature. But Donny was too preoccupied by Melanie flicking her long dark hair over her shoulders to notice a large-framed man stood watching him from the other side of the bar, clocking his every movement.

As Melanie watched Donny approaching with the drinks, he blushed slightly; her steady gaze made him feel nervous. He sat down next to her. 'I've been gagging for a beer all day. The wife is out with her mate so there's no rush to get home. I've got a nice chilled night planned, footy, a few more beers and bed.'

Melanie dropped her eyes low, started to play with her long, slender fingers. Had he said something wrong, upset her?

'I've not long split up from my partner, so nobody's waiting for me at home anymore.'

Donny sipped his pint. He didn't really know much about Melanie, only what he needed to know about her teaching background. Her personal life was none of his business.

She toyed with her drink, still not meeting his eyes, but seemed eager to talk all the same. 'My ex is a nightmare. I've told him there is no going back this time, but he keeps turning up wherever I am.' She continued talking in a whisper as if he might be able to hear her – wherever he was – her eyes darting around the room just in case. 'He said if I get somebody new, he'll cut their balls off. He's a total headcase, got a screw loose.' The hairs on her arm were standing on end. 'And he would you know, he's got a terrible temper and he doesn't know when to stop once his cage has been rattled. I asked him to get help, you know, but he point-blank refused, told me I was the one with the problem not him.'

Donny wasn't quite sure how to respond. 'He sounds like a right one. How did you end up with somebody like that? You seem like you've got your head screwed on. Men with tempers like that are trouble. It starts with words, but that's not usually where it ends.' He paused. 'Did he hit you too?' He realised that maybe he had overstepped the mark with his last question. He should have been more cautious, though it didn't seem to faze Mel, who carried on talking as she nervously twiddled the ends of her hair.

'Donny, you don't know the half of it. He's done some bad things to me; sick, twisted things. He thinks he's untouchable. I've been out on a few dates since we split up and he always gets wind of it and turns up and warns them off. It looks like I will be single for ever, well, at least while he's still around,' she paused as if unsure whether to carry on. 'You see, the thing is, he's a copper. So, it's not like I can report him, he's got the boys in blue looking after him. They all piss in the same pot. I did phone them when he first started hitting me and nothing was done. It's a waste of time. It's like pissing in the wind.'

'You should ask to speak to someone else, go higher than him, that will fuck him up.'

'He *is* one of the higher-up ones, Donny. He's older than me and he still thinks I'm some sort of kid. We got together when I was sixteen and he sort of looked after me when I was in a bad place. But I realised too late he liked the power. He's a bully, Donny. A control freak.'

Donny didn't know what to say to that. Why hadn't she kicked him to the kerb and sent him packing years ago? He'd never understood why anyone would stay with an abusive partner and struggled to find the words she was clearly wanted to hear.

Melanie took another sip of her wine and sat back in her seat, clearly deciding it was time to change the subject before she got upset. Donny could already see her welling up. 'So, tell me a bit about you. Obviously I know you're the headteacher, but I don't really know anything more about you.'

Donny's mobile started to ring; he stared at the screen and stood up. 'I just need to take this call.' He held the phone to his ear and started to walk away, but Melanie still caught snatches of the conversation. 'I'm busy at the moment, but I'll catch you later tonight, just crack on and I'll ring you back soon.' Donny ended the call and walked back to his seat. He raised his eyebrows and sighed. 'Sorry about that, just a mate who needed a favour.'

Melanie smiled softly. 'You're a friend to everyone, aren't you, Donny? The main reason I took this job was because of how you are with people. You have a great outlook on life and I'm glad to be a part of your team.'

Donny was chuffed. 'It's hard graft but I get so much more from the job. These kids need us, not just to teach them, they need to feel part of something. Sure, a lot of them will still face a few bumps in the road when they leave us, I'm not going to pretend we've never had a former pupil end up in jail or get pregnant underage, but lots go on to bigger things and sort themselves out. One lad who used to come to our school has his own business now. He owns a café in Miles Platting. On my life, he drove into the school car park one morning and told me. "Come and bring the kids to my café, it's on the house." Ten students and four staff went for lunch and he fed us all for free. He told the kids about how he started out and how he got to where he was today. It made me choke up really, it was so good to see someone that had been to our school make something of themselves. If I'm being honest a lot of the kids won't even sit their exams, so if I didn't step in they'd leave school with no qualifications, nothing. But I have a lot of work placements set up in the area, local businesses and that – the kids who aren't academic, I'll send them there in hope they might get a decent job at the end of it.'

Melanie seemed impressed. She looked him directly in the eyes. 'You really are a knight in shining armour, aren't you, Donny?'

He was lapping up the words. Melanie moved closer, whispered in his ear. He could feel her breath hot on the side of his neck; it sent shivers down his spine. What was she playing at? He pulled away. Maybe the wine had gone straight to her head. His phone was ringing again, Susan's name flashing across the screen. But there was no way he was answering the call now, no way in this world. She had a sixth sense for working out when he was around other women. Instead, Donny picked his drink up and took a large swig. He loved his wife and there was no chance he was jeopardising what he had at home for a quick knee-trembler with one of his staff in a pub toilet. Melanie couldn't have made it more obvious; she was there for the taking if he wanted her. But he didn't. Back in the day he wouldn't have thought twice, but not now, he was a changed man.

Donny knew he needed out; he faked a yawn, stretched his arms above his head before glancing down at his watch. 'I'd better be off. The missus will be home soon, and I want to have stuff sorted for her when she walks through the door, a nice warm bath, candles and that.' There you go, the signals sent out loud and clear: he was not a cheater, he was a good husband. Susan was his soul mate and he had vowed he'd never do anything that would hurt her again. He'd learned his lesson. Sure, Melanie was sexy, and he was flattered, of course, but the snake was staying in the cage.

Melanie knew a knockback when she saw one. She threw back the rest of her drink, looked at the table, a bit embarrassed. 'Don't suppose you could drop me off at home, Donny?' That was all he needed, he just wanted to be home now. But what could he say, he was the one that had offered in the first place. 'OK. You ready?'

Melanie nodded, reached over to grab her handbag, giving Donny a look at her slim thighs in the process. She wasn't making it easy for him. He stood up, anxious to get going. Note to self, do not take Melanie for a drink again. She was clearly a woman who knew what she wanted.

———————

It was already dark as Donny drove down the dimly lit side street, unaware of the black car that had been trailing him – always at a safe distance – since he left the pub. Melanie was applying lipstick using a mirror she'd fished out of her bag. It was like she was going for a night out, rather than heading home.

'What number?'

'Oh, sorry. Erm, number twenty-five. Just carry on up past the lamp-post and I'm on the left.' Donny drove a few yards further and pulled up outside the house. Behind him the black car pulled over too, still far enough away not to be noticed. Melanie was in no rush to get out. She sat looking at him and Donny started to worry she was going to go in for a kiss. Fuck, fuck, fuck. That was all he needed. He braced himself to push her away, but now she was looking out of the window, clearly nervous about getting out – he could see that her hands were trembling. She looked back at him once she'd completed her recce of the dark street. 'At least he's not about tonight, stalking me.'

Donny found himself looking in his rearview mirror to check there was no one lurking. 'Go on, quick, get inside. I'll watch til you're in safely.' She opened the door slowly. 'You're OK. I'll be fine. I'll see you in work tomorrow, Donny, and thanks for the drink. Maybe we can do it again sometime?'

Donny just wanted to get out of there. He tried not to let his impatience show. 'Yes, yeah, great, see you at school. Night.' At last she was gone. He pulled away quickly; she didn't seem to be in any hurry to get indoors. As he looked back through his wing mirror, he could see her still stood on the street watching him drive off. 'Bloody hell,' he mumbled under his breath. 'That was a close one.'

As Donny headed home, he turned up the stereo; his tunes were pumping and he was singing his head off, lost in the lyrics. His phone was ringing again but he ignored it. Whoever it was could wait. He was going home and putting his feet up, chilling. Today had been a long day, a very long one indeed.

As soon as he let himself in the front door, Donny spotted Susan's car keys on the hall table. He was confused; hadn't she said she was meeting up with Sadie? He walked into the kitchen and saw his wife sat at the table drinking a glass of red wine. She looked stressed.

'Hello, baby, I thought you was doing counselling for your nutty mate tonight?'

She ran her finger slowly around the top of her glass and lifted her eyes up to meet his. 'I changed my mind, couldn't face it. Just rang her instead. Where have you been anyway?'

Donny thought on his feet. She'd go ape if she knew where he'd really been. He avoided eye contact. 'I had a few things to catch up with at work, you know, emails and that, remember I said this morning?' She narrowed her eyes, watched him carefully as he walked across the kitchen to get a glass. 'I phoned you, you never answered.' He still couldn't look at her and dipped his head in a cupboard.

'I was going to ring for a takeaway – you hungry?'

'No, I feel a bit sick if I'm being honest,' Susan said quietly. He knew before he looked at her that something was wrong.

'Are you alright? You seem a bit pissed off, have I done something to upset you, babe?'

Her lips started moving but no words were coming out. He sat down next to her, gave her a hug and she could smell perfume on him, the smell of lies and deceit. 'I'm just due on my period, my head is banging, and I've got terrible cramps.'

He snuggled his head next to hers and kissed the side of her cheek – like that would make everything OK, the Judas.

'Tell you what, take a couple of tablets, go and get in bed and I'll order us some food and then I'll make you a hot water bottle.'

Susan tried her best to smile but she was struggling. She stood up. 'OK, I'll go and get in my pyjamas,' she said as she left the room.

In the bathroom she bolted the door with trembling hands and stood with her back to the door. 'Bastard, bastard, bastard,' she muttered under her breath. Her husband was a lying, cheating rat and it seemed that her fears were true. Well she'd show him this time. Susan walked over to the bathroom mirror and stared at her reflection. She smiled, nodded her head slowly. It was showtime.

Chapter Eight

G ed kept his head low as he walked down the busy Rochdale Road. It was cold tonight and the wind was biting at his ears. He felt a bit anxious. Maybe he should have put his big coat on, it was freezing. His mam had bought him the coat last year; she'd treated him with her work bonus money. Two hundred quid she paid for it, nearly the whole bonus. He never really wore it, kept it for special occasions and there weren't many of those. Ged carried on walking, constantly looking around him, jumpy. He hated the dark; even now in his teens he always kept a small light switched on in his bedroom at night – not that he'd ever have admitted it to anyone. He didn't really go out much; bit of a home bird. Friendships were much easier online, anyway. He liked his own company, didn't mind that most evenings were spent in front of a screen. He could entertain himself – being an only child had probably helped with that, no siblings to wrestle with, to play hide and seek, to sit and talk with. He'd got so used to being a loner he'd forgotten how to do anything else.

He picked up speed. He didn't feel safe – maybe he should just turn round and go home. He could make an excuse to Frankie, tell him something had come up that he needed to deal with. He swallowed hard as he spotted Eastford Square in the distance. It had six shops and some landmark thing set in the middle – God knows what it was, some big grey concrete slab just plonked there. All around there were noises, people talking, cars flashing by. A motorbike screeched past too close, his heart was in his mouth, racing, he was shitting himself. What the hell had he said yes for? And then he heard a voice shouting his name in the distance. Ged turned his head quickly and could see Frankie waving over at him. Too late to bottle it. He walked towards him slowly, eyes down.

Frankie was sat with three other lads, all about the same age, shady-looking, all in black with baseball caps pulled right down so you could barely see their eyes. Dodgy for sure. Ged watched cautiously as Frankie dug into his jacket pocket and passed something to one of the others. He couldn't see what it was. The guy just walked away, never said a word. Frankie rubbed his hands together, blew on them to try and warm them up a bit. 'I thought you was going to ring me when you was on your way here, Ged?'

'I forgot, soz. But I can find my way OK.'

Frankie urged him to sit down. 'I'll get us some scran in a minute. The jerk chicken from the Spice Rack is to die for. Do you like jerk chicken?' Ged nodded, even though the only chicken he'd ever eaten was what his mother had cooked – a Sunday roast. There was no money in their household to be eating takeaways, they were too expensive.

'Yeah, I like it. I'm starving too.'

Frankie looked over at some more lads stood near him. 'Right, you should be getting off. I'll catch you later, ring me if you need anything else,' he told them. Ged watched them walk off and started to head towards the takeaway with Frankie.

'I'll get you the same as what I get. I'm a regular here and they know my order soon as they see me.'

Ged followed, aware of a strong smell of weed. His mother was always on about drugs – when they walked down the market on a Saturday, she would always go off on one when they passed someone smoking it. Ged had never tried anything. He was a good kid underneath the moods and the lip, had never really got caught up in that world – you didn't get into trouble if you barely left the house.

Frankie ordered and leant over the top of the counter watching the food being dished up. He licked his lips before passing Ged's food over with a plastic white fork. 'Go sit at that table near the window, quick grab it before someone else does. I don't fancy standing up eating, you don't enjoy it the same when you're stood up.'

Ged carried the polystyrene tray over to the table, it smelt lovely, rich and spicy. His eyes focused on every scrap of food there, it looked like nothing he'd ever eaten before in his life. He sat down and put a piece of chicken in his mouth. *Oh my God*, why had he never tasted anything like this before? The spices jumped about on his tongue and he had to open his mouth up wide to help it cool down. Frankie joined him, sat facing Ged and started to tuck in too. He never flinched as he ate his chicken. Clearly had an asbestos mouth.

Frankie's mobile started to ring; he answered the call with a mouthful of food, listening to the caller for a few seconds before he replied. 'Take two brown and a white to the bridge. Don't be letting him have any on tick either. He's a cheeky fucker. Tell him he pays what he owes otherwise I'll snap his jaw.' He carried on talking while Ged sat staring. He was confused what the call was about and it showed on his face. Frankie looked at him, kept his voice low. 'That's how I earn my money, Ged lad. How do you think I get all the top clothes that I wear? My mam and dad are skint. I just sell a few bits to keep me ticking over.'

'Bits of what?' Ged asked.

'Fuck me, don't you know the script around here or what?'

Ged could feel his face burning up. He didn't even know there was a script, let alone what it said.

'Mate, most of the lads sell a bit of weed around here. It's easy money if you keep your head down.'

Ged freaked out a bit inside but did his best not to show it, to act cool. 'Yeah, a few lads who I know sell it too.' He was talking out of his arse again. He didn't know anyone who sold drugs.

Frankie shovelled in another mouthful of food. 'You can start earning if you want?' His mouth was open, Ged could see the bits of chicken half chewed. 'Start off small and keep it on the low. No pressure, just saying.'

'How would I do that? I don't know what to do?' Ged was an innocent – why had he even come here tonight? He'd have been much safer sat at home just playing on his Xbox. He didn't know much, but he did know that this world was

77

bad, dangerous. He needed out of it before he got in any further.

'You leave all that to me. Let's say I'm in the know. Eat your food and we can talk about it later.'

Ged couldn't argue with that. He didn't have to say no, he just had to find a way not to say yes, he told himself. And so he tucked in, enjoyed every morsel. He was soon full; he couldn't eat another mouthful. His phone vibrated with a message. Bloody hell, he never got calls or messages and now it was glowing again with another message. He pulled the phone out, checked the screen.

Hi Ged, what you up to? Love Nancy

He showed Frankie – at last, something to make him look cool.

'No flies on that Nancy. I didn't have her down as being that forward.' Frankie handed the phone back and chuckled. 'The girls these days are dirtbags. Trust me mate, stay single and play the field. Having a girlfriend is nothing but stress, I know.'

Ged pocketed the phone, sticking to the role of cool guy. He'd always been quiet because he didn't know what to say. Now he realised he could make silence powerful. Better to be a man of few words than say the wrong thing and risking letting Frankie see the nerves and questions he felt inside.

'Yeah, I'll text her later, no rush is there?'

Frankie's phone rang again, and he barked out another message to go to the bridge. Then silence for a few seconds before he spoke again. 'So, who do you live with?'

'Just my mam, my dad's in the nick, but he's home soon. I can't wait. We've got loads of things planned. He said he might get me a motorbike. He rings me when my mam's at work, she doesn't even know I speak to him, she would shit a brick if she knew.'

Frankie raised an eyebrow, intrigued. 'What's your old man in the slammer for?'

'Armed robbery, assault, some other stuff.'

'Fuck me, so your dad had a shooter. I want a gun. You need one when you're in this game.'

'He's said he's sorting his head out and going on the straight and narrow. My mam won't have him near us though, she said he'll never change.'

Frankie stroked his chin. 'It's hard to change when you've been involved in that kind of a world, mate. Who's going to get a job paying two and half hundred quid a week when they can earn grands doing a few grafts?'

Ged was wishing this conversation over; he hated talking about his dad, how his life had turned out. Things could have been so different if he'd only kept his head down, got some decent work. But it was always one shit job after another with his dad, one last chance to get enough money to support his family, so they wouldn't want for anything in their life again.

Frankie scraped the last bit of food from the white tray. He opened the can of Coke and downed nearly all of it in one go. A massive burp. Ged grinned, glad to be off the topic of his dad. And he could see why Frankie ruled the roost at school – he had confidence, certainty and, yes, this kid was funny. A good friend to have onside.

'Who's in your gaff now, Ged, is your mam in?'

Ged shook his head. 'Nah, she won't get home till midnight. She works in a bar until late, so I won't see her until the morning.'

Frankie looked surprised. 'Shite that, mate. So, you're in all night by yourself?'

'Yep, on my Jack all the time if I'm being honest.'

Frankie seized his chance, draped his arm around Ged's shoulders. 'Come on then, let's chill at yours for a bit. I'm freezing my nuts off standing out here all night. You've got FIFA, right?'

Ged could barely speak. A real life mate, coming to his house, someone to hang with. Maybe actual friends were more of a laugh than online ones…

'Yes, sure. I'm top at it too, I should warn you, if you fancy a game?'

'Game on, mate, come on let's do one.'

The two of them set off along the main road, just another two kids out too late, traffic speeding past, police sirens blaring in the distance.

Chapter Nine

Tina sat in front of the TV with her husband. She'd finished all her chores, and this was her chill time. Finally. She was watching the end of *Coronation Street*. Like every night it was on, she'd got her stall set up before her favourite soap started. She loved the northern humour. There were always dramas on the street and for the thirty minutes it was on, it took her away from her own problems. Chris wasn't keen on the soaps – if he had his way, he'd be watching a nature programme, not what he called 'this bag of shite'. But she knew if he had his programmes on, claiming it was something educational, he'd still be ignoring the telly and mucking about on his phone. Not so bloody educational, really.

Tina raised her eyes to the ceiling, it was like a herd of elephants was running about upstairs. Nevaya, her stepdaughter, was a noisy cow at the best of times. No doubt she was getting ready to go out, so it would be the works – a full face of makeup, hair straightened, the lot. Chris's kids had lived with them since they were small. Their mother just turned up one day, left them on the doorstep like an unwanted parcel. 'You've taken my husband, now take his kids, you slut,' she'd yelled as she'd dumped them in the doorway.

Tina had been a bit shellshocked at first, but, after a time, was happy enough to take on the role of surrogate mother. How hard could it be? She did all the stuff you were supposed to; read bedtime stories, baked cakes, mopped up tears when they were upset, cleaned the puke when they were ill. Truth be told, it had been easy enough when they were little but now they were teenagers it was a very different kettle of fish. No gratitude for everything she'd done for them, anything she did for them, no thank yous or appreciation. And it seemed to happen overnight. They went to bed as normal children and got up the following morning spotty, hormonal, ticking time bombs. Nightmares the both of them. Charlie seemed to have decided that he was the man of the house, and started testing Tina at every opportunity. She'd tried speaking to Chris, of course, but he never really saw the digs, the pushing at the pecking order of the household, so he mostly just ignored it and carried on as normal.

Bone idle, Charlie was, he had never done a tap in the house, always 'busy' whenever she asked him to do anything. After everything she'd done, he could have pulled his finger out now and then instead of sprawling on the sofa the whole time, playing deaf. But now, she'd realised that lazy was easier to cope with than bolshy.

Charlie's sister was even more of a piece of work. Nevaya was a right handful, she never wanted to spend time with Tina anymore. No more girly pamper nights, no duvet days at weekends watching chick flicks together – it had all gone. If she wasn't at school or out with her mates, she was dossing in her bedroom, on the phone to them. She only appeared when she wanted something. And the mouth on her. Tina felt like she'd lost a friend – just another blow for her to take. Maybe if she could have had her own it would have been different, but she'd never know now, would she? The thought that she would never hold her own child in her arms killed her.

Chris didn't really get it. Why would he? He had two kids, didn't know how it felt to be what her mam's generation had always called 'barren'. The horrible word kept coming back to her now, haunting her as she tried to come to terms with the fact she would never feel a life growing inside her, a baby kick. He was a man; he didn't understand how deep-rooted her need for a baby was. She'd always imagined her life with children, she loved children. Even when she saw a baby on the television her heart melted, she wanted to smell them, feel their little fingers and hold them close to her heart. After the hysterectomy her world fell apart – it had destroyed her. She cried non-stop for days, sometimes she couldn't even get out of bed. Chris was her rock at first, but, as time went by, his wife's pain seemed to wash over him. Of course he cared, he even offered to buy her a puppy to try and take the pain away, but she refused. How could the aching in her heart be taken away by a daft bleeding animal? He just didn't get it.

Tina lay on the sofa watching the events on the street unfold while munching on snacks. Crisps were her downfall – she didn't want to count the number of packets she could get through in a night while she was watching TV. She ate the last one then poked every finger inside her mouth in turn so she could suck off the salty flavouring. At least the comfort eating kept her away from the booze, she figured.

Behind her the door was flung open and Nevaya stormed into the room, up in arms about something, ever the drama queen. She was shrieking at the top of her voice and it took every ounce of Tina's self-control not to read her the riot act. She wouldn't stand for this at school – why should she have to put up with it at home? Who the hell did she think she was talking to? There was really no need for this. Nevaya carried on shouting and poking her finger towards her stepmother.

'Have you used all the conditioner? I have to wash my hair tonight and it's all gone. Every Tuesday and Friday I wash my hair, and you've used it all again. You're a selfish bitch. You've done it on purpose.'

Chris sat up, his hair was stuck up all over the place. He'd been having a snooze, hand stuck down the front of his shorts. He sat up swiftly, and looked over at his daughter.

'Oi, watch your mouth. Don't speak to Tina like that or you'll get a clip round the ear.' Really helpful. Tina sighed. He should have been up out of his seat and ragged her up to her room, grounded her, taken her mobile phone away. Something to make the kid actually listen. She stood up; there was no way she was being spoken to like this, no way in this world. She eyeballed Nevaya. 'Right, young lady. And who the hell do you think you're talking to? Sort your attitude out and speak to me with some respect. I'm not one of your friends from the streets, and we never brought you up to have a mouth like that.'

Nevaya kicked off again, didn't give a shit. 'I'm sick of this bloody house, sick of you too, Tina. All you do is moan.'

Chris was studiously ignoring them, suddenly fascinated by *Corrie* in a way he never had been in all the years. Tina had to bite her lip before she said something she'd regret. She sat back down on the edge of the sofa and folded her arms tightly around herself. 'Just go back upstairs and have a look in the drawer. There will be a new one in there. You're horrible lately. I don't even know you anymore.'

Nevaya put her hands on her hips and glared. 'You don't know me because I don't want you to. You're not my mother. I have my own, so back off.'

That was below the belt. After she'd given up so much to take on these kids. Where was the respect? Tina could have married a man without any baggage, without any problems, but she chose to give everything to this family, to help them stay together. Maybe she should have told her that, knocked her off her high horse. Ever since Chris's ex, Wendy, had come back on the scene again, it had all gone steadily downhill. It was a joke – not a word from her for all those years and then she decided to rock up like nothing had happened. Where had she been when the kids needed her most? She didn't deserve to be a mother. She was just a woman who had given birth and then abandoned her family when it suited her. What kind of woman did something like that?

Tina took a deep breath and looked over at Chris, hoping he'd back her up. Nothing. It was like his eyes were welded to the TV. Her blood was boiling now.

'Are you really going to lie there and say nothing? Can you not hear how she talks to me?'

Chris sighed and scratched his head. Bloody hell, all he wanted was a bit of peace and quiet. Was that too much to ask? He was tired and in no mood for all this drama.

'Nevaya, say you are sorry. And don't talk to Tina like that. She's always been good to you, never let you down. Your mam has been back on the scene for two minutes and suddenly you think the sun shines out of her arse. She dumped you both here, left you, are you forgetting that?' There, that should do it. But his words had the opposite effect.

Nevaya paced up and down the living room like a headless chicken. Forget the bloody conditioner – this was her mother's honour she was fighting for now. She looked at her dad, bent towards him as she spoke. 'So what, she made mistakes, that was then, and this is now. Anyway, she told me the real reason why she left, and it was because you were shagging her sat over there, dear father,' she pointed over at Tina. 'Mum loved you, Dad, and you broke her heart. What did you expect her to do?'

That was it. Chris was on his feet now, roaring so loud the walls shook. She had no idea what really went on, he shouted. How dare she speak to him like this, believe her lying bitch of a mother who wouldn't know the truth if it hit her full on in the face.

'You're talking out of your arse. Why are you even listening to her bullshit? She's a born liar. I'll tell you what, shall I, get your arse back up the stairs and stay there. You're grounded.'

Tina had had enough too. No more playing good cop, trying to keep the peace. 'If I was a different woman, I'd slap the living daylights out of you. Whatever happened between your parents is none of your business. And I met your dad *after* he'd split up from your mum, so put that in your bleeding pipe and smoke it,' she yelled into her stepdaughter's face. 'And, if we're being honest here, I'll tell you what actually happened between Wendy and your dad, shall I?'

The colour had drained from Chris's face. He had to stop her before she went too far, but it was already too late. Tina was on a roll now, so much for his private life staying private. He groaned and put his head in his hands.

'Your mother was sleeping with anybody who would have her. It was your dad who was the injured party here not her. Every bloody night she left you and Charlie so she could go off with one of her fancy men and it was your dad who stayed home and looked after you both. Go on, Chris, tell her. That's the truth, so don't be letting her paint some romantic portrait of that old tart.'

Nevaya ran at Tina and curled her fingers deep into her hair, yanking, pulling, then pushing her about, shaking her. This was her mother she was slagging off, she wasn't going to get away with this. How dare she?

Chris knew he had to do something. He leapt to his feet and yanked them apart. 'Whoa, turn it in now!' The room was suddenly a war zone, his wife and daughter trying to rip each other's eyes out.

Tina was fuming, this had been a long time coming and she was holding nothing back. This should all have come out years ago and there would have been none of this. She backed off and stood opposite her stepdaughter panting like a dog on a hot day. She kept her eyes on Nevaya, ready if she decided to make another move.

'Your mam come home one night and packed her stuff, said she was making a new life with whichever bloke it was that week. She didn't want any of you, all she cared about was dropping her knickers. And you can tell her I said that too because it's the truth. She's a total slag and had been cheating for years,' Tina yelled, going for gold. She puffed up her chest, ready to deliver the final blow. 'She was a desperate woman and she'd sleep with anyone who'd give her the time of the day.'

'Enough,' Chris screamed at the top of his voice. This had all gone too far. 'Let's all just calm down, I've heard enough, had enough. Day in and day out you two are fighting and bickering, it needs to be sorted out before I lose my head. I want a quiet life, not this.'

'It's her, Dad, not me. She's slagging my mam off and expects me to sit here and say nothing. But we can all tell the truth though, can't we?' Her eyes sparkled with fury. 'Is it not right that you were her friend, and our babysitter? Yes, I thought you'd change your tune now. Look at you, lost for words. My mam told me all about you too. You were her mate, she trusted you and you two were having it off behind her back. OK, she messed up, but what you two failed to mention is that she caught the pair of you having sex. Yes, in her bed. So don't you dare come across all high and mighty and try and tell me that my mother is a whore. She's worth ten of you, Tina, and you know it. That's why you've never even spoken to me about her. Did you think I would just forget her?' She started to back off, heading towards the door. 'Well, I'll never forget her, she's my flesh and blood, not a plastic pretend mother like you are.'

Chris flung the remote at Nevaya. 'Go now, get out of my sight before I say something I'll regret.'

Tina was ready to run after her, but Chris dragged her back by her arm. 'Turn it in, love, leave her to it. If she thinks that much of her mother, then she can pack her bags and go and live with her. I've had enough. Wendy won't give her the time of the day in a few months' time, you mark my words. She's always let her down, she'll never change, ever.' A ball of misery choked Tina. Scrapping like one of the kids from school – how had it come to this? Yes, she'd always wanted her own child but it hadn't stopped her giving Nevaya and her brother all the love and support a kid should have. And this was the thanks she got for always being there. You could bet she was the one who would always be there, not her goddamned mother. 'All of this because she couldn't be bothered to find the new bottle of conditioner. She's not on, Chris. You need to support me on this.'

Chris walked out of the room, came back a few seconds later with a can of Foster's. 'I need a drink. Fuck only knows what the neighbours think. It never used to be like this.'

Tina stood with her hands on her hips, her bottom lip quivering. He still hadn't answered her question. She reached for her handbag, pulled out her cigarettes and stuck one in her mouth before walking to the back door and opening it wide. If he wasn't going to calm her down maybe nicotine would do the trick. She stepped outside, took a long drag – it seemed like forever before she blew a thick grey cloud of smoke from her mouth. She stuck her head round the door, 'I've a good mind to go and see Wendy, find out what her game is. I was never her friend, the lying bitch. And you two were well split up when we started sleeping together. Why is she poisoning the kids against me?'

Chris rubbed his hand on the side of the sofa. 'I don't know and to be honest I'm not arsed, Tina. It's ancient history. Just forget about it. I'll have a word with Nevaya tomorrow and make her apologise. I'm stressed with it all, look at me drinking on a weeknight.' There was silence. Tina stepped back inside the house, fag in her hand.

'Are you for fucking real, Chris? This goes a lot deeper than a bottle of bloody conditioner. She hates me. Otherwise why has she just said all that?'

'Stop overreacting. It's a disagreement. Shit happens, just move on and get on with it.'

Tina flicked her cigarette butt into the garden and slammed the door. Chris was meant to be on her side. He'd barely had to lift a finger raising the kids and keeping the home since she'd come on the scene. A bit of loyalty and gratitude was long overdue. He was getting told.

'No, you listen Chris, I've been putting up with her attitude for months and you've done jack shit. Don't think by having a quick word with her that it'll all be sorted. You heard what she thinks about me, go on, tell me that's bloody normal behaviour?

'I'm saying that I will sort it out. For fuck's sake, Tina, don't you think I've enough on my plate without this? Turn it in and sit down.'

Tina ground her fingers into her palms, her knuckles turning white. She couldn't believe he was playing the bloody victim. 'You've had fuck all on your plate compared to me, Chris. I'm the one who is struggling each bastard day, not you. You are aware that I've not long had major surgery which means I will never be a mother, aren't you? Tell me you know that, and you haven't forgotten.'

But the stress was getting too much for Chris. He let rip. 'For crying out loud, I knew it wouldn't be long before that was brought up. Like you'll ever let me forget it. How did I know that it would all come back to you in the end? It's not my fault Tina, it's nobody's fault, it's just life and we have to deal with it.'

This was bad, it took a lot to get a rise out of her husband, but she wasn't backing down.

'Piss off, Chris. You never really wanted another baby. I bet you're relieved that I can't have one, aren't you?'

'Don't go there, Tina. I'm in no mood to be fighting with you too. We both need to calm down. Go and have a lie down or a hot bath.'

'No, Chris, I won't. Maybe I should go to my mam's. At least there I will feel loved and supported.'

Chris sat back down on the sofa. 'Do whatever you want. I'm watching the football.' He grabbed the remote and changed the channel.

Tina couldn't hold back the tears now. 'Like I said, you don't care. I'll get my stuff in the morning and leave you to it.'

Chris watched her leave the room and exhaled slowly. She wouldn't go, she never did.

Tina slammed the bedroom door shut behind her and stood with her back resting against it. Her chest was heaving, she could feel the start of a panic attack building. Breathe, breathe. She sat down and gripped the edge of the white cotton duvet, took a few more breaths before reaching down to pull a small suitcase from under the double bed. She slowly unzipped it, pulled something out.

Tina ran a single finger softly over a white hand-knitted cardigan. It was so small, so tiny. A woman had been selling them on the local market the year before and she just couldn't help herself, she had to buy one. She went back every week after that for months: bootees, mittens, all matching sets. And for what? Tina held the cardigan to her cheek and stroked it softly. Maybe she should have given them away instead of tormenting herself whenever she was upset or feeling down.

She could hear someone on the landing and quickly put everything back and pushed the case back under the bed. The bedroom door opened slowly, the bright light from the landing making her screw up her eyes.

'Are you alright? I don't want to argue with you, Tina. I love you.' Chris stood shadowed in the doorway. She sniffed and lay down flat on the bed, dragging the duvet over her body. Her voice was low.

'I'm a good person, Chris, I never hurt anybody. I just feel like a failure.'

He moved further into the room and sat on the edge of the bed, putting his hand on top of hers. 'I know, love. Come here and let me hold you. I hate seeing you upset. You've been through so much lately. Come here.' Chris pulled her towards him and looked deep into her eyes, wiping the tears away with the corner of his shirt. 'It's all going to be OK. Honest, love, we will get through this.'

Tina started to cry again. 'I'm broken. I can't explain what is happening to me. I just feel empty all the time. Will this ever pass?' Chris looked at the ceiling. It was not a conversation he wanted to get into – he was hurting too; she just never saw it.

'Shhh, baby. It will all be fine, hush now.'

Chapter Ten

F rankie looked around Ged's front room. 'It's an alright gaff that you have here, Ged, pretty smart.'

Ged plonked himself down on the sofa and flicked his shoes off as he set the Xbox up. 'My mam is a right clean freak; she hates any mess. I swear if I fart, she's there with the air freshener two seconds later.'

Frankie nearly pissed himself laughing. He stared at Ged. 'You're an OK kid, you know. Me and you are going to be good mates. What if I get my head down here tonight, will that be OK? My mam knows I often crash with mates.'

Ged nearly passed out: a sleepover? A mate staying at his house. He didn't have to think twice. 'Defo, you can top and tail with me, or kip on the floor. Like I said, my mam isn't in until late and she'll be glad that I have some company. She's always telling me to get out more.'

'Sorted then,' Frankie said, as he kicked his shoes off too and the games began. They never stopped laughing. Ged kept them fed with whatever he could find in the cupboard

– crisp butties, biscuits. Suddenly he was the hostess with the mostest.

Halfway through the evening, Frankie stretched his arms above his head and suddenly looked concerned. 'Fuck, I might have to go actually. I'd forgotten I've got some weed and that still on me and I need to stash it somewhere safe.'

Ged was torn. He didn't want to get involved in that side of things, but there was also no way he was going to lose his new friend after the laugh they had had together.

'You can store it here if you want. There's a loose floor-board under my bed, you can put it there. Nobody ever comes in my room, only my mam and she won't look down there so it will be as safe as houses.'

It was clearly exactly the answer Frankie was looking for.

'Top one, mate. Show me where it is so I can get it hidden away. I don't want your mam finding it, do I?'

As Ged stood up he looked over at Frankie. Fucking hell, he was rolling a spliff. Ged was speechless. If his mam'd walked in right now, she'd have slung Frankie out by the scruff of his neck. A spliff in her front room! She'd do her nut. And then give him the same old lecture about how only fools took drugs, they ruined lives.

'Have you ever been stoned?' Frankie asked.

Ged could have lied but the question took him by surprise. He froze. Frankie burst out laughing.

'Stop being a soft lad, everyone blazes a bit of bud. It chills you out. I'll light it up when we go to bed. I always smoke a zoot before I go to sleep, it relaxes me.'

Ged figured it would be safer to get it out of sight in his room rather than making the lounge stink of the stuff, and showed Frankie upstairs to his room. He was just helping a friend out, there was no harm in that was there?

———————

The next morning, Clare opened Ged's bedroom door and stood gawping. It was hard to make out in the winter morning gloom but it looked like there was someone else in her son's bed with him, she wasn't sure. She edged further inside the room and took a closer look. Surprise hit her like a truck, she barely managed to get back out onto the landing. She looked like she'd seen a ghost. She made it to her bedroom, where she sank to the floor. It all made sense now; the moods, the secretiveness, the aggression. Why had she not seen what was right in front of her eyes? Maybe he'd been trying in his own way to tell her, but she never had the time to listen to him – she was always so busy. She was a bad mother, she'd failed him. Clare pulled her phone out of her cardigan pocket and started typing into the Google search box. 'What to do if your son is gay'.

Was this down to her? Had she made him feel like he couldn't tell her? He'd had to find love wherever he could because, let's face it, she worked long hours and his father wasn't around. Who did he have to show him affection? Who did he have to comfort him? Clare had a single tear running down the side of her cheek, a big, fat one. Could she have loved her son more, showed she cared more? Yes, she could have. A gay son didn't bother her but his dad would disown him, she bet. He was always slagging off anyone who dared do anything a little bit different, couldn't get his head around how two blokes could love each other, he said. Sausage jockeys he called them. Clare read through the pages on her phone – she didn't know any gay men. Had no one to ask for advice. How should she act towards him now? She sat staring into space, thinking, stressed. Maybe she could phone a helpline to discuss this with them.

Ged rolled out of bed around ten o'clock. It was the weekend and he liked to have a lie-in when it wasn't a school day, but he was up earlier than usual today. Frankie was still well away, snoring his head off. Ged looked over at him and smiled. He'd got stoned for the first time and they'd talked for hours. Frankie was even going to go with him to the big house so he could see his dad. How cool was that? His dad would be buzzing to see him. He'd only ever visited once before with his mam, years ago, it scared the living daylights out of him. Screws everywhere, body searches, so many criminals under the one roof. It wasn't a nice place to be. Frankie said he'd do the journey with him, hang around while Ged saw his old man, show his mum he was old enough to see his dad by himself. He said he was going to buy some new trainers for Ged too, said he'd hook him up until he got some cash of his own. Ged had confided in him that he was on his arse and he wouldn't be able to pay the money back any time soon, but his new friend insisted – he was helping a mate out.

Ged sauntered into the front room in his boxers, bare-chested. His mam rushed in from the kitchen, scanning the room as if she was looking for somebody. She was acting strange, he noticed it straight away.

'Do you want a brew or some breakfast?'

Ged slumped onto the sofa, pulled the cushion up over his chest. 'Nah, not hungry.'

Clare sat down at the other end of the sofa, fidgeting; she couldn't keep still. What was up with her? Ged could feel her looking at him, she was doing his head in, making him paranoid. 'What's up, why do you keep staring at me?'

Clare swallowed. 'No reason,' she paused. 'Erm ... I came in your room earlier, who's that in bed with you, Son?'

Ged played it down, didn't want his mam to know how grateful he'd been to find someone to talk to, to hang out with. He picked up the control for his game and turned the TV on.

'That's Frankie, he got his head down here last night. He's a mate. He's sorted, he looks out for me.'

Clare's eyes were wide open. What was that pop group back in the eighties called? Frankie Goes To Hollywood. There you go. She studied her son as he set the game up. She had to know. 'So, where has this Frankie come from? You've never mentioned him before?'

Ged kept his eyes on the screen; he was in no mood for a full-blown interrogation. 'Fucking hell, Mam, he goes to the same school as me. I've already told you he's sound. Why, is there a problem?'

'No, stop being snappy. I just asked a simple question, that's all. No need to speak to me like that, is there? And sort your language out, how many times have I told you about swearing?'

'Wow, you always peck my head when I've just woken up. God, I had a friend stay over, it's not a big deal.'

Clare steeled herself. She needed to know if her son was into lads. She needed to ask the question. Had to go for it.

'Are you gay, Ged?' she blurted out.

Ged turned his head slowly, as if he wasn't sure what he'd just heard. 'You what?' She repeated herself and held her breath waiting for the answer with one hand held to her chest. She'd already decided she was going to be understanding, she was going to support him, she just needed to know.

Ged looked confused, then pissed off. 'What the fuck, Mam? Have you really just asked me that?'

She sat up straight and put her hands on her knees. 'Yes, well, I go into your bedroom and you've got a guy in your bed. You've never mentioned him before, so what am I supposed to think?'

Ged laughed. 'OMG, you are off your napper, you, Mother. Frankie asked if he could stop over. It was late and we were chilling on the game. I like girls so stop thinking random shit like that about me. Wow, you need to get more sleep or something. Why on earth would you ever think I like guys, tapped you are, Mother.'

Clare gasped. 'I've been out of my mind, I've even researching it online. I've been that stressed out I can tell you – I thought you were keeping secrets from me, that I didn't even know my own boy. I don't care if you're gay, I just want you to be happy – but I want you to be able to share stuff with me, love.'

Ged laughed out loud and even Clare started to see the funny side of it.

'You are on another planet, Mother. You come out with some shit sometimes you do.' It was nice to see his mother laughing, she looked so pretty when she smiled. It was a shame she didn't do it more often.

At that moment, Frankie walked into the room and nodded at Clare.

'All right? Nice to meet you. I'm Frankie.'

Clare returned the greeting while surreptitiously looking him up and down. He had that kind of confidence some kids seem to carry off. Why on earth was he bothering with her son? With the best will in the world, Ged was a geek, a gamer, a loner.

'Do you want some breakfast Frankie, or a drink?'

'Nah, I don't do breakfast. I'm going to get off soon. I've got a few things to do. Are you coming, Ged, or are you staying here?'

Ged didn't need asking twice. Dead right he was going with him. 'Yeah, I'll just get some clothes on.' He ran to get ready, which gave Clare the opportunity to grill their guest.

'Where do you live Frankie?'

'Collyhurst. Lived there all my life. It's quiet where we are. A good neighbourhood.'

Clare stuck a fag in her mouth and sparked up. 'Ged said you go to the same school as he does.' There was no point beating around the bush. 'Why was you kicked out of mainstream school, then?'

Frankie knew she was interrogating him. But he had the gift of the gab, had no problem making sure he ticked all the boxes.

'I'm not really academic. Never have been. So I never paid attention in class till I got to Second Chance. I like hands-on stuff. I've got a work placement at a garage and hopefully I should have a job at the end of it.'

Clare was impressed. She'd been worried about the types of student Ged would fall in with at Second Chance. But this kid had goals at least, maybe even a job soon. This was just what Ged needed in his life. Somebody to help him, show him the way. The interview seemed to be over. Frankie followed Ged upstairs while Clare sat smoking, looking out of the window. She dipped her hand in her purse and pulled out a fiver. She'd made some good tips last night and she was happy to be able to pass some of her good fortune over to her son when he came asking for money.

Ged rushed back into the living room clutching his trainers. This was the quickest she'd ever seen him get ready; usually he would doss around for hours. He sat down on the sofa and started to put his shoes on. Clare chucked the note over to him, happy that she had money to give for a change.

'I've got a fiver for you here, son. You can grab some food when you're out.'

Frankie stood in the doorway and smiled. 'It's my treat for food today. No need to give him any money. You save it for yourself. I'm taking Ged down the market to see if he can get some work too. I work there helping the traders, unloading and packing away, and I'm sure I can get him on. It's good money and it's only a few hours after school each day.'

Clare couldn't have been more delighted to hear this. Seemed this Frankie was a great role model for her son, just what he needed in his life right now.

'Oh, that would be great, Frankie. I've told him before to look for work but he's never off that bleeding game. You've done me a favour. I'll tell you, most days I need a crowbar to get him up off that bed. No motivation that one.'

Ged was mortified. Why did she need to be going on like that? He had to shut her up and quick.

'Mam, go and get back in bed and stop waffling. I'm looking for work so you can relax. You might even get a little treat if I get a job.'

Clare arched her eyebrows. 'I won't hold my breath. The proof is in the pudding, son, seeing is believing.'

Ged was ready to leave. Frankie gave him the nod then turned and faced Clare. 'Nice meeting you. I'll look after your boy, don't worry about him, he's in safe hands with me.' He walked towards the door, Ged right behind him as Clare shouted, 'No kiss then?'

Ged stomped back and pecked her on her cheek. *Mothers, eh?* They were so fucking embarrassing.

Frankie kept his head down low as they left the house. He was edgy, looking over his shoulder and checking everything out. 'So, what time are you going to see your old man, then?'

'The visit is two o'clock, but I have to get there at least half an hour before.'

Frankie nodded. 'I know a few kids who are in the big house too. Johnny Weston got five years shoved up his arse last month and Roy Jennings got an eight stretch. They're both in Strangeways too. You might even see them. Top lads they are too, fucking ruthless.'

Ged was intrigued. 'What did they get sent down for?'

'Drugs, they got caught, banged to rights, they were lucky with their sentences too, they could have got a lot more time. They got off lightly if you was to ask me.'

Ged walked at Frankie's side, following his lead and looking behind him every now and again. Frankie moved in closer and spoke.

'I'm going to get you started up with your own phone later on. You'll be smashing it in a few months. You might need to go out of town though. That's where the money is. You can take some gear with you and meet my team in Blackpool. They will give you some wedge to bring back too.'

Ged was confused. 'What do you mean? What about the work at the market?'

Frankie brushed his question off. 'I'll tell you properly later, but for now we're going to get you some new clobber – trainers and a trackie. You're one of my boys now and you need to look the part. You can bin them old trainers, I'm not being funny but they're shite.'

Ged nodded his head in agreement. This was music to his ears. New clothes were something he only got on birthdays and at Christmas. He wasn't turning his nose up at any free ones, no way in this world. Maybe he'd been too quick to think he couldn't run in Frankie's world. After all, he was a mate now.

Frankie was as good as his word; the two of them were in the city centre at a sports store. Frankie knew what he was looking for and led Ged to the trainers. He pointed at the rack of sport shoes. And not the ones with the sale stickers where Ged would have looked.

'Check them out, fucking mint mate, do you want a pair of them?'

Ged picked them up and clocked the price tag. One hundred and seventy pounds, surely Frankie didn't know what they cost. Ged whispered over to him. 'Have you seen how much they are?'

Frankie nodded. 'Yes, pretty cheap if you ask me.'

Ged was used to spending sixty pounds on his trainers, seventy at a push. These sneaks were something he'd only dreamed of. Frankie took the shoes from him and shouted the assistant over.

'Yo, boss, have you got any of these in a size,' he nudged Ged, 'what size are you?'

'Eight.'

Frankie continued talking to the assistant. 'A size eight, mate.'

This was really happening, Ged was getting kitted out just like Frankie had promised. They both sat down and waited for the shoes to arrive. Frankie turned to face Ged, his expression serious. 'You tell fucking no one who bought you these. This is kept on the low. Tell your mam you got a job, hide the sneaks for a few weeks and blend them in with your old ones. In fact, tell her I give them you. The last thing we need is anyone asking questions.'

Right then, Ged would have agreed with anything Frankie said as he tried the trainers on. He was buzzing.

Frankie nodded. 'So, no time like the present. After we've been to see your old man you can get the train up to Blackpool and drop some gear off. The lads will pass you some cash and your job is to get it back here to me without any bother. Easy-peasy really, isn't it?'

Ged was still focussing on the trainers. 'Yeah, sure,' he mumbled. He didn't have a clue what was going on, he was lost in the moment and admiring his new Nikes in the mirror. His dad would be impressed; he'd show him that he could fend for himself. He needed nobody to look after him anymore, he could make his own way in life now that he was going to be grafting and earning a few quid. A chip off the old block.

Fifteen minutes later, Ged carried his new gear in his bag; a black Nike tracksuit as well as the trainers, even some new socks and boxers. He felt like a million dollars. His confidence was sky high – for the first time in his life he felt like a somebody. He no longer wanted to be invisible, he wanted to stand out from the crowd and let people know that he existed. He had a voice now, and people would listen and take notice of him. He was one of Frankie's boys now. One of the crew.

———

As Ged sat waiting for his name to be called in the prison visitor centre, some of the morning's confidence began to wear thin and the nerves kicked in a bit. He was jumpy, on edge.

'Ged Grey…'

At last it was time to go over to the main jail along with the rest of the visitors. Bleeding hell, there were some sights here today. The women were dolled up to the nines, short skirts, caked in makeup, stinking of perfume. They looked more like they were on a night out. Ged walked over towards the main building with caution.

There were a couple of men in front of him, he'd seen them while they were hanging about outside. Frankie had elbowed him, 'Couple of junkies them two. I bet they are doing a drop.'

Ged didn't have a clue what he was talking about.

Frankie realised that he would have to explain what he meant – the kid was so wet behind the ears, it was untrue, he seemed to know nothing about the real world and how things worked. 'They'll be bringing drugs into the jail. Usually the inmates pay someone to bring some shit in. These crackheads don't give a toss about their freedom and they are willing enough to get slammed in jail for a few ton. Honest, you mark my words, keep an eye on them.'

Ged steered clear as he entered the main jail. There was an eerie silence as the visitors got searched. Shoes off, belts off, watches off. Fuck me, he thought, what a palaver. You would have thought the visitors were the criminals here today. Ged showed his ID, went through the metal detector, looking flustered as he came eye to eye with one of the screws. The officer had disposable gloves on, and asked Ged to stand on a wooden box so he could search him. He never spoke a word as he felt up and down Ged's body; you could see he was on a mission and he was going to let nothing get past him today.

'It stinks in this place,' one of the women said loudly. The visitors had gathered in another room. There was just one last search by the dog and then they would be free to see their loved ones. Ged could hear it barking in the distance. He loved animals, was intrigued how they could be trained to smell drugs on a person, couldn't get his head round it.

'Aww, it's a springer spaniel. I love them dogs. Look at how giddy it is, I defo want one of them when I get my own gaff.' It was the loud woman again.

'Nah, fuck that, you need a pit bull or a staffy; spaniels are for pussies,' the bloke next to her replied.

Ged kept quiet. He liked spaniels best of all. His nana had had one when he was a kid. They were loyal, easy to train. He knew what Frankie would say though, he'd said it when they passed a dog earlier. 'Pit bulls every time – keep you safe. If someone's trying to boom your front door down, you want an animal who will rip the fuck out of them, don't you?'

Ged had never thought about stuff like that. He could see Frankie's point, but who would ever be kicking his front door down?

As Ged walked into the visitors' room he looked up and down for his dad. He could see a man waving his hand up in the air at the back of the room – his old man. He swallowed hard trying not to cry. Bloody hell, his pops looked rough. A big bushy ginger beard, and hair stuck up all over the show.

His dad was on his feet now, couldn't wait to hold his son. It had been too long since he'd seen his boy. You could see the pain in Kevin's eyes as he gripped Ged tight; he was emotional, a lump in his throat.

Ged wriggled free. 'Come on, Dad, you never used to be like this, stop embarrassing me. Sort it out.'

Kevin ruffled his son's hair and sat back down. He was happy now, never took his eyes off Ged. 'You look the business, mate, you're really filling out. You've gone taller too. I'll have to watch myself now, you'll be knocking me out if I give you any shit, won't you?' Ged threw his head back and laughed out loud. His dad was proud of him and that was all he wanted.

Ged was excited to tell his dad about his new best friend. 'His name's Frankie. He goes to my school and we watch out for each other. He's a top lad and you should see him on FIFA, he's mint.'

'Good lad, keep him onside, make sure he don't let any pricks fuck with my boy. I worry about you all the time. The world is getting worse every day that passes – you need to be able to look after yourself. I'll be home soon and then I can do the job myself, but it's good to have a mate who's got your back. Tell me about school. Been in any trouble?' Ged felt his cheeks redden. He didn't say anything. Kevin chuckled. 'Take after your old dad, do you? I used to go from zero to sixty in seconds, but I've had some anger management sessions in here so hopefully I can control my shit when I get rattled in the future.' He changed the subject quickly; he hated talking about his mental health. 'How's your mam, is she still saying she hates me or what?'

'Dad, you know what she's like, one minute she hates you but then she's telling me stories about you. Just give her time and she'll come round. You two need to sort your shit out together, it's not up to me to do it.'

'What I need to know is, do you think she'll let me move back in?'

Ged laughed. 'Bit of a big ask, Dad, but let's see.'

Kevin looked around the room. His voice was soft and his eyes filled up as he reached over and touched Ged's hands. 'I've had enough of jail, son. I'm getting too old for all this shit now. I want to go straight and settle down and get a job. You have so much time on your hands in this shit-hole to think about stuff. You can put the world to rights when you're behind your door each day, let me tell you. You can see everything that matters, I mean really matters.'

His dad was speaking to him man to man now, Ged appreciated that; he was growing up and it was about time everybody stopped treating him like a kid. Before he knew it, the screw shouted that visiting time was over. This was the hardest part of seeing his dad; it was a struggle to leave his old man behind.

Kevin reached over and gripped his son in a bear hug. 'Mate, I'll be home before you know it and then me and you can make everything work together. You've missed out on so much because of me and all that I can say is that I'll make it up to you. My hand on my heart, son. I'll do right by you and your mother from the minute I get home. You just watch. I'll make everything right.'

Ged choked up. This was not the time or place to break down. He was a big boy now and he held back the tears. His words were sincere and from the heart. 'Dad, just keep your head down and get home. Don't be getting in any bother in here and getting time added to your sentence. I want you home now. I want us to be a family again.'

The screw was beside them now and he shot a look over at Kevin. 'Visit over,' he spat. Kevin eyeballed him, his nostrils flaring. This guy was known throughout the whole nick as a hard-nut and very few prisoners dared to mess with him. Kevin squeezed his son one last time and they said their final goodbyes. As he walked out, Ged didn't look back once.

Chapter Eleven

Nancy stared out of her bedroom window, a single finger pressed against the cold glass drawing shapes. It was raining outside, dark clouds hanging in the sky. Not really the weather to be going out in. The pale flesh of her arm showed scars old and new. Deep white lines engraved on her skin. Nancy held a small metal nail, dragging it deep into the inside of her forearm, pain in her eyes as the small sharp point pierced her skin. Bright red blood dripped from the new cuts, dribbling down her arm. Nancy had been self-harming for a few years now, and she couldn't explain to anyone why she did it. She just did. Maybe she was unhappy with her life, maybe it was a cry for help. She didn't know anymore. She paused, could hear someone coming up the stairs. She yanked her jumper down over her arms and threw the nail under the bed. Nobody could see this, nobody would understand. She was good at hiding things, very good indeed. The bedroom door creaked open and her uncle stood there, just looking at her. He was a shady one, that was for sure. Her Uncle John had lived with her family since she could remember, but that didn't mean she had to like it.

'What do you want? Get out of my room!' John was a mess, as ever, he could have done with a good scrub. His shoulder-length hair was greasy, his skin had a greyish sheen.

'No need for the attitude, gobshite. Your mam asked me to check you were OK. Just doing her a favour really. I couldn't give a shit if you was alive or dead, to tell the truth.'

Nancy could give as good as she got. 'Well I am alright so close the door and leave me alone. Go on, fuck off instead of standing there gawping.'

When Nancy was in a mood like this she had a foul mouth on her. But in truth, she was all over the place. Was it any wonder that she'd just walk out of the house and go on the missing list for days? She'd never been able to really explain why. She said it was just the way she was. She'd been to see enough specialists about her mental health problems, but none of them would put a label on her. Maybe she was bipolar, ADHD? Consultants and counsellors had suggested all sorts, but would giving the way she felt a name actually help? Or maybe one day they'd go with her suggestion: she was like she was, just because her life was shit.

John ignored her invitation to fuck off and instead edged closer, keeping his voice low. He was a creepy bastard and he stank of stale tobacco. Her stomach turned as he came towards her. He gripped the side of her face, squeezing her cheeks so hard the skin turned white. 'Listen up, you cheeky cow, carry on talking to me like that and you'll get a good arse kicking. I don't know who you think you are...'

Nancy knew when she was beaten. Her expression changed, resignation clouding her eyes. 'Do whatever you want to me, do I look bothered? You can't hurt me anymore. How many times have I told you that you mean nothing to me, you're not my family, you're just a prick.'

John was nose to nose with her now, his stale breath hot against her face. She looked away but he turned her back to face him. Slowly he pressed his dry, cracked lips to hers, shoved his tongue into her mouth. Nancy tried to pull away then, but he yanked her back by the hair. He checked the door to make sure they were alone as he whispered, 'I'll be back to see you tonight, we can have some fun, you like that don't you?'

Nancy didn't dare flinch, though hate filled her eyes and the hairs on the back of her neck stood on end. Slowly, he backed off and left the room. She could hear him laughing under his breath. She lay on her bed for a few minutes, gripping the duvet, squeezing it between her fists. Her eyes prickled with tears and, one by one, they slid slowly down her cheeks. Why had she never been able to tell anyone what was going on? Maybe if she had it could have been stopped. Her uncle would have been banged up and slammed in the nonce wing in the big house. Maybe then people would have understood. But the words would never come.

Nancy got up and put on an extra-thick woollen jumper. She didn't know where she was going to go, but wherever it was, she wanted to make sure she'd be warm enough. She walked around her bedroom picking things up and shoving them in her pockets. It was time to go again.

Nancy sat on the concourse at Piccadilly station; noises, talking, people rushing all around her. But she just sat there on a bench, looking around at the passers-by as they headed who knows where. Maybe she would dress like these women one day, smart and professional. But right now, no one gave her a second glance, a fifteen-year-old girl, huddled over her phone like any other teenager.

She often came here, sat for hours just watching people go by. Somehow the station made her feel like she was going places even without moving an inch. This was her safe place, where nobody could touch or hurt her. Nobody ever questioned her either, she kept herself to herself and bothered no one. Nancy sat crunching her way through a packet of crisps; she'd robbed twenty pounds from her mam's purse. She was always dipping her when she was skint; she knew it was wrong but never cared enough to stop.

Suddenly she sat up straight and brushed her hair out of her eyes. Was she seeing things or what? She pulled her hood up, looked closer. It was him, she wasn't imagining it. What on earth was Ged doing here? Nancy stood up and slowly made her way down the platform, ducking and diving behind people and luggage so he didn't see her – she wasn't sure yet if she wanted him to. Nancy had often jibbed on the trains, it was easy; she just kept her head down and walked through the turnstile and nobody ever seemed to notice. If she got caught, she would just lie and make up a story about falling out with her boyfriend, they would never charge or fine her when she worked her magic on them and gave them her sob story. She could cry at the drop of a hat, a performance that any leading lady would be proud of. Give her an Oscar.

Ged looked like he was out of his comfort zone, you could tell he didn't really know what he was doing. He was like a fish out of water, looking around, his head twisting one way then another so fast it was a wonder he didn't fall over. He kept checking the ticket in his hands over and over. Nancy watched him board the train and quickly jumped on after him, making sure he still didn't clock her.

Ged shoved the ticket in his pocket and sat down. He pulled his hood up and dropped his head against the window. How hard could it be? Just a quick train journey out of town that's all, nothing to worry about. Frankie was his mate, would never put him at risk, would he? Easy money he'd said. Frankie had made it sound like he'd come too but Ged sat here now feeling just as alone as ever.

Nancy sat as close as she dared, watching Ged through the gap in the seats as the train moved off. His mobile started to ring; she could see the panic in his eyes as he fumbled in his pocket trying to find it. She could hear every word: 'Yeah, I'm on the train now, tell them to meet me at the other end,' he said. The call went on for a few minutes. He looked nervous, couldn't keep still, fidgeting.

Half an hour later and he'd still never looked up. Nancy was bored. She stuck her head between the seats; she'd had enough of being by herself and she knew him, so why wouldn't she say hello? She stood up and made her way down the carriage.

'Where you off to then?'

Ged nearly choked as he spotted her. 'Fucking hell, Nancy, what are you doing here?'

She sat down next to him.

'I always take myself off to different places when I'm bored. It's just something I do. I go all over.'

Ged had gone pale and he checked around to make sure no one was watching them.

Nancy asked him again. 'So, where you off to?'

He swallowed hard and she could tell by his body language that he was up to no good.

'I've just got to take some stuff to someone. I'm coming back later tonight. It's just a favour for a mate.'

Nancy looked him right in the eye; did he think she was green or what? She knew what was what – he needed to stop trying to pull the wool over her eyes. She was way more intelligent than he was giving her credit for.

'Ged, stop talking out of your arse. I'm not daft you know. If you don't want to tell me then that's fine, but don't lie to me.'

Ged cracked his knuckles, looked around again to make sure nobody could hear them. He wasn't going to admit he was shitting himself and seeing her made him feel a bit better. And could she be trusted? He reckoned she probably could. He kept his voice low. 'If you have to know, I'm dropping some stuff off for Frankie. He's been great with me and sorted me out with some new gear and that so it's the least I can do to pay him back, isn't it?'

'Stuff like what?'

'Just a few parcels,' he whispered.

The penny dropped. 'So you mean drugs?'

Ged's eyes opened wide as he nodded slowly. 'Yeah, fucking hell, keep your voice down will you?'

Nancy was way more streetwise than her new mate and knew more about this stuff than she'd ever let on. It was crystal clear what Ged was up to. County lines. Surely he wasn't that thick that he didn't know how this was going to end up? Nancy's brother Graham had been done for the same thing a few years back and he was still in jail serving the rest of his six-year stretch for his part in the whole thing. This was a fool's game. The top men got richer and richer and the pricks at the bottom end of the ladder got slammed in jail with not a penny.

Nancy had idolised her older brother and since he'd been in jail nothing had been the same. John would never have dared lay a finger on her when Graham was about. If he knew what was going on now, he'd have knocked ten bags of shit out of him given half a chance. She'd been so close to telling him the last time she visited, but as usual the words just wouldn't come out. And what could he do when he was locked up in jail, anyway? Nothing. The time would come though, and the tide would turn. It was just a matter of time before John got what was coming to him.

Nancy started to tell Ged about her brother, explain exactly what it was that he was getting himself into, but he just brushed it off.

No way was he having this girl telling him what to do. He was one of the boys now, he could do whatever he wanted. Ged wished she'd just bugger off, he was not in the mood for her chatter. But Nancy wasn't giving up.

'So, can I come with you once you've done what you are doing? We can go into Blackpool and have a bit of fun if you want?'

Ged hadn't left Manchester in years. The last time he'd been to Blackpool was with school when he was ten. He would love to go to the Pleasure Beach, ride the roller coasters and eat candy floss. Carried away with the memories of being a kid, he softened.

'Yeah, alright. But keep this to yourself, you tell nobody what I'm doing, do you hear me, fucking nobody.' Ged didn't get Frankie's operation, but he knew enough to understand that if this went tits up, he'd be in deep shit.

Nancy, on the other hand, was happier than she'd been in ages. Something interesting was happening in her life for a change. Usually she'd just walk about on her own for hours, speaking to nobody. Now the pact was made, and she crossed her heart and hoped to die if she broke his trust.

'I won't say anything to anyone. I promise. I'm just glad we get to hang out.'

Ged couldn't help grinning, this girl was off her napper, but he liked her, something about her just made him feel better. He looked out of the window and watched the landscape speeding by. They'd be in Blackpool soon and then he could get rid of the gear and start to relax. He'd tell Frankie when he got back that this was a one-off.

Nancy sat eating her way through a Mars bar; she broke a piece off and passed it over to Ged with a smile. The rich, creamy caramel oozed from the chocolate and she thrust it at him.

As they left the station, Ged kept his head down. Frankie had told him to use his eyes, make sure nobody was following him. There were some shady bastards hanging around train stations this time of day. Tramps, drug addicts, prostitutes, traffickers, you never knew who was hiding away in the dark shadows. And then there was the undercover dibble. Fuck, fuck, fuck.

Nancy was at Ged's side taking it all in her stride. She'd been up here lots of times and seemed to know the place like the back of her hand. As they walked away from the station Ged stayed alert, constantly looking left and right. Frankie had said there would be a white car waiting when he got there, but he couldn't see one anywhere. This wasn't good – maybe they'd been arrested and the police were now sat waiting for him to make his move. His heart was beating rapidly and he had started to sweat. Nancy just wanted him to deliver the parcel as soon as possible so they could go and have some fun. But if she was going to help, she needed some details: who, what and where.

'Who is your man at this end?'

'Mathew, he's called. Frankie said he would pick me up from here. Maybe he's spotted you with me and thinks it's on top.' He scratched his head and kept walking up and down.

'Tell you what. You wait here and I'll have a walk about and see what I can see. I'll come back for you once it's sorted.'

Nancy wasn't up for being left on her tod. 'How long are you going to be? Don't leave me here on my lonesome. I don't see why I can't come with you anyway. It's not like I don't know what's going on.'

Ged was insistent. 'Wow, I'm stressed as it is, don't you be adding to it too. For fuck's sake, just chill here for a bit. And stop being annoying.'

'Just saying,' she whispered under her breath.

She spotted a bus shelter and started to walk over towards it. 'I'll be here waiting, don't be long.' But Ged wasn't listening – all he wanted to do now was get rid of the gear. He headed up to the end of the street and crossed the road, his head low and his hands deep in his pockets. He'd only been walking a couple of minutes when he heard a car engine roaring behind him. His heart was in his mouth. Now what? He wished he'd never come. The car slowed down alongside him.

'Oi, Ged, right?'

Ged nodded and walked over to the driver's side window. 'Yeah, Frankie said you'd be waiting for me. Mathew, yeah?'

Mathew was a big strapping lad, around eighteen years old. He looked hard as nails. He checked Ged out from top to toe. Ged could smell weed coming from inside the car – the guy in the passenger seat was blazing a zoot as he looked over at him.

'Get in then, I'll take you to the gaff where you'll be staying tonight.'

Ged looked puzzled.

'No, I'm just delivering this and taking some money back. No one has mentioned me staying over.'

'Change of plan. The money won't be in until late, so you're not travelling back tonight. Frankie knows the score.'

Ged swallowed hard. His mam would go sick if she knew he wasn't at home. What on earth could he tell her? And then there was Nancy. He just couldn't leave her, he had to come clean.

'I'll have to go back up the street, my girlfriend has come down here with me so I don't look suspicious, so she'll have to stay with me too. I can't just leave her, can I?'

Mathew shook his head and drummed his fingers against the steering wheel.

'For fuck's sake are you some kind of baby or what? I'm not running a fucking nursery here,' he let out a laboured breath. 'In future leave her at home. This is no place for any girl, surely you know that?'

Ged acted cool; he chewed slightly on the side of his lip. 'Yeah, it's a one-off. And, like I said, nobody told me the plan was to get my head down up here.' He opened the car door and climbed in. The smoke was thick in here, stinging his eyes. He coughed and pulled his coat up over his nose, then sat forward in his seat and pointed in the direction he wanted them to go. The tunes were turned up, bass pumping as they drove along the road. Surely these idiots should have been keeping a low profile, not bringing attention to themselves? *Knobs*, he thought. Acting the big men, but they were just jumped up kids.

Ged walked into the terraced house cautiously. It stank of wet dog. The wallpaper was hanging off the walls and the paintwork was yellow. Mathew had gone in ahead of him and now stood talking to another man in the dark hallway. 'Ged's here for the night, make sure you look after him and his girl. I don't want to hear you've been trying to have his eyes out, because you know what will happen, don't you?'

The guy seemed to be propping himself up against the wall with his hand. He was skin and bones, so thin that if a gust of wind come along it would have swept him away. His voice rasped. 'As if, I'll look after him like one of my own. I wouldn't mess with you lot, you know that. You just keep me sweet like we agreed, and it'll all be good.'

'Squeaky, I always look after you, remember that.'

Squeaky chuckled, showing off his stumpy teeth. Ged shuddered; the guy was rancid. He reeked. Nancy, as ever, not shy at coming forward, decided to make herself at home. She went straight into the front room and threw herself down on the sofa, taking in her surroundings. It was clear this wasn't going to be the cleanest place she'd ever stayed, but it was better than sleeping on the streets like she'd done before. The sofa arms were ripped and stained, overflowing ashtrays littered every surface, and the dark brown curtains hung precariously from a piece of string across the bay window. Ged sat down next to her and whispered under his breath. 'Fucking stinks in here.'

Mathew just nodded across at Ged.

'Right, I'll be back later. Here's the phone. Make sure you answer it and tell them where to go. Don't fucking fall asleep either, because if the phone's not being answered then none of us are earning any money.'

Ged caught the phone in his hand; he was about to say something but thought better of it. This was a piss-take. It was not what he signed up for.

Squeaky followed Mathew back into the hallway and let him out. Once the front door slammed shut, he came back into the room and sat down to make a roll-up. His fingers were yellow at the end – you could tell just by looking that the guy was rotten inside and out. Ged watched him like a hawk as he slid his tongue along the edge of the Rizla.

'You know how all this works, don't you?'

Ged was on the spot. He didn't have a clue – but he didn't want to show it, wasn't going to let this clown, this tramp, call the shots.

'Yeah, so don't be trying to have me over or I'll cut you up.'

Nancy's eyes couldn't have been wider; this wasn't the Ged she'd seen so far, the gawky, nervous kid who couldn't have been less streetwise if he'd tried. Where had that come from? She decided to add her two penn'orth while she could.

'It's not just him you should be scared of, mate, any shit and the crew will be up from Manchester, trust me, you don't want them down because they'll mess you up proper. Twisted they are, fucking nutters.'

Squeaky wiped his mouth with the side of his hand and sucked hard on his fag. 'I'll get this lot bagged up then. That phone will be on fire soon and we need to make sure we're ready. I'll give Dino a bell and tell him to get his arse here ready for work.'

Ged sat watching as Squeaky took the drugs from the package and started to weigh them out into small bags. It was the first time Ged had seen exactly what he'd been carrying up from Manchester. Fuck's sake. That wasn't weed. It was smack, fucking heroin. Class A stuff. Ged's jitters turned into full-blown panic. Nancy didn't seem bothered in the slightest. She kicked her shoes off. This was a great adventure for her, way better than hanging out on her own at Piccadilly station. She'd ring home though and say she was staying at a friend's, all she needed was her mam ringing the rozzers reporting her missing.

The mobile Mathew had given Ged started to ring.

'Go on then,' Squeaky said.

Ged fumbled about with the buttons to answer the call. He had no idea how this worked; he'd have to play it by ear. Squeaky was getting impatient.

'Mate, answer the fucking call. We're losing money if you don't.'

'Hello,' Ged's voice was barely audible. There was a silence. It was clear he had been bluffing. Squeaky walked over and grabbed the phone from Ged's hand.

'Yo, mate, what d'you want?' Ged could hear the voice at the other end of the phone though not what it was saying. Squeaky listened for a moment before replying.

'Right, be at the bridge in ten. And make sure you're on time because our guy won't wait about there for long. There's been a few old bill knocking around there lately so make sure you're on the ball.'

The call ended and Squeaky chucked the phone back at Ged. 'So, it's the first time you've managed the line then?'

Ged had no idea how to reply. It was clear he'd already lied and he didn't reckon he'd get away with it again. Nancy could see he was on the spot and answered for him.

'He doesn't usually do the phones, he's more on the transport end of things, but he's doing the phone tonight as a favour. You just fill him in on how things work and he'll take it from there, he's a quick learner.' Nancy nudged Ged and looked at him encouragingly. 'That's right, isn't it, Ged?'

He nodded, finding his tongue. 'Yeah, that's right. Just give me the lowdown and I'll be sorted.'

Squeaky laughed out loud and shook his head. 'For fuck's sake, I should get a raise for all the fucking training I do.

You're not the first one they've sent me who doesn't know the script.'

Ged's cheeks were flaming, the beetroot red clashing with his hair. 'Just cut the shit and tell me what to say,' he snapped. 'You only need to tell me once then I'll be fine. Is that alright with you or should I ring Mathew and tell him you're giving me shit?' Smart move. Squeaky relented, cracking his knuckles and tried to backpedal.

'Nah, nah, I'm just saying is all. You just don't know my sense of humour yet. It's all good, our kid. So, when they ring, just ask what they want. It's usually white or brown they ask for. All you need to do is tell them to go to the bridge, they know where it is, and then fuck them off. Don't let them keep you on the phone either. And no cash, no drugs, simple. A few of them try and get tick and promise you the world in return but give them fuck all, just tell them that's the rules and that usually shuts them up. Oh yeah – don't use your name, change it, don't want nobody knowing who you are.'

It was a lot to take in, seemed like it was a big operation. The phone started to ring again. This time Nancy took the call.

'What d'you want?' she asked in a confident voice. 'Yep, go to the bridge and they'll be with you shortly.' She ended the call and smiled over at Ged.

'Induction over, you're ready to go. Squeaky, three brown. Get your lad ready to go.'

Ged was sweating, his hands were clammy. Squeaky was on the blower giving his orders to the foot soldiers and he could see it was going to be a very long night indeed.

Chapter Twelve

It was a Monday morning and Donny was in early as usual. He sat in his office sipping at his coffee, the hot steam rising from the mug. Rita was in early too and didn't seem her usual self. Today she was all smiles and laughter, rather than her standard mardy mood. Donny studied her and grinned.

'Rita, have you come to tell me you've met a new man or something, because there's definitely something going on. Come on, spill.'

Rita turned to face him and shrugged. 'I wish, look at me, who'd have this?'

Donny rolled his eyes as if he was humouring her, but couldn't help thinking she wasn't far off the truth, not that he'd ever tell her that. Anyway, sometimes it was nice to make people feel good about themselves.

'You're a great catch, Rita. If I wasn't a married man, I'd be all over you like a rash. On my life, you're a prize that any man would be proud to have on his arm.'

Donny was so smooth he was even impressing himself. She flicked her hair over her shoulder and smiled. 'Do you really think so, Donny? I've kind of given up on ever finding a man at my age. I just seem to scare them off.'

Donny looked at her, pressing his lips firmly together to keep the truth sealed firmly in his mouth. She was no oil painting, there was no getting away from it. But he kept the platitudes coming; he hated seeing anyone down in the dumps. 'There's someone out there for everyone, Rita. What do they say? A lid for every pot? It's just a matter of time before Mr Right comes along and sweeps you off your feet. And what a lucky man he'll be.'

Rita looked like the cat that had got the cream. She pushed her chest out.

Yeah, and maybe start with a decent bra, thought Donny. He said nothing as she yanked her leggings up higher to cover her midriff.

'Stop it, Donny, stop giving me hope,' she said, but she was smiling.

Tina walked in, looking surprised to see Rita in at this time of the morning and not looking miserable either. She checked her watch. 'Bleeding hell, Rita, what's got into you?' To be fair, turning up before her shift had started was not something Rita was known for.

Donny rocked back on his chair and looped his hands behind his head. 'She was here before me this morning, Tina, she'd opened the main gates up and everything. And then she's in here all smiles, handing me a hot cup of coffee. Not that you'll hear me complaining. Feel free to come in early every morning if you're going to do that, Reet.'

Tina took her coat off and sat down heavily. 'I swear to you, Nevaya is doing my head in. The last couple of weeks she's worse than ever. You should have heard her this morning, talking to me as if I was a piece of shit on her shoe.' She'd never been good at holding things back. 'I've told her again to go and live with her mam, hopefully she'll take my advice and piss off there before I get home. Chris is a bloody waste of time; he lets her get away with it time after time. I can't anymore. I just want to punch her lights out and I'm not even a violent person. She's pushing me over the edge, let me tell you.'

Donny sighed, there was always something going on with Tina. Nothing was ever plain sailing in her life.

Rita headed for the door. She had enough problems of her own, couldn't be doing with anyone else's.

'Tina, do you want a nice hot cuppa? You sit down there, and I'll do you a few bits of toast and something to drink. Maybe that'll help.'

Tina sighed. 'I need more than a bloody cup of tea to sort me out, love. A couple of diazepam and a stiff brandy more like it. But, aye, thanks, Rita. A cup of coffee'd be a start.'

When he was sure Rita was out of earshot, Donny turned to Tina. 'Something strange going on with that one. Keep a close eye on her, Tina, she's up to something. She's never nice to anyone without wanting something in return.'

Tina agreed. 'Yeah, she's never ever offered me a drink in all the time I've known her. Maybe she's had a win on those scratchcards she's always doing.'

Tina switched her computer on and scanned through her emails. 'We've got a meeting with Ged's mother, says he's been acting up. She seems quite concerned about him. His dad's due out of jail soon too and she reckons the shit is going to hit the fan when she tells Ged that she doesn't want him home. Maybe that's what all this is about. It's his dad at the end of the day. No surprise that he's kicking off.'

Donny shook his head. 'This job is more than just being a teacher, Tina, you know that as well as I do. Parents come to us for support both in the education of their kids and their home life. That's what makes this school different, we care about the students' whole lives – not just the hours they're with us. And that's why we do things differently too, you know that. Look at what happened a few weeks back, when I had to go round to Jacko's house and take his PlayStation out of his room. After he smashed the school TV up I told him that I would take something of his until he could get it fixed so I had to follow through on it. His mam was right behind me too. Jacko lost it big time when he realised that I'd actually done it, been round his house and taken it.'

Tina laughed. 'You're something else you are, Donny. And the kids rate you, even if you are a right bastard sometimes. You'll have to give me a few tips to help me deal with them kids I've got at home before I swing for them, though. I can cope with anything this lot do in school, but not when it's under my own roof.'

'A good kick up the arse is what they need. I told you months ago to stop pussyfooting around them and tell them straight, didn't I?'

'I'm not like you though, Donny. You're a hothead. You'll just go for it when it kicks off. It's not in my nature to shout and scream. You should have heard me the other night though – I was like a woman possessed.'

'Works for me. I treat the kids here like they're my own and if they're acting like little bleeders then they'll get told. Anyway, what else do we have on today?'

Tina looked at her screen again. 'A couple of other meetings too and the new kid coming in for a look around.'

Donny reached into his drawer and grabbed his fags.

'Right, I'm going to get a cig before the mob starts to arrive. If you need me, I'll be outside.' As he walked towards the door, Donny's mobile started to ring. He didn't recognise the number, left it to ring; whoever it was he wasn't in the mood right now.

In the kitchen, Rita sat at the table with her head in her hands, a letter at her side. The smiles from earlier had vanished. The door opened and one of the students walked in, made her jump. She quickly wiped her eyes and sat up straight.

Amelia studied Rita and started to take her coat off. She wasn't much of a talker and it was clear she didn't know quite what to say. Rita stood up quickly and walked to the kitchen side, took a deep breath. 'Amelia, do you want any breakfast? Toast, or cereal?'

The girl shook her head, she hated eating in front of people and she would rather starve than sit eating in front of a member of staff. A lot of kids were like that. *Funny fuckers they were*, thought Rita.

Amelia sat down at the table and stared at her fingers. Rita thought it was best to leave her to say whatever it was she wanted to say in her own time. She went back to pottering about the kitchen, slamming cupboards shut and banging pans. Seemed a nice enough kid, she just didn't fit in anywhere, or that's what she'd told the school. She was pretty too, long dark hair past her waist, big green eyes, clean, fresh skin. She was certainly popular with the lads here in school – word on the street was that she wasn't scared of putting it about, especially when she was drunk or off her head at the weekend. It was funny really, to adults she seemed shy, lacking in confidence, but to her peers, she was loud and daring. You picked up a lot about these kids watching them in the lunch queue.

Rita stopped for a moment and gazed out of the window, the troops would be here soon, she needed to get her head in gear and be ready for them. She glanced over at Amelia, who looked like the colour had suddenly drained from her cheeks. She noticed her waft her hand in front of her face, like she'd been overcome with a wave of heat. Sweat prickled on her forehead as she stood up and wobbled, had to hold the table to steady herself. Rita was right there, helping her back into the chair.

'Are you alright there? You look like you're going to spew your ring up.'

Amelia loosened her black cardigan and pulled her T-shirt up over her nose, exhaled slowly. 'I'm fine, just leave me alone, will you?'

Rita had plenty to do, wasn't going to waste her time if this was the thanks she got. 'Suit yourself, you try and be nice in this place and all you get is abuse. Stay there on your own then, see if I care.'

Amelia stood up and walked unsteadily out of the kitchen, heading for the toilets. As soon as she reached the cubicle she slammed the door shut and fell to her knees. She held her head over the toilet and a rush of stinking green bile sprayed into the bowl. She was burning up, sweat pouring from her. She rested her head on her arms for a moment, before another torrent gushed from her mouth.

The minibus pulled up in the car park and, as per usual, the students were loud; so much noise. Robert Sinclair had just parked up and was eager to get inside before getting caught up in the rabble. Chelsea spotted him getting out of his car. Too late – the pupils were off the bus.

'Sir, your car's a piece of shit, how can you drive around in it? It's like a pensioner car. There's no way I would be seen driving about in that old banger.'

Sinclair sighed, a few minutes earlier and he would have avoided all this. But there was no way Chelsea was going to get away with embarrassing him in front of everyone.

'Right, Chelsea, what do you drive?' She walked over to his car and kicked his tyre.

'I don't drive, sir, I'm a kid, durrrrr.'

'Exactly. You don't even have a car, so when you do have one then you'll understand how much they cost to run. It gets me to work and that is all that matters.'

Chelsea was unruffled, the rest of the students in her

thrall as usual. 'Oi, you lot, get a look at sir's motor. Tell him it's a rust bucket. I would rather walk than drive about in that shed. Sort it out and get something decent. I mean, look at the way you dress, you've not got nothing going for you, sir.'

The students were sniggering as they started to walk into the building. Sinclair shook his head. Best to ignore her, to walk away before he said something he would regret. He looked down at his old tan shoes and his black trousers. Maybe she had a point, he could do with a shopping trip to revamp his wardrobe. Damn you, Chelsea. He was annoyed he'd let her get to him. It wasn't like she had anything much going for her. She wasn't academic and he'd have put good money on her landing herself in jail when she was older. He knew they were meant to find the good in every student, but on days like this, he had no time for her, none whatsoever.

The students gathered in the main hall as they did at the start of every school day. As the kids found their seats, Donny answered a call from Susan.

'Hi babe, morning assembly in a minute, I'll bell you later.' There was clearly something up – he could tell just by a few words. He ended the conversation quickly, before he got drawn into an argument, and strode into the room.

Donny stood at the front; he didn't look like he was in a good mood but he made sure his presence was felt in the room. The teachers stood against the wall, waiting to take the students off to their various lessons. Tina was in the corner of the room texting – Donny glared at her, and she quickly shoved her mobile back in her pocket. The rules were there for the students and staff too. No mobile phones to be used throughout lessons or in morning assembly. He watched as she edged out of the room and headed for the toilets.

Donny welcomed his charges like he did every morning. Working in a school like Second Chance meant the place was small enough to know each pupil properly – and each teacher. Melanie stood to his left and he could feel her eyes on him. He blushed slightly as he caught her gaze. 'Good morning, everybody.' There was no reply. Donny raised his voice higher and repeated himself. 'I said, good morning everybody, can nobody hear me or what?'

Chelsea was first to respond. 'Good morning, sir, why are you shouting? Take a chill pill. Don't take your moods out on us.' She had an answer for everything, could never stay quiet. At least Donny had their attention now.

'Guys, some of you have lost your breaks today. I'll read your names out at the end of assembly. It's your own fault, if you go on the system for your behaviour, you know the consequences, so deal with it.'

A few of the kids were complaining all the same. One girl, Annie Watson, folded her arms in front of her and made sure everyone could hear her.

'I hope I'm not on the list?' She shot a look over at Melanie and gritted her teeth together. 'That silly bitch over there probably put my name forward, she's got it in for me. Her lessons are boring, and, just because I told her I wasn't doing any of her shit lessons she got all arsey.'

Donny cut her short; this kind of talk was not acceptable. 'Annie, rein it in. In fact, go up to my office and wait for me there. I don't know who you think you're talking to. Miss

Peters is a member of staff and I won't have you speaking to her like that. Do you talk to your mother like that?'

Annie stood up and her cheeks were red with angry defiance.

'My mam gets told too; you can say what you want to me. I'm not arsed, her lessons are still shit.'

Donny blasted his voice over at her. 'My office, now!'

Chelsea turned to Nancy and smirked. 'You tell her, sir,' she piped up. 'No respect, that's her problem and that's why she'll end up getting a slap from me if she carries on with her attitude.'

Donny snapped. 'Shut up, Chelsea. Stop making it worse for her.'

Annie stood with her hand placed firmly on her hip. 'Sir, she's just a daft slag who I don't listen to. She's just a sperm bank. Ask any of the lads, they'll tell you.'

Chelsea bolted up from her seat and ran at Annie. She was screaming at the top of her voice, ready to knock ten bells out of the girl.

'We'll see who's a slag when I knock you out. Just you wait until after school when these knobs are not here stopping me. I'll rip your fucking head off.'

This was not a good start to the morning. The staff were all over Annie and Chelsea and separated them quickly.

'Mr Sinclair, take Annie to my office and stay with her until I get there.' Donny kept Chelsea by his side. 'Teachers, please take your students up to lessons. I'll come and see them all soon.'

As the crowd dispersed, Chelsea was still fuming, pacing up and down and not shutting up. 'I swear to you now that bitch is getting wasted. Who does she think she's talking to?'

Donny blocked the door by standing in front of it. 'You're going nowhere. You'll be in isolation now all day until I've sorted this out. You can't just threaten people, you know that as well as anyone.'

'Sir, don't you dare try and blame me for this. That slapper started it, you heard her, she's the one who's got attitude.'

'Yes, just like you. You're the one who made threatening remarks, remember?'

Chelsea clenched her fist tightly. 'We'll see then, won't we? She'll get what's coming to her. I don't know where she's got her balls from, talking to me like that.'

Donny let out a sarcastic laugh. 'Who the hell do you think you are? Everyone is equal, you can't call the shots around here.'

Chelsea slouched down on the nearest chair and sat biting her fingernails. 'I need a cig. Sir, you can let me go out or I'm getting off on my own. Trust me, I'll be gone.'

Donny could see she was stressed out. Although there was no smoking policy in school, he knew perfectly well that most of these kids stood chugging on cigarettes all the way through their breaktime. After all, he did the same if he could find a corner where he wouldn't get seen. There wasn't much he could do about it either – most of them smoked in front of their parents anyway, so threatening to tell them was pointless. He looked over at Janice, the teaching assistant who'd stayed back to see if there was anything she could do to help.

'Miss Ellis, can you escort Chelsea off site while she has a bit of time out. Then bring her straight back and take her upstairs to isolation – I don't want her mixing with the other students today.'

Chelsea stood up with a cocky swagger. 'Bothered?' she hissed as she walked out of the hall with Janice close behind her.

Donny sighed. What a morning. Hopefully the day would get better, but he wasn't holding his breath.

Donny was pacing up and down the side of the building, where no one inside would see him. His phone was pressed to his ear and his voice was low; he seemed stressed, looking around him before he spoke. 'I said, I'll be there later, fuck me, how many times do I have to tell you not to ring me when I'm in work?' His nostrils flared as he sucked hard on his cigarette. As the call ended, he stood with his back to the wall for a few seconds, thinking. A few of the kids from the local high school walked past and Donny looked over at them. These were the 'normal' kids, the full uniform, homework done brigade. Arse lickers, he liked to call them. He watched them go by and smiled at them. The kids from his school had had plenty of beef with this lot before now and he'd had to come out of school to stop his pupils starting on them. As he headed back to the fray, he spotted Melanie sitting in her car. Trying to get a moment's peace between lessons no doubt. This was his cue to go back inside; there was no way he wanted to get caught up talking to her on his own. Best to keep giving her a wide berth for sure.

Donny made for the door; he could see her using her rear-view mirror to reapply the candy-pink lip gloss she never seemed to be without. He picked up his pace but too late, she'd spotted him.

'Hello, boss, have you been waiting for me?'

Donny was cornered. He smiled at her though it didn't reach his eyes. He was making an effort, didn't like to appear rude.

'Hello, Mel, you're looking well. Did you have a good weekend?' She locked her car and leant against the door.

'You're joking, aren't you? I had the ex on the phone half the time. After he heard somebody had dropped me off that night after the pub, he hasn't stopped giving me the third degree.'

Not what Donny wanted to hear. It wasn't like there was even anything going on. Even so, if his missus got wind of this, she would scratch her eyeballs out and cut his balls off.

'Just tell him it was a work thing; you work with me. If he needs to speak to me about it, then fine.'

Melanie burst out laughing, pulling her coat tighter around herself. It was cold again. 'Are you having a laugh or what? He's a total head-the-ball. Trust me, you want nothing to do with him.'

She followed Donny as he headed inside. 'I've told him a hundred times you're a happily married man, but he said he doesn't believe me.'

'He sounds like a right one. Surely there's somebody who can get him off your back?' Donny pulled the door open and let Melanie go first; he thought she pushed herself against him suggestively as she brushed past him – or maybe he was just imagining it. 'I'll see you later, I've got a pile of things to get through.' He left her in the corridor and headed for his office.

Tina was stood by the staircase, on her phone again. 'Chris, are you really going to keep pretending that nothing's going on? She's making me ill. I was awake all night again thinking about the things she's been saying. I'm the innocent party in all this. I've only tried my best. Please, sort it out.'

Donny edged past, tried to give her some privacy, though airing her dirty linen in the middle of the school corridor wasn't exactly ideal. He paused at the door; was that alcohol he could smell on her breath? That was all he bloody needed. Tina had been on the bottle before she went off sick, but, when she came back, she promised she'd knocked it on the head. Clearly not. Donny sighed. This needed nipping in the bud. A pissed-up teacher was something he really didn't need in his school right now.

As he sat down, his phone started ringing again. Susan.

'Babe, I was just about to ring you back, you wouldn't believe the shit that's been going down here today.' He dropped the pen he'd been fiddling with. 'What? You're outside school? What for? Why aren't you at work?' He was already pulling his coat back on as he left the office and started to walk back down the stairs. 'I'm coming out now, just wait there.'

Donny took the stairs two at a time and then headed outside. He could see his wife straight away. He marched over to the car and opened the passenger door. 'What's up? Is something wrong?'

Susan kept her eyes focused on the steering wheel. 'I can come and see you, can't I? Do you have a problem with that?'

'No, why would I? It's just funny you turning up, that's all.'

With perfect timing, Melanie appeared – she must have left something in her car. She didn't even seem to be able to walk across the car park without wiggling her arse. Naturally Susan clocked her straight away. Her nostrils flared.

'Who's the dolly bird?'

Donny swallowed. 'Oh, that's just Melanie, one of the new teachers.'

Susan watched her like a hawk, never took her eyes off her. 'Pretty little thing, isn't she?'

Donny reached over and touched her shoulder. 'Babe, I only have eyes for you. I'm not interested in any other women.' His words bounced off her like water off a duck's back.

'I've only come to see if you wanted to meet up for some lunch later. We don't get any quality time together lately and I want to make an effort to keep the spark alive.'

Donny was confused. 'We're sweet, Susan. Saturday night showed we haven't lost the spark, and it was good, wasn't it? I can't see any problems.'

Susan watched Melanie as she headed back into the building. 'I just want to make sure I'm being the wife you want me to be, that makes you happy.'

Donny looked at her. 'Susan, what the fuck is going on with you? You've been acting strange for a while now and fuck knows what I've done. If I've upset you or not done something that I should have, please just put me out of this misery and tell me what it is?'

Susan started to straighten her hair, didn't look him in the eye. 'There's nothing. I'm fine, Donny, completely fine. If you've not got time for lunch shall we book a table for a pizza tonight?'

He knew that the easy option was to agree, but he'd got nothing done so far today and didn't want to fall further behind. 'Babe, I'm rushed off my feet. School reports need sorting out and stuff for the education authority, can't we just get a takeout? We can cuddle up on the sofa after if you want, watch a film. Maybe something to get us in the mood if you're up for it?'

She smiled at him, a strange smile, he still couldn't work out what was happening here.

'Whatever makes you happy, Donny.'

His phone started ringing again. 'Fuck's sake, I've only been out of the bloody building five minutes … Listen, let's speak later on when things calm down here. I've got to go back and sort that lot out, honest, today is something else, the kids are all over the bloody place. So, is that a deal, we sort something out later?'

She nodded and watched him as he scrambled out of the car. He turned back before disappearing back into the building.

'Love you, babe, speak later.'

There was no reply.

As soon as Donny was gone, Susan started the engine and made a call, put it on loudspeaker before she drove out of the car park. 'John, I can't take this much longer. Something's going on and I need to show the bastard exactly who he's messing with. I'm going to start taking money out of the joint account like you said. I want to leave him with nothing, do you hear me, fucking nothing.'

John agreed. 'I hear you.' Nobody messed with his sister, nobody.

Ged looked like a different kid with Frankie at his side. Thick as thieves they were now, brothers-in-arms. Frankie steered him away from the other students loitering outside and kept his voice low.

'So, you're on it again tonight? I've got another parcel that needs taking up to Blackpool. I could do with you staying there for a few days to be honest, make sure them bollock heads are not having our eyes out. Let's say the count was a bit low with the last lot.'

Ged was distraught. 'I never touched a penny, I wouldn't take the piss out of you when you've done so much for me.'

Frankie nodded his head. 'Yeah I know, I'm not saying you would have me over, it's them pricks up there. They think I'm green. Maybe I need a trip up there myself to tell them straight. I'll kick fuck out of each and every one of them if it happens again, so make sure you tell them that. Another thing while we're on the subject; you need to fuck Nancy off. She's a liability and I don't want her knowing shit about what we're doing. I let it go before because it was your first time up there, but that's the end of her. Cart the cling-on and tell her you don't do drops anymore. Nancy's got problems, she's well known for going missing. The dibble will be all over you if she's chilling with you. Think about it, it will be on top.'

Ged was gutted but hid it well. He liked Nancy, enjoyed being with her, she made him laugh. She also seemed to know more about this job than he did. But there was more to it than that. They'd slept together too, that first night in Blackpool, but there was no way he was admitting that to Frankie. Especially when he was always slagging her off. But Ged had been walking on air since and Nancy would go sick if she knew what Frankie was saying about her – there definitely didn't seem to be any love lost between them. Ged slowed down as they neared the door.

'My mam said she was coming into school today. To talk about my progress and all that.'

Frankie pressed his lips together. 'Yeah well, make sure you tick all the boxes, don't start having this lot on your back and involving any third parties, like social services. Just agree to anything they suggest.' He kicked the floor as he stood on the spot. 'How's your mam been with you, is she still pecking your head?'

Ged sighed. 'You can say that again. Every fucking night she's asking where I'm going and what time I will be in. She's doing my head in. She needs to chill the fuck out and leave me to it. It's not like she can check if I'm in the house when she's at work all the bastard time anyway.'

'Just keep her sweet like I said.'

As they headed back into school the minibus was just pulling up – a group of students had been off site at the gym. Ged and Frankie turned round when they heard the noise. Ged blushed furiously when he spotted Nancy hanging out of the window shouting his name. Frankie nudged him and whispered into his ear.

'Sort it out, mate, cart her before she starts blabbing our business to every Tom, Dick, and Harry.'

'Yeah, yeah. I will, leave it with me, she'll be gone don't you worry.'

Later that afternoon, Ged sat next to his mother on the small grey sofa in Donny's office.

Donny put Ged's file on the small table between them and sat back with his legs crossed. Tina was first to speak.

'I feel Ged's making good progress in most of his subjects and if we can get him to study just a bit more, I'm sure he could get some decent grades when he sits his exams.'

Clare didn't give a flying shit about his exams right now, they were the last thing on her mind. She jabbed a finger in her son's direction. 'Something's up. He's turned into a cheeky little bastard, his attitude stinks. You should hear the way he speaks to me at home now. He sits here in front of you two like butter wouldn't melt in his mouth, but he speaks to me as if I am less than a stranger in the street. That's when he's even at home, not off hanging out God knows where. He was never this bad, he's changed, and most of the time I don't even know him anymore. I need help with him before I lose the plot.'

Ged was trying his best to hold it together, but he was struggling, temper rising. Donny clocked the signs instantly.

'Ms Grey, just calm down. I know you're angry but let's keep our voices down and try and deal with this the best we can…'

But Clare was livid; she'd started and there was no way she wasn't going to finish. 'I work all the hours that God sends, so he can have a good life and when he is actually home, all he does is moan or play on that game all night. His bedroom is a shit-tip and he just treats the house as if it's a bleeding hotel—'

Ged had had enough, she was doing his head in. He didn't care who else was in the room.

'Mam, wind your neck in. How embarrassing are you? Shut up, will you?'

That was it. Clare was going for gold. She sprang to her feet, ready to throttle him. 'You see what I have to put up with? He needs anger management. It was bad enough before. But now it's like he's changed overnight. One minute he is the son that I love, a decent lad. Now he's just a cheeky bastard who doesn't give a toss about anyone but himself.'

Tina took control of the situation. This wasn't how she had planned the meeting at all.

'Ged, would you agree that things haven't been that good at home? You can see how upset your mother is.'

Ged didn't get why he was the one at fault. 'She's the one who started it. Every time I speak about my dad, she disrespects him and calls him a fucking idiot. Go on, Mam, tell them you said he was just a sperm donor, that he's never been a dad.'

Clare raised her hand to her throat, his words choking her. Donny sent Ged across to the other side of the room before they started laying into each other. He meant business now; this was his school with his rules, not a bleeding boxing ring. No wonder the kids here had problems when their parents were just as hot-headed as their children. Tina poured Clare a glass of cold water.

'Here you go, it will help you calm down. Might I suggest that we just have a five-minute breather so everyone can calm down?'

Donny nodded. 'Come on, Ged, let's me and you go and grab a bit of fresh air for a few minutes. We'll sort this mess out, don't worry.'

Ged stood up – it was clear he was about to snap. 'Just get me out of here away from her. It's her fault winding me up all the time. She's a crank.'

'Come on, let's get that fresh air,' Donny steered him out of the room.

Tina sat facing Clare and passed her some tissues; she was sobbing now. She lifted her head up and looked at Tina directly. 'I love Ged with all my heart, but I can't cope with him anymore. He's started coming home at all hours and some nights he doesn't even bother coming in at all. My nerves are shattered with him. I keep thinking I'll get a knock at the door telling me he's been found dead in some alleyway or something. The streets are dangerous, and I don't want him getting mixed up with the wrong kind of people. His dad was the same; he was a follower and look what happened to him. I don't want that for my Ged. I want him to get a good job and make something of himself. I don't want him ending up in jail.'

Tina was sympathetic. God knows she knew how hard bringing up a teenager up could be. 'I agree with you. Ged's got so much going for him. Like I said, he's doing OK and if he gets his head down, he will get decent results. Do you think a lot of this anger is to do with his dad? I know it's hard to admit, but sometimes we have to let our children see for themselves what the other parent is really like.'

If only she could have followed her own advice, Tina thought. Maybe it was time to take the gloves off and encourage Nevaya to have a proper relationship with her birth mother. Maybe then she'd see what she was like with her own two eyes and then it could be put to bed once and for all.

Clare dabbed the crumpled white tissue into the corner of her eyes. 'Kevin is out of jail next week and I'm scared to death of what will happen. Ged loves his dad, but he doesn't know him like I do. He'll let him down, he always does.'

Sometimes silence was for the best. Tina knew the value of that bit of thinking time that slows the heartbeat down and lets people gather their thoughts together. Clare had clearly been struggling with all this for days, maybe weeks, and now that she'd got it out, she would feel that maybe something could change. Mothers who came into school were usually like that; they'd shout and scream but after they'd said their piece and felt like someone had actually listened to them, they'd start to calm down. Tina had seen this situation time and time again. The kids were growing up, finding their own paths in life. It was scary for them too, hormones flying all over the place, they didn't know if they were coming or going either.

Clare looked out of the window and sniffed. 'I don't know what to do for the best. I feel like a failure as a parent. I've let him down. I should be at home with him every night making sure he's safe, but I have to go to work, I have to pay the bills. It's just me on my own, nobody else, just me.'

Tina was aware that she'd have to mention to Clare that as Ged was a minor, she shouldn't be leaving him on his own every night, but for now she put it on the back burner.

Outside, Ged walked away from the school with a fag hanging out of his mouth. The nicotine seemed to be calming him down.

Donny's voice was low and steady as he walked with him. 'So, do you want to tell me what's going on? Are you blazing the bud or what?'

Ged knew Donny was a straight talker and didn't see the point in dodging the question. 'I just have it to calm me down. I need it when she's doing my head in.'

Donny edged closer to him and looked him straight in the eye. 'Are you selling it? I'm not being funny but looking at the some of the clobber you've started wearing – it's either that or you've won the lottery or something. Those clothes cost money, mate, and as far as I can see your mam isn't the one who's coughing it up. Low-paid jobs, bills, rent...'

Ged had his answer ready. 'They're not my clothes; my mates borrowed them to me. Like I could afford a Canada Goose coat. They're about eight hundred quid, where would I get cash like that from?'

Donny nodded. A calculating look came into his eyes. 'Just checking. A lot of kids your age get mixed up with drugs

– selling and taking them. I just want to make sure there is nothing that I'm missing here.'

Ged flicked his cigarette to the floor and ground the butt into the tarmac with his heel. 'Nope, you're barking up the wrong tree with that. I chill at my mates and get stoned, sure, but I'm not doing anything else.'

Donny rubbed at his arms. He should have put his coat on. It really wasn't the weather for a short-sleeved shirt. 'Shall we go back in now? Listen, Ged, your mam loves you and maybe you should start showing that you appreciate her too. You should be glad she cares about you. Do you know how many kids I deal with whose parents are not bothered where their kids are or what they're doing?'

Ged sighed and kicked the pavement. More anger. 'I just want my dad to come home. Everything was great when he was with us. My mam didn't have to go to work all the time and it was good having two parents at home.'

'Lots of kids just have one parent who cares for them. If I'm being honest, I'd say over seventy-five per cent of kids coming to this school only have a mum at home, some kids don't even know who their dads are. Imagine that, not knowing who your old man was?'

Ged digested what Donny had said. He was quieter now. 'She has to realise that I'm not a kid anymore. I want to live my life and if I make mistakes, then I'll have to deal with the consequences myself, not her. She's not stopping me from having a relationship with my old man, no fucking way in this world. He's looking forward to spending some time with me. He's told me how sorry he is for the way things have turned out and I believe him. My mam just needs to give him a chance. He still loves her; he's told me he'll always love her. It's just her being a stubborn cow.'

Donny realised that this went a lot deeper than he'd first anticipated. He could give all the advice in the world, but it seemed that this had the potential to get a lot worse before it got any better. 'Come on then, let's go and face the music and see if you can patch things up with your mam. Remember what I've just said. Your mother only cares about you, that's why she's stressing.'

Ged remained silent as he followed Donny back into the building.

As Donny walked back up the corridor with Ged dawdling behind him, he spotted a woman sat on one of the chairs in the reception area, with a young teenager next to her. She seemed familiar, but he couldn't quite place her. He turned to Ged to hurry him along. 'Come on, lad, you'll have it dark.'

As Donny and Ged returned, Tina could tell by the head teacher's expression that there would be no more shouting and screaming in this room today. She pointed to the chair facing her and asked Ged to sit back down. The ball was in his court now and it was up to him to make the first move. He coughed and sat forward in the chair, nervously playing with his fingers.

'Mam, I'll start to clean up my act and speak to you better. I need to talk to you about my dad when we get home, not here, that's our business. I don't think you know how much it's affecting me; it hurts.'

Clare looked at him. Her son was right, this was nothing to do with school; it was a private matter, nothing really to do with anyone except the family. 'OK. I just don't want any more shouting and screaming. It's making me ill. We need to sit down and speak to each other with a bit of respect.'

Donny raised his eyebrows at his colleague. Tina started to talk about the subjects Ged was struggling with and by the end of the meeting a new learning plan was put in place. Hopefully, when the two of them got home they would talk about Kevin's release from jail without it turning into another dog fight.

When Ged had gone back to class, Donny and Tina walked Clare to the door. After the enforced intermission they were already fifteen minutes late for their next meeting. Tina nudged Donny.

'I'll go and get the new kid and his mam from reception. Follow me up when you've finished.'

Donny pulled her aside. 'Do us a favour. I have to nip out, can you take the next meeting? I just have to drop some money off for Susan.'

Tina nodded her head. 'OK, but you owe me one. Go on, get gone, before I change my mind.'

Donny patted her on the arm and hurried off. He could hear Tina's heels clipping down the corridor as she headed to the reception area to meet the new pupil. He wondered what their story would be. No one – teacher or pupil – wound up here without a tale to tell.

Chapter Thirteen

Donny walked into Susan's salon and took a seat in one of the silver crushed velvet bucket chairs. He smiled as he looked around, silver glitter walls, huge silver mirrors, proper glamorous. The girls loved it when Susan's husband came in – he was great with the banter. Chrissy the receptionist smiled at him.

'I'll let her know you're here, she's just doing a spray tan.'

Donny crossed his legs and unwrapped the tin foil containing his lunch.

'I've told the missus that I will do all the spray tans in future but she's having none of it. I don't know why, but I reckon I would do a better job than she does. I've creosoted a fence before – same thing, isn't it?'

Chrissy burst out laughing. 'You're a rum bleeder, you are, Donny. I don't know how she puts up with you.'

He took a large bite of his food and carried on. 'She loves me, that's why. Look at me, who wouldn't love this face?' Chrissy shook her head. So much confidence – mind you, he was the full package, good looking, good job, great body, what more could a woman ask for? Chrissy walked to the end of the salon and knocked softly before opening the door slightly.

'Sue, Donny's here.'

'Can you make him a coffee, Chrissy? Tell him I will be with him shortly.'

Chrissy closed the door and walked back to deliver the message while Susan left her client to dry off and went into her office where Sadie was looking through a magazine. They both looked through the small window at Donny talking to the girls; he was like a kid in a sweet shop.

Sadie shook her head.

'He's a cheeky fucker, look at him acting like he doesn't have a care in the world. Fucking ruin him, Susan. It's about time us ladies showed these men that they can't walk all over us. I'm sick of them taking the piss, destroy him, take him for every penny.'

Susan nodded. 'Don't you worry, love, he's going to think he's been hit by a two-ton bus when I've finished with him. I've already got plans for his Rolex – it's his pride and joy. The moment he puts it down, it's going missing. Trust me Sadie, this is just the start of it. If he thinks he can have me over again, then he's got another think coming. I swear to you, I don't know how I've held myself back. I know something's up, I just need proof. Then – boom.'

'You show him Susan, I've never liked the cocky fucker anyway. He's never really had the time of the day for me. It serves him right and I can't wait to see the arsehole fall off his pedestal.'

Susan checked her hair in the mirror. 'Come on then, I'll walk you to the door. Remember, act normal, don't give anything away.'

'My lips are sealed.'

Donny watched Chrissy make his drink and smiled. His wife ran a tight ship here and it was a successful business. Of course, he'd funded it at the start. His wife had always wanted her own salon and as soon as he'd saved enough money, her dream was the first thing on his list. Her brothers threw a few quid in too, they were always willing to help out, and they liked a good investment. Donny would have much preferred they stayed out of it but, as always, they had to stick their noses in where they didn't belong. He messed around on his phone as he waited. Not much on the news. He clicked on Facebook. A friend request from Melanie. What the hell was she playing at? Like he'd accept. His wife was on the ball, she knew the friends on his list. Apart from when she'd seen her in the car park, he'd never said a word about Mel to his wife. If she had even the slightest idea that she was trying it on with her man, she would rip her to shreds. Susan would take no shit. If she thought it, then she said it. It was like she had no filter sometimes. And now she'd seen what she looked like he had no doubt that she would put two and two together and come up with six. He knew he'd given her reason to doubt him in the past. But he'd put that behind him. He had other things on his mind.

He saw Susan and stuffed his phone in his pocket. He'd delete the friend request as soon as he could.

'Two minutes, baby, and I'll be with you.' Susan shouted over.

Donny finished his food and threw the rubbish in the bin.

'No worries, love, whenever you're ready.'

Chrissy passed Donny his coffee. 'There you go, is it still no sugar?'

He patted his hand on his stomach. 'Does this body look like it has sugar, Chrissy, come on love. My body is a temple.'

Donny leant back in his chair. The smell in this place was lovely; sweet, floral. His wife was into all this aromatherapy stuff – it was the same at home. Susan re-emerged with her client and walked her towards the door, with Sadie close to her side.

'See you soon, honey, and remember, no shower til tomorrow. Let me know how your date goes too, I hope you like him.'

The middle-aged woman looked optimistic. 'Thanks so much, Susan. I feel amazing. I hope he likes me too. I need a bit of a tan to cover everything up!'

Susan put her hand on her client's shoulder. 'You stop that negative talk right now. You're lovely and this man is lucky you are even giving him the time of the day. You get out there and show them all what they're missing, lovely. Too many men these days take us ladies for granted, so if he's not ticking the boxes, cart him.' She darted a look at Donny, making sure he'd heard every word. Donny whistled at the woman.

'You look stunning, love. Like my wife said, any man should be happy to take you out.'

The woman blushed. 'Oh stop it. I'm not used to all this attention. My head will burst if you carry on.'

Susan waved her client off and turned to Sadie. 'Right, my love, you keep your chin up too.'

Sadie nodded. 'I'll ring you later and thanks for listening, as always.'

The two of them shared a hug before Sadie left. Donny kept his mouth shut; he knew it would only end in tears if he slated his wife's best friend again.

Susan sat down next to her husband. 'Poor Amy, that last client, has had a bad time lately. She got divorced last year and she's not been herself for a while. I think she's been a bit depressed. Anyway, she's joined a dating agency and she's got her first date tomorrow night.' There's a lot to be said for these agencies. A few people I know are using them to find a partner. I suppose if you work all the time you never get the chance to meet someone new, do you?' Susan looked piercingly at her husband.

Donny tried to look sympathetic and thought that buttoning his lip was the best way to avoid trouble.

Susan still looked at him directly and kept a poker face. 'If we ever split up, I'll be signed up to an agency within the week.'

Donny couldn't keep a straight face any longer – he reached over and prodded her in the ribs. 'Lining up my replacement already, are you?'

Susan burst out laughing and everyone in the shop looked over at them.

'Donny, I was joking, you're the only man for me, honest. I could never love again after you.'

Donny didn't seem too sure – he could feel a coldness beneath his wife's joke.

'Good, the thought of you moving on without me does my head in. Until death us do part, remember?'

'Yes, until death do us part.' Susan held his gaze.

Donny looked serious now; the laughter seemed to have disappeared. He would never again risk losing his wife he thought. He'd been stupid in the past. Now everything he was doing wasn't just for him – it was for them. He wished she knew how much he meant that. She was his rock, the person who fixed him when he needed fixing, he could never truly imagine his life with anybody else.

Susan reached over with her hand and stroked the side of his cheek gently. 'I love you, baby. As long as you're faithful to me then you have nothing to worry about.' She still didn't take her eyes off him. There it was, that was all he needed to hear, he was fine. He needed to lighten the mood.

'Babe, I've left Tina in a meeting. I've not got long. I just wanted to make sure you're alright after this morning. You've been a bit off with me lately and all I want you to know is I do love you. Oh, and I've got a little something for you …'

Susan stood up and beckoned for him to follow her. This was a private conversation and she didn't want her staff listening in. She led Donny into her office and made sure the door was closed behind them. Donny reached inside his jacket and pulled out a white envelope.

'I couldn't give this to you at school. There's two grand in there. Put it through your books like normal and get it in the bank, would you?'

Susan looked troubled. 'Maybe you need to stop the gambling, Don. I love it when you win, but this streak won't last forever, so lay off it while you're ahead.'

He got it. 'Stop worrying, will you? It's just a bit of stress relief. You can't do a job like mine and not need a way to let off steam. And this is win-win. I get to forget about school for a bit, and you get a nice little wedge of cash into the salon, and back into your purse. Nobody knows and that's the way I want it to stay, that's why I want you to put it through your books. I don't want to ever have to explain to anyone where my little bit extra comes from – you and I deserve our little luxuries, and we sure as hell wouldn't get them just on my headteacher's pay.'

Sue edged closer to him and touched her soft red lips to his. 'Can your lovely missus have some new shoes then? They're three hundred and fifty pounds but they're worth every penny – I love them. Please, pretty please?'

Donny grinned. 'Depends on what you can give me in return.' He poked his tongue into the side of his cheek and looked at her lasciviously, pulling her into his arms. 'So, what do you think?'

Susan snuggled against him. A blow job was the usual price tag for any favours and it looked like today was no different. 'I'll put your name down in my book for one, Donny, new shoes for me and a gobble for you. See, we're both happy.' She ran her hand down his chest. He'd have been up for it there and then if she'd let him.

She leant in to him, forgetting for a moment all her doubts and fears and just feeling his solid chest against hers. That was the problem with Donny. Even when she hated him, she loved him too.

They heard a voice outside the room and pulled away from each other. Susan pointed at her husband's crotch.

'Quick, cover that up before you poke someone's eye out with it.' Donny looked down and placed his hand over his erection.

'Whoops,' he sniggered. 'Right, I'll see you later, sexy. I'll get us a takeaway tonight for tea like I promised. I want you to relax, especially if I'm on your good list.'

Susan said nothing; now she had control of herself again the spell was broken and doubt came rushing back in.

Donny, oblivious, placed his hands in his pocket and checked it was safe to leave now. He kissed his wife and left the room with a smile on his face.

———

Back at school all seemed quiet. Donny went back upstairs to his office where he found Tina tapping away at her computer. She looked up.

'It was all fine with the new kid. He starts in a few days. Seems alright, usual story – acting up in his old school, no respect for boundaries – nothing we haven't seen before. I don't think he'll give us any trouble. Oh and his mother said she knows you from when she was younger. Pearson, she's called now, I'm trying to remember what she said it was then.'

Donny shrugged. 'I knew a lot of girls back in the day. Did she have a crush on me? I bet she did.' He chuckled.

Tina was thinking back. 'That's it. Her maiden name was Greggs. Bethany Greggs.'

Donny blanched, could feel his knees go weak. Gobsmacked was an understatement. Tina didn't seem to notice, just carried on talking. 'Nevaya has texted me to say sorry. But I know Chris has made her do it to keep the peace.'

Donny was still lost in the past, trying to push thoughts of Bethany Greggs as far down as he could.

'Nevaya's up to something, Donny. She's a snake in the grass. I need to be careful, she's all cloak and dagger that one is.'

Donny nodded in agreement, only half listening. 'Yep, watch her like a hawk, Tina, never take your eyes off the game when you have beef with someone.'

It was sound advice and Tina knew more than anyone that the fight with her stepdaughter was far from over. Donny coughed and cleared his throat, tried to sound casual.

'So, tell me more about this new kid and his mam.'

'The woman seemed edgy. I got the feeling that something wasn't right with her. She was a bag of nerves and kept asking when you'd be back. The lad, Dan, was nice enough though. A good-looking lad. I can see a few of the girls lining up to get to know him, trust me, he's every teenage girl's idea of eye candy.'

Donny was impatient to know more. 'Did Bethany say anything else, like how she knew me?'

Tina was busy now reading her emails, and didn't even look up. 'No, she never said.'

Chapter Fourteen

Nancy walked down the road with her coat zipped up tightly, she was always cold. Her cheeks were bright red and the end of her nose was chapped. Even so, she seemed happy for a change. Her hair looked neater and she'd paid more attention to the way she was dressed. She walked down the path and knocked on Ged's door. She liked it here, she felt safe, could let her guard down. Nothing. She lifted the letterbox flap and peered inside, then stood back and looked up at the windows. Ged was probably in his bedroom messing around on his phone. After a few seconds she knocked on the door again. Bloody hell, it was cold tonight and if he didn't hurry up and answer the door she was going to freeze to death. A light came on in the hallway and a shadow approached the front door. Nancy stared at Ged as he stood looking at her; he looked bothered, not himself. She pushed past him into the hallway.

'Are you deaf or something? I've been here ages freezing my tits off.'

Ged shoved his hand down the front of his tracksuit bottoms and scratched his nuts. 'I was half asleep, I didn't hear you. I thought I told you to leave it tonight, I'm knackered.'

Nancy headed into the front room. She kicked her shoes off and made herself comfy on the sofa. His comment went over her head.

'I got some money from my mam so we can order some scran if you want?'

Ged hovered near the door; he had something on his mind, he seemed edgy.

Nancy patted the space next to her. 'Come on then, sit down, we can find a film to watch.'

Ged sat down next to her but he was still acting strange. Nancy studied him for a few seconds. Maybe she was being paranoid, she wasn't sure.

'Are you alright?' she asked.

Ged bit his lip. 'Yeah. Tired. But I'm glad you're here. I need a chat with you.' Nancy sat up straight. This was it; he was going to ask her to be his girlfriend. After all, she'd had sex with him and he did tell her how much he liked it, so of course, this was the next step. Maybe he'd bought her a promise ring. Lots of girls had them, so why not her? Her heart was thudding.

'Nancy, I've got a lot of shit going on at the minute as you know,' he began. 'And I don't really have time for a girlfriend. You're lovely, but it's all come at the wrong time for me when my head's all messed up.' This was not what Nancy was expecting, not what she wanted to hear. So that's all she was, a quick leg-over, a sack emptier? She was wounded and wasn't going to take this lying down. She made sure he was looking at her.

'What, so you're binning me? We've had sex, I thought we had something. I don't sleep with just anyone you know – I'm not a slapper.'

'I know. And yes, that night was great, but it's not about that. It's about all the stuff I've got going on in my life.'

'I thought we had a connection, or was you just blagging me to get my knickers off?'

Ged was getting agitated, this wasn't going the way he planned. 'Of course not. I enjoyed everything – not just the sex – but for now I think we should knock it on the head.'

Nancy was distraught. 'What about the laughs we have when we go out? What about Blackpool, who's going to go there with you, eh?'

Ged tried to remember what Frankie had told him to say; he kept his cool as the lies kept on coming. 'I've carted that too. It's on top and I'll end up getting sent down if I get caught. My dad's home next week, and I want to be around to help him as much as I can. It's going to be hard for him to adjust when he gets out.'

Nancy swallowed hard. She liked Ged, she really did, and without him she would go back to feeling crap. There had to be something she could say to convince him not to finish with her. She hung her head low and closed her eyes.

Ged wasn't ready for this, he never expected her to cry. For fuck's sake, what could he do now? He wasn't a horrible person, he had to comfort her. He reached over and moved the hair that was stuck to the side of her cheek.

'Don't cry, Nancy. I'm not good at stuff like this. You're a lovely girl and you're right we did have a buzz when we were in Blackpool, but like I said, I'm not doing it anymore. I need to get my life back on track and sort my family out. My mam said she's not having my dad back here, so the guy's going to be homeless. I've had pure shit with my mam going on, we're arguing all the time and it just feels like my head is going to explode with all the shit I've got resting on my shoulders. I can't breathe, honest, I need a bit of time on my own.'

Nancy used her knuckles to wipe the tears away. 'I can help. You even said when you're with me that I chill you out. We can roll a zoot up, get stoned. You're just having a bad day. I have them too. I do some horrible things when I'm not thinking straight. Go on, skin up and let's relax for a bit.'

Ged sighed, Frankie would go sick if he didn't follow orders and he didn't want him on his back, no way. He had to man up and put this to bed. He had to show he was a man, not a soft arse kid.

'Nancy, you can say what you want but it won't change my mind. We're done. I mean, fucking hell, we only slept together a few times it's not like we're married. I don't want to be in a relationship. I'm staying single.'

His words stabbed her deep in her heart and the tears stopped. She looked hard suddenly. 'You're a daft prick, Ged. I helped you out in Blackpool when I could have left your sorry arse to crash and burn. You're full of shit you are. I thought you were different, Ged, but you're not. You're a sly, shady dickhead.'

Ged screwed his face up. He wasn't listening to any more of this, not in his own house anyway. She was getting flung.

'Come on, you can fuck off. I tried to be nice but you're being a knob. Get your shoes on and do one.'

Nancy reached down and started to put her shoes on. 'You're a user, cheeky bastard you are. I wouldn't piss on you if you was on fire anymore. You do what you've got to do but don't come crying to me when it all goes tits-up. I thought we were friends, Ged, but obviously not.'

Ged could feel his rage building. No girl should talk to a lad like that, no matter what had happened. 'Do one,' he snarled.

Nancy stood up. She could see how angry he was and there was no point. Ged watched her leave and shuddered as she slammed the front door shut. He paced around the room for a bit; his temper had got the better of him and he was finding it hard to cope. He walked over to the table and rolled a joint. His hands were shaking and he was ready to snap. He punched the wall a few times and kicked the door. 'Fucking hell!' he screamed, but there was no one to hear him.

The weed helped; Ged had calmed down a bit. He lay on the sofa staring into space. This stuff was strong. 'Star-dog' was what all the kids were smoking, it just knocked them out, sleeping all the time. But Ged fought the urge to shut his eyes and instead picked his phone up and started to read through his messages. Nancy was going to town on him. Each text was as long as the next, slagging him off one minute and then telling him how much she was gutted the next. The girl clearly didn't know if she was coming or going. He scrolled through his contacts until he reached Frankie's number; he needed to tell him that his mission was complete.

———

Ged tossed and turned all night long. The last message from Nancy had spooked him. It had ended with, 'You'll be sorry'. What did she mean by that? Was she saying she was going to grass him up, was she going to hurt herself, he wasn't sure?

Tomorrow was going to be a long day. It would be the first time he'd be going out of town on his own, usually he'd have Nancy or one of the crew with him. But he knew the basics now. He was going to make a name for himself, show everyone that he wasn't a nobody. His eyes closed slowly, and he drifted off to sleep. Fuck Nancy, she wasn't his problem anymore.

———

Nancy sat on the train with her head pressed against the window. It was nearly midnight and she should have been at home tucked up in bed. What was she doing out at this hour? She twisted her cuff and pulled at the skin around her nails. Her eyes were red; it was clear she'd been crying. Sometimes you were safer when you had nothing – at least then you had nothing to lose. But she knew she was vulnerable and bad people could smell it like blood in the water. It wasn't safe out there for a lost soul like her.

Chapter Fifteen

Tina stood in the bathroom and looked at herself in the mirror above the basin. She looked old and haggard with dark circles under her eyes. All this drama was doing her no good at all. She opened her makeup bag and pulled out a few things to try and make herself look half decent. Her skin was red and blotchy and her hair was limp, no real style to it anymore. She'd been drinking last night – more than usual – the hangover wasn't helping. It must have been a bad night because she'd necked a half bottle of brandy. Nobody at home knew she was drinking; she hid it away from them all, but she was worried the word was out at school.

Chris came in and stood behind her, his hands on her shoulder.

'Good morning, my love, how did you sleep? It felt like you were restless all night – kept me awake. Are you OK?'

This was the time to open up to him, to put her cards on the table instead of pretending everything was hunky-dory. Why did she keep pretending she was coping? Surely if he knew, he could help? Tina carried on applying her makeup trying to find the words. But then a wave of defeat hit her. Telling him wouldn't change the facts.

'I've got stuff on my mind. You know I'm always the same when things are bothering me.'

Chris edged her to the right and started to brush his teeth. 'Nevaya has said sorry so what's there to worry about? It's all fine now. Don't kick the arse out of it, love, it's over now, move on.'

Tina walked over towards the door. 'It might be fine in your world, Chris, but it's crap in mine. So don't paint it as perfect, when it's far from over.'

Chris sighed and shook his head. He couldn't face another argument, he just wanted a bit of peace. And it would all blow over given time.

Tina headed to the bedroom and started to get dressed. When she was done she walked over to her wardrobe and knelt down beside it. Her hand rummaged through the stacks of shoes and boots and bags until she found what she was looking for. She pulled it out, checking behind her to make sure nobody was about. She pressed the lip of the cold glass bottle to her lips and gulped. The brandy steadied her nerves, sent a flood of warmth through her when everything else was cold.

A noise behind her. Somebody was coming. She panicked and wiped her mouth with her hand, then chucked the bottle back into the cupboard. This was her secret, and nobody could ever know. She only drank to take the edge off things, anyway. A few sips here and there, and it wasn't every day. Where was the harm?

Nevaya came into the room and stood there looking at her with her usual cocky smirk. Tina raised her eyebrows questioningly. 'Did you want something?' Her tone made it clear that she was still upset with her.

'I'm going out with my mam tonight for something to eat. I've told my dad and he said it's alright with him, but I have to run it past you first.' Nevaya waited for a reply. Tina stood up and straightened her clothes. There was no way this kid was ruffling her feathers again. She put on her best poker face.

'You don't have to tell me anything, do whatever makes you happy.'

Nevaya shook her head. Here she was trying to make amends and this stubborn cow was still being a bitch. She turned to make sure nobody could hear her. 'Correct, I don't have to tell you anything. I'm just keeping my dad happy. You just stay out of my way and I'll stay out of your way too. Simple, isn't it?'

Tina didn't need this shit first thing. 'Listen, you cocky bitch, one day someone is going to wipe that smile right off your face and I hope I'm there to see it. Piss off out of my room and do what you want.' She wasn't proud of losing her rag but she just wanted to be left alone.

Nevaya walked out and slammed the door shut behind her. There was no love lost here today, none whatsoever.

Tina pulled up in the school car park and sat with her head resting on the steering wheel for a few seconds. From the corner of her eye she saw somebody running past her and heading for the alleyway. It was one theirs, she was sure of it. Nobody was about, and she knew she would have to deal with it.

'For fuck's sake,' she whispered under her breath as she got out of the car and clicked the lock.

Tina pegged it down the alley but soon ground to a stop. She stood there gasping for breath; it had been a long time since she'd set foot in the gym and to say she was unfit would have been an understatement. She squinted as she tried to make out shapes at the bottom of the path but then realised someone else had stopped halfway along. She moved closer, dodging dog shit and rubbish. It stank of bin juice and piss and she had to watch every step. Somebody was slouched against the wall a few feet away from her.

'Are you alright?' Tina waited until the girl lifted her head. 'Amelia. What are you doing down here, what's wrong?'

Amelia had been crying, her eyes were red and swollen.

'Just leave me alone, will you? Fuck off, just fuck off.'

Tina was in no mood for more of this kind of behaviour today. She'd just left one moody teenager at home, she didn't need another pecking her head at work. 'There is no need to speak to me like that. You're clearly upset. Do you want me to ring your parents?'

'No! Just leave me alone!' Amelia screamed at the top of her voice and banged her head against the brick wall behind her. 'Nobody can help me, and certainly not them. Go away and just leave me here, I need to be alone.'

Tina was concerned and intrigued in equal measure. The kid never really caused any trouble in the school, usually just kept herself to herself. Sure, she had a bit of a reputation, but so did half the other girls in the school. Tina stood for a few seconds thinking.

Judging by the state she was in there was clearly something very wrong. And given her age it was going to be a safeguarding issue. As the lead safeguarding officer at the school she knew she couldn't just walk away and leave the girl on her own. What if she went missing? What if she harmed herself? No, she had to stay.

'Can you at least come inside where we can have a proper chat? Honest, if I stay here any longer, I might puke. I think that's a dead rat over there. Come on, let's go inside.'

Amelia lifted her head up to see the brown furry rodent on its back not far from where she was standing. If there was one thing she hated, it was rats. 'I feel sick.' She jumped to her feet. Her cheeks filled up like she was holding a ping pong ball in each side. She sprinted out of the alleyway and straight into school, making for the toilets. Tina wasn't far behind her, though she could barely breathe. Bleeding hell, the school day hadn't even started yet and there was drama and an unwanted workout.

Rita was stood in the corridor; she watched Amelia and the deputy head rush by, trying to get a better look at what was happening. Amelia didn't look good. She was pale and sweating and liquid began to spray from her mouth even before she made it through the door. Tina blocked the toilets off while she was dealing with this emergency. That was all she needed – an audience. Given half a chance, the kids would be all over it, making things ten times worse than they already were. Gossip spread round a school like wildfire.

Amelia raised her head weakly from rim of the toilet bowl. 'I've been like this for days. When will it ever stop?' Tina was trying to clean the floor while getting her breath back. This job was grinding her down, drama after drama every bloody day.

'Have you eaten something that doesn't agree with you?'

It was clear that Amelia was struggling to get her words out. Tina helped her up and sat her down on a chair. 'Come on, take deep breaths. I'll get you a cold drink of water and you might start to feel a bit better.'

She was back in a couple of minutes with a full glass. Amelia sat sipping it slowly as Tina watched her.

'How are you feeling now?' Amelia put the glass down and dropped her head into her hands, mumbled under her breath. Tina struggled to hear what she was saying and asked her to repeat herself. Amelia looked up.

'Miss, I think I'm pregnant. I've missed my period and I'm puking every morning. You need to help me. My dad will leather me if he knows I'm knocked up. Please, Miss, help me. Make it go away, do something. I can't have a kid. I can't even look after myself properly, make it stop, take it away.'

Tina groaned inwardly. It wouldn't be the first pregnancy test she'd bought for a pupil at the school. The girls were always thinking they were with child in this place. She thought of what her own mother would have said if she'd come home knocked up. She'd always warned her not to have her knickers up and down like a yo-yo. Little did she know then that getting pregnant was never going to happen.

'Right, let me go and drop my bag off upstairs and then I'll call the clinic. I can go with you.'

Amelia was distraught. 'No! Are you not listening? I said nobody can know about this. I don't want a clinic to go on about my "choices". If I'm pregnant then I'm getting rid of it. I don't want a baby at my age. How the hell will I cope? I can't do it.'

The irony of the situation had not escaped Tina. Her cheeks burned. Here she was desperate for a baby and this young girl was desperate not to have one. Life really wasn't fair.

'OK, OK, just relax.' Tina walked up and down dragging her fingers through her hair. She had to think on her feet. 'Just stay there for a minute, let me go upstairs and speak with the head. I'm not going to tell him what's happened. I'm just going to say you need some sanitary pads for now. No one asks questions if you say that.'

Amelia sat with her arms wrapped around her body, shivering, sobbing. 'Just hurry up. I don't want to be on my own. My head's going to burst if this isn't sorted. I need help. Just help me, will you?' She was desperate.

'I'll be back, just stay put.'

As soon as she heard Tina leave, her heels clipping down the corridor and up the stairs, Rita crept into the toilets.

'You don't look well, Amelia, are you alright?' There was no reply, but Rita wasn't leaving it at that. 'I heard you being sick. That's not right, is it? Do you need to go to the doctor's?'

Amelia stood up and went back inside the cubicle and locked the door. She didn't want to talk about it and this nosy cow didn't seem to be moving for love nor money. She pressed her back against the toilet door. 'It's period pains, miss. I suffer with them every month. Just leave me alone will you?'

'Do you need some tablets, a paracetamol or something?'

'No thanks,' Amelia replied. Tina rushed back in with her car keys in her hand. She shot a look at Rita and told her she was no longer needed.

'It's alright, I'm dealing with this, Rita, you can go back to work.'

The cook raised her eyebrows but slunk off. Tina had her black leather handbag on her shoulder and clutched her keys tighter. 'Come on then, let's get this sorted out. Dry your eyes first though. I can't take you anywhere looking like that. You look like you have done ten rounds with Tyson Fury.'

Amelia walked to the mirror and dabbed the crumpled white tissue into the corners of her eyes. 'Please miss, promise me you won't tell anyone about this?'

Tina knew she couldn't promise her anything, she'd have to report it. 'Come on. We can talk about this more when we know what's happening. You might not even be pregnant and then you'll be worrying for nothing. Let's just get a supermarket test first, then we can talk about next steps.' Tina started to walk out of the door with Amelia behind her, her head down low. She looked like she had the worries of the world on her shoulders. A door slammed shut behind them. Tina looked round immediately, but nobody was there.

The deputy headteacher stood outside the cubicle once she had passed over the test and gone through what Amelia had to do with it. She stood now biting her nails, waiting for the old lady who was taking forever to wash her hands to leave the toilets, then banging her fist on the door. Her voice was low. 'Have you done it? Pass it me, hurry up.'

The door creaked open and Amelia handed the white plastic stick to Tina. The teacher looked at it as tears filled her eyes; she knew she would never experience this for herself, she would never have a positive result on a pregnancy test. She would never have the joy of knowing that a child was growing inside her. She would never rush home to tell Chris that he was going to be a dad again. No one would ever call her Mum. The sadness hung in her chest like a lead weight. 'Miss, miss, what does it say?'

They walked out of the toilets before anyone else came in. 'Just get in the car, we can talk about it there. You can't wash your dirty laundry in public – let's keep this to us, not the world and his bloody wife.'

Tina could barely speak. She sat in the car, with her head resting on the steering wheel. Amelia watched her impatiently, desperate to find out if she was tubbed.

'Miss, come on, just tell me and put me out of my misery.' Tina lifted her head up slowly. She had to put her own issues to the back of her mind and deal with this situation professionally.

'Amelia, it's a positive result.'

The girl swallowed a large mouthful of air – she looked like she was choking. She reached over and gripped her arm. 'Just breathe, take deep breaths.'

Tina reached to her left and pressed the button for the electric window. Some fresh air would help. The cold breeze drifted in. Amelia gritted her teeth together tightly. 'Forget what I said earlier. Take me straight to the clinic. I want it gone today; can they do an abortion today?'

Tina squirmed; she wasn't comfortable with this one little bit. 'Listen to me, Amelia, you're just panicking at the moment. You're not thinking straight. Let's go back to school and have a chat about your options.'

Amelia smashed her fist against the car door. 'Fuck off, will you? You don't know my life; you know nothing about me and what my family is like. My dad will do me in.'

'What about the father of the baby? He might want to support you and the baby. You should talk to him first.'

'I don't even know who he is, miss. I've slept with a few lads over the last month.'

'Well, you could have a DNA test when the child is born but let's worry about that later.'

'My dad thinks I'm a virgin, miss. Imagine telling him I don't even know who the dad is, he will shit a brick. Miss, I know what I want to do. Don't try and persuade me to keep it. If you don't help me, I'll do it myself. I'll drink vodka and get a coat hanger or something. That will do it, won't it?'

Tina was alarmed. 'What about all those people who can't have children? You could have the baby and put it up for adoption, make someone's dream of having a child come true. Don't rule that out.' Tina welled up and a single fat tear rolled slowly down her cheek. She couldn't help herself. 'Amelia, you might as well know – I'm one of those women. I can't have a child and do you know how hard it is for me to sit here and listen to you? It's selfish, very selfish.'

Amelia stared at her. Then she punched the dashboard. 'You fucking have it then, go on, you have it.'

Tina retaliated. 'Have you no feelings, Amelia? This is a child we are talking about, not a bleeding pair of trainers or something. You just can't make a decision like this in a few minutes. You have to think about it properly.'

Amelia turned her head towards the window and sucked in large mouthfuls of the cold air. She slowly calmed down. 'Miss, I'm sorry but I really, really don't want a kid. Maybe if I was older and had a partner, things might be different, but look at me, Miss, I've been thrown out of mainstream school and let's face the facts: I'm never going to finish school with any qualifications, am I? And certainly not if I've got a baby to raise. The best thing to do is to get rid of the baby. Go on, what other options do I have?'

Tina answered without even thinking, the words leaping from her tongue before she could hold them back. 'Then maybe you're right. I'll have the baby. If we're careful, nobody has to know that you're pregnant. When the time comes for you to give birth I will stay by your side and take the baby when it's born.' Tina was completely caught up in the moment. Why shouldn't she have a baby? Turn this unwanted pregnancy into a longed-for child?

Amelia reached over and squeezed the teacher's hand. 'D'you mean it, miss? If I have the baby you'd take it? And it will be our secret; nobody will ever know? How would we manage that? It'll be months.'

Tina was in deep now. What was she thinking? How would it work? The logistics ... She had to tell the girl that it wasn't possible. But she couldn't do it. Where was her head at? There were laws about this sort of thing, procedures to follow. She needed to tell Amelia this instead of getting involved in some ridiculous web of deceit. But she couldn't let go of this dream. Tina turned the key and closed the window.

'I do mean it, Amelia. But this has to be our secret. I will find a way to look after you until the baby is born but you mustn't tell a single person, not a living soul. Because, if anyone finds out about this, we would both be in trouble, deep trouble.'

She had no idea how it was going to work, but she'd find a way. Tina smiled. She would be a mother after all.

Chapter Sixteen

Ged rolled a spliff and passed it over to Frankie. Now that Nancy was out of the picture things were back on track.

'I need you to get on the seven o'clock train to Blackpool tonight, mate. This is the biggest load you've taken so you need to be extra cautious. Just get up there, drop it off and bring the money straight back.'

Ged nodded. He took a deep breath before he spoke. 'This is the last run I'm doing, Frankie. My old man is out of the nick this week and I want to keep him on the straight and narrow and how can I do that if I'm dabbling in the world he's trying to leave behind?'

But Frankie was having none of it. 'Nah, you can't just stop. You're quids in and you are earning. You'd be a fool to give that up, wouldn't you?'

Ged sucked hard on the spliff and exhaled before he answered. 'It's just the way it is. I need to think about my old man, don't I?'

Frankie wasn't impressed. You could see the cogs whirring. 'Do whatever then, mate. Just get your arse up there tonight and sort it out.'

Ged looked relieved. He'd been dreading telling Frankie that he was stopping. It had gone better than he'd feared. He looked at his watch and closed his eyes. One last job and this would be over for good and he could go back to his normal life without all the stress and worry hanging on his head. He'd saved a few hundred quid now, so that should help him out for a while. Well, until his dad got back into work and back on his feet. Frankie stood up and scouted the area. He seemed agitated, like he had something on his mind. 'Pick the gear up from the usual place and let me know when you're on the way back and I'll meet you. Like I said, don't fuck this up. It's a good wage for you to finish on.'

Ged pulled his jacket down. 'Oh yeah, Frankie, before you shoot off, I want to thank you for all you've done for me. You hooked me up and sorted me out. Cheers for that.'

Frankie didn't seem to be arsed with his mate's thanks. He was already walking off, never turned back once or said a word.

––––––––––

Ged sat on the train looking out of the window, lost in a world of his own. A final trip, then it was over. Bright lights in the distance, the noise of the speeding engines. This was his last drop, the end of feeling anxious, the end of putting himself at risk. He patted his coat pocket and closed his eyes for a few minutes. He'd be in Blackpool soon and his plan was to get in and out as quickly as he could. There would be no staying over at the trap gaff, he was just doing his job and bringing the cash back. Then he'd put this life behind him. He wasn't a thug, a gangster, who was he trying to kid? Ged opened his eyes quickly as he felt the back of his seat move. He could feel someone's warm breath; the hairs on the back of his neck stood on end and a cold rush of adrenaline flooded through his body. His knife, where was it? He rummaged in his coat pocket. Voices behind him, whispering. Ged gripped the handle of the sharp metal blade inside his pocket, and braced himself to plunge it deep into anyone who thought they could have him over. He jumped up and looked behind him, meeting the eyes of two teenagers, both dressed in black with hats pulled down low. He stepped out into the aisle and headed to the toilets still clutching the blade. He was probably being paranoid, but those two guys seemed shifty as fuck.

Ged stood in the toilet and checked his watch, he'd be in Blackpool any minute now; he relaxed a little. He turned left out of the toilet rather than right and went to sit somewhere else, looking back as he moved along the aisle. The two lads had gone, nowhere to be seen. He was spooked though, his breathing getting faster and his heart still thumping. He looked around again just to double-check. Nothing. He let out a laboured breath and found a place near the doors ready for a quick exit. He perched on the edge of the seat, trying to make sure he had a good view of the areas around him. If anybody was coming for him, he would be ready for them. He reached into his coat pocket again and gripped his knife again. Frankie had given it to him and he never thought he'd actually have to use it but God help anyone who fucked with him – they were getting it dug deep into their flesh.

Ged kept looking over his shoulder and as soon as he left the station, he got on his toes. His heart raced; he still had a gut feeling that something wasn't right. Was the dibble on his case, was he being watched, was something happening? The night was cold and seemed darker than any other, pitch black. He dipped his head low and cautiously set off on his usual route before picking up his pace and breaking into a jog, still looking over his shoulder every few seconds. It was like his mind was playing tricks on him. He could hear footsteps behind him as he cut through a housing estate. He started to sprint. His breath was ragged as he ran through the dark entry.

Rustling, banging, shouting.

Ged fell to the floor as the first blow hit his head. Noises, frantic voices, hands rummaging in his pockets. He lifted his head up; his vision was blurred, all he could see was silhouettes. Feet booting him, his body curled up in a small ball as he tried to protect himself. 'I've got it, sorted,' said a voice somewhere above him. Ged rolled onto his side, blood seeping out of the corner of his mouth. His fingers splayed across the cold grey concrete flags as he tried to lift himself up from the floor. There was a burning pain in the side of his stomach like someone had poured boiling water over him. A pain like he'd never felt before. It felt like a hot poker had been shoved deep into his flesh He reached down and touched it. His fingers were wet, covered with bright red claret. He'd been stabbed.

Ged could barely make it onto his feet, his fingers clasped the cold wall. He didn't seem to be able to speak or call for help. It was like someone had locked his words inside his mouth. He looked down the entry; he could see a figure approaching. For fuck's sake they were coming back to finish him off. It was no use, every bit of strength from his body had left him, he was a sitting duck. He covered his head and sank to the floor and prepared himself for more beatings.

There was silence, nothing was happening. Then a soft voice. 'I knew this was going to happen. I seen them following you when you got off the train. You've been set up.' Ged lifted his head and tried to focus on the face he could see in front of him which was swimming in and out of focus. It looked familiar. It looked like …

'Nancy,' he managed. 'They've stabbed me, get me home, please get me home.'

Nancy tried to help him to his feet. 'You need to go to the hospital, Ged, the blood's pumping out of you. Let me tie this around your waist to try and stop it.' She pulled the black scarf from her neck and lifted up his T-shirt, her eyes wide open with shock. 'Fucking hell Ged, it's deep, blood's gushing out all over the place. They've sliced you up good and proper.'

'Get me back home, Nancy, it's not that deep. Stop overreacting. I'll go to the hossy in Manchester. I need to get away from here, please just help me to get home.'

Nancy hovered over him. She owed him nothing – the way he'd treated her she should have left him to rot. Not so much of a big boy now, was he? Ged's mobile started to ring, but he ignored the call; his life was at risk here. He knew it was touch and go whether he'd make it or not. He could take a turn for the worse any second, he just needed to get home. Nancy hooked his arm over her shoulder, and she started to walk back towards the train station. She was strong this girl was, and she was doing a pretty good job of supporting him.

'Ged, are you sure you can do this? I'll get a taxi if you want?' He didn't reply. His body was weak and all he wanted was to go home. Nancy was his only lifeline.

She knew, when they got back to the train station, that he needed to act normal. If anyone even suspected that he'd been knifed they would ring the police at the drop of a hat and he'd be arrested and have the book thrown at him.

'Ged, try and stand up properly, we're nearly there. Please. Trust me, you need to act normal if you want me to get you home.'

She pulled his hood up over his head and he walked as tall as he could to the platform. 'Just get me home, please. I want my mam,' he sobbed.

Ged doubled up in pain as he sat on the train. Beads of sweat were visible all over his forehead, he was burning up. Nancy held scraps of tissue in her hand, patting his forehead to try and cool him down. She seemed to have stopped the bleeding from the stomach area, but he was in so much pain. He needed to get to the hospital as soon as they reached Manchester.

Ged's phone was ringing again, and it took all his strength just to pull it out of his pocket, only to see Frankie's name flashing. He held a single finger to his mouth and urged

Nancy to be quiet. He looked around and made sure he was safe to talk before he answered the call. 'I've been had over Frankie, they took the fucking lot, bruv.'

Nancy could hear the cursing and shouting down the other end of the line. She pulled a face, ready to take the phone from Ged's hand and tell the prick how badly his so-called mate was hurt. As the call ended Ged dropped his head back, his eyes closed and his bottom lip trembling.

'Frankie is going sick, he said it's up to me now to pay the money back. It's five fucking grand, Nance. Where the fuck am I gonna get five K?'

Nancy shook her head and gritted her teeth. 'Is he for real or what? It's not your fault you got had over. Tell him it was you who put your neck on the line, not fucking him. He's a cheeky bastard. Did he even ask how you were or where the hell you was?' The blood started to seep through the scarf again; she knew he was on borrowed time.

'Nancy, shut the fuck up. I don't need you chipping in right now. What the fuck were you doing up here anyway?' His words were slow, his face paler than it was five minutes before. He needed to rest, save any energy he had.

Nancy looked at him slowly. She'd just saved this lad's arse and now he was on his way home he was getting mouthy with her. 'It's a free country, I can go wherever I want. It's a good job I was there tonight, or your sorry arse would be six foot under. I spotted you leaving the train when I was on the platform. I wanted to see where you were going – thought maybe we could chill for a bit.'

Ged clenched his fists; he wasn't listening to a word she was saying. 'I knew those two muppets behind me on the train were up to no good. I could sense it. I had a gut feeling I should have listened to it instead of carrying on. I should have stayed in the station for a bit longer to make sure they weren't on my case.'

'That doesn't matter now. The most important thing is to get you looked at. Frankie can whistle for his money if you ask me. He's a prick saying it's your debt now. What happened to him having your back, best mate, brothers-in-arms and all that? He was talking through his arse if you ask me.'

Ged wasn't talking anymore; he was getting weaker, and struggling for breath. For the rest of the journey he kept quiet. His head was battered, and he knew this shit just got real. He had a debt to pay, a lot of money to find to pay for his mistake. He couldn't walk away now, however much he wanted to. He had to stay in the game and work his debt off. He knew the rules.

Chapter Seventeen

Nancy stayed by Ged's side all night long. She did all the talking in the hospital, told them that Ged was jumped as he walked down the canal with her. The police would be here soon, and they would want to know every detail of the attack. But she was on the ball this girl was, and she'd already hatched a plan to get Ged off the hook.

Ged lay in the hospital bed and lifted the white sheets up to look at his battered and bruised body. He'd had six stitches in his stomach and the doctor had told him he was lucky to be alive. Every move he made hurt like hell; you could see the waves of pain soaring through his body in his eyes.

Once Nancy had made sure Ged could get the story straight, she told him to ring his mother. When she arrived, she stormed into the room, though once she spotted her son laying in the bed, she nearly folded in two.

'Ged, fucking hell, who would do this to you? Where was you, what was you doing?'

Nancy was the one who answered her. 'We were walking along the canal and we spotted two lads coming towards us. I think they were high on spice or drunk or something because they didn't seem right, they were loud and throwing stuff into the water. I knew they were going to kick off because I heard one of them say he was going to twat Ged on the way past. There was nothing we could have done, it all happened so quick. All I can remember is seeing Ged on the floor and the lads running off laughing.'

Clare clutched her son's hand and stroked his fingers. She was crying. 'You could have died. Oh my God, what would I have done then if that had happened? Ged, oh my God, son. I'm so glad you are still alive.' She started sobbing even louder and Nancy had to comfort her.

'The doctor said he's going to be fine. Hopefully, the lads who done it will get caught. Ged's the innocent one in all this. He was just in the wrong place at the wrong time.'

Clare stroked her son's face gently. 'Son, bloody hell, my baby.' The door swung open and Frankie marched in. How he'd got past the nurses was anyone's guess. His mouth was moving rapidly as he chewed on gum. He glared at Nancy. 'What are you doing here?'

Clare looked over at Nancy; she could tell right away these two had beef.

Nancy sat up straight and faced him. He didn't own her, who was he to tell her who she could speak to? 'I'm here for the same reason you are. I care about him.'

Frankie edged closer. 'You can get off now he's fine. I'll sit with him, you get yourself off home.'

It was clear to Clare that there was no love lost between them and she decided she had better get involved. Teenage feelings ran deep, she knew that much. 'Frankie, Nancy was the one who brought him to the hospital. I'm sure Ged wants her here, don't you?' Ged's eyes looked more swollen with every second that passed, deep purple bruising, puffy and sore. 'She can stay,' he croaked. Frankie sat down. You could have cut the atmosphere with a knife.

Clare stood up. 'I'm going to speak with the medical team. I want to know what they're doing for him. You could fall apart in this place and nobody would notice, they're stretched so thin. All these NHS cuts are showing now. I knew they would in the end. What did they expect when they are cutting jobs all the time?'

She reached over and kissed her son on his forehead. 'I won't be a minute, son, I'm just going to have a word with the doctor and make sure they've examined you properly. You might need an X-ray, maybe there's broken bones. I mean, you have to check, don't you, who knows what internal injuries you've had?'

As she left the room, Frankie followed her with his eyes to make sure she was gone. Nancy, in turn, was watching him like a hawk.

'Fuck me, mate, they messed you up good and proper, didn't they?'

Ged winced as he replied. 'I knew things didn't seem right. There were two lads on the train – they looked shady. I moved away from them and sat on my own up the carriage.'

'Dirty bastards they are. Stabbing you up too, why didn't they just give you a few digs and take the gear?'

Nancy listened to the conversation sitting forward in her seat. 'The lads must have followed him up from Manchester, I mean, they must have had some inside information that he was carrying, otherwise how would they know?'

Ged looked at her. 'She's right. They must have been on to me from the start and moved up the carriages when we were nearing Blackpool.'

Frankie didn't make eye contact. 'Nah, I reckon they just got lucky that's all. It happens all the time.'

But Nancy wouldn't let it lie. 'No Frankie, it's a set-up for sure. Who knew he was taking gear up tonight? You must have told somebody, otherwise how come he got jumped?'

Frankie had had enough. He'd never liked Nancy and wanted to make sure she knew that meddling in his business would get her hurt. He checked the door was shut properly. 'What the fuck do you know about it all, you ugly cunt? Why was you with him, anyway? Ged, don't tell me you took her with you when I told you to cart her?'

Ged didn't have chance to reply, Nancy was right in there. She didn't need anyone to fight her corner. 'So, it was you who ruined things between us? I knew it wasn't Ged. I was there because I was watching his back, unlike you. Ged didn't even know I was on the train. You use Ged to do your dirty work and make him think that he's one of your boys. Go on, Frankie, tell him the truth: you don't really give a flying fuck about him, it's all about the money.'

Frankie gripped her by the scruff of her neck, spittle landing on her face as he pulled her up close. His teeth were clenched tightly together as he spoke. 'Who the fuck do you think you are, you daft rat? Ged got rid of you because he had other girls on the go, pretty girls, not munters like you. Go home, little girl, before you get hurt. There is nothing here that concerns you, fuck off home.' He released his grip and flung her back in her seat.

But Nancy was never one to take things lying down. 'You're lucky I'm not telling the police about you. I've seen the way you get the lads involved and don't think I haven't. Leave Ged alone and go and get one of your other muppets to do your dirty work. Trust me, you don't want to mess with me. I'm not scared of you or any of your boys.'

Frankie pursed his lips and spat in her eye; Nancy flicked it away with the ends of her fingers. 'You don't scare me Frankie, not now, not ever.'

Clare walked back into the room with an update and the others fell silent. 'I've spoken with the doctor and he wants you to stay in for a few days to keep an eye on you. At least you will rest here because I know if you were at home, you'd be doing everything to go out. I'm just going to find the toilet. Back in a minute.'

Frankie, meanwhile, was furious, his face red with anger. He pulled his cap down low and ignored Nancy altogether.

'Ged, I'm getting off, I'll call tomorrow. Let me know if you need anything bringing up.'

Ged nodded weakly.

Nancy tilted her head towards Frankie. 'Prick,' she mumbled under her breath as he left.

Ged groaned as he tried to find a comfortable position. He looked directly at Nancy, his eyes wet with tears. 'Thanks for helping me. I dread to think what would have happened if you wasn't there. And as for Frankie, leave him to me. He's a hothead and you just need to know how to handle him.' He broke off as his phone beeped. He reached over with difficulty and looked at the text, his eyes growing wide as he read the message.

> You're a daft prick getting jumped. You owe me
> five grand remember. As soon as you're out of
> there you better get grafting and pay the
> money back. You fucked up, it's your problem
> not mine.

Ged deleted it and put the phone face down on his lap.

Nancy could see something had upset him even more. 'What? What is it?' she asked.

'I'm up shit street, that's what,' Ged whispered under his breath.

Nancy reached over and held his hands. 'We're in this together Ged, if you fight, I fight.'

Chapter Eighteen

*D*onny *was in a foul mood this morning*, thought Susan. He stormed around the bedroom, behind schedule, which didn't help matters either.

'Susan, where the hell is my good white shirt? The fitted one with the long sleeves?'

Susan rolled over and dragged the duvet over her head. She was having a lie-in for once and was pissed off at being woken up. Her words were muffled. 'Check the wardrobe properly. If it's been washed, then it will be there. Shut up anyway, I'm trying to sleep. You should have got your clothes ready last night for work instead of pissing off down the boozer with your mates.'

'Do I need this moaning so early in the morning? Simple question, that's all, I don't need a fucking lecture.'

Susan peered out from under the duvet. 'What's the matter, Donny, did you lose this time? I know you've been at the casino again, you're always like this when you've been there thinking you can win big. It's a loser's game. I've told you time and time again, you'd be better off staying away from there. There is only ever going to be one winner, and it's not going to be you. You're a mug.'

She pulled the duvet back over her head; that was it, he could piss off now and go to work without a kiss goodbye. He was a moody fucker and he needed to learn the hard way. She'd show him she could be a pain in the arse, too.

Donny perched on the edge of the bed and put his socks on. 'I'll wear my blue shirt then, shall I? Sorry I bleeding asked. And I can't find my watch either. Have you seen it? I swear I put it on the bedside table like always, but it's not there.'

No reply.

He pulled his phone out of his pocket and checked through his messages. Whatever he saw there didn't make him happy. He was in a bigger rush now. There was no sweet talk for his wife this morning, no coffee, no sitting by the fire, he was proper stressed out.

Susan sat up as she heard the front door slam shut. She brought her clasped hand out from under the covers and unfolded her fingers one by one. She smiled as she looked at Donny's Rolex.

'Revenge is sweet, Donny, very sweet indeed.'

Tina pulled up outside Wendy's house. Apparently, it was her job to pick her stepdaughter up and take her to school from there. Nevaya had stayed at her mother's house last night, yet somehow it seemed that Tina would be the mug who had to scurry around after her doing all the fetching and carrying. Why Wendy couldn't take her to school was beyond her – she had a car, what was the problem? Tina texted Nevaya.

I'm outside. Running late so don't be long.

She hit Send and shoved her phone back into her bag. She kept the engine running and tapped her fingers on the dashboard, waiting. She was on edge today, even more than usual; twitchy, licking her lips a lot. It was the first time in a long time that she'd not reached for her secret booze stash to give her the kick-start that she needed to help get her through the day. She could do this, she told herself; she was no alcoholic. Everything was going to change for the better and once she had a baby in her arms her life would be complete. She just had to come up with a plan, find a way to get Chris on board. Tell him it was a private adoption. Something like that. He said he loved her, so surely he would want her to be happy? Together they could get through this. He would understand, he'd support her and everything in the garden would be rosy again. He'd just be happy that she was happy, and she would have the one thing her body had craved for so long, a child.

Tina twisted the blue plastic lid from her water bottle and took a large mouthful, wiping her mouth with the side of her hand. Where the hell was Nevaya? She checked her watch again and sighed. Her patience was running out. She banged the flat of her palm against the horn. So what if the neighbours were pissed off, looking at her through their windows, she was going to be late. 'For crying out loud…'

Nevaya finally appeared at the gate looking as cocky and

full of attitude as ever. Tina sat up straight in her seat, her hands gripping the steering wheel tighter as Wendy was walking behind her. She gritted her teeth. If the witch wanted beef, she'd give it her, the mood she was in. What the hell did she have to say for herself?

Nevaya opened the car door but made no move to get in, just stood talking to her mother; chit-chat, nothing of any importance. Tina was sure they were doing it just to wind her up. She sighed loudly, not one bit arsed if they heard her. She didn't have all day.

Nevaya finally looked round, bending slightly to meet Tina's eyes. 'What's up with you? I'll be with you in a minute. I'm just saying goodbye to my mother.' She stressed the word mother too. Like she was rubbing salt in the wound. Enough was enough, fuck that.

'I'm going to be late, some of us have to get to work. If you're not ready now, then you can make your own way to school. I'm not a bleeding taxi service. Or better still get your mother to take you.'

And suddenly there she was, mouth almighty – it was never going to be long before she made her presence felt. Wendy moved her daughter out of the way and stuck her head inside the open car door. 'Don't you be speaking to my daughter like that. No wonder she can't stand the sight of you, acting like you're her mother when the truth is, you haven't got a maternal bone in your body.'

That was enough for Tina. She unclipped her seatbelt and leant over into the passenger side so they were face to face. The long months of frustration came rushing to the surface. Wendy was trouble, always had been.

'Listen here, fucking Mother of the Year. Nobody asked you to poke your nose in, so take your sweaty arse back into the house and leave me to be the mother you could never be. You've been back on the scene for five minutes and already you're causing grief, so stop filling her head with shit and crawl back under the rock you came from. Don't mess with me, Wendy, because I'll take you to the bleeding cleaners. Trust me, I'll ruin you if you mess with me.'

Tina hadn't finished yet. 'And you, Nevaya, are you getting in or am I going without you? You're either in or out.' Wendy was doing her best to come back with some verbals of her own, but Tina wasn't giving her any airtime. 'Last chance, I'm going,' she yelled.

Nevaya slouched into the car, clearly fuming. 'How dare you talk to my mam like that? Who the hell do you think you are? You just wait until my dad hears about this, he'll pull you down a peg or two, just you wait and see.'

Tina turned the radio up full blast and pulled out. Wendy was still stood on the pavement shouting abuse, but she rammed two fingers up at her and drove off.

What was happening to Tina? She never used to be like this. She was always so mild-mannered and good-natured. Maybe it was a case of if you can't beat them, join them. Months of abuse from her husband's kids had finally taken its toll.

Nevaya sat with her arms folded tightly across her chest, leaning against the passenger window, keeping as far away from Tina as she could, as if she was diseased. She was furious. The journey continued in complete silence. Not a peep out of her, nothing until Tina pulled over outside the school.

'Money. I need some dinner money,' she mumbled.

Tina huffed and dragged her handbag from the back seat. 'I thought your mother would have given you your dinner money?'

'I didn't ask her for any, otherwise she would have. Listen, just give me the cash and I'll be out of your face.'

Tina opened her purse and pulled out a fiver. Nevaya went to snatch it from her hand but Tina held on to it as she stared her stepdaughter out. 'I can carry on like this for as long as you want, young lady, so be my guest. I'm prepared.'

Nevaya swallowed hard as she looked at Tina. Locked eyes, no words. Tina reached over and dropped the note into her lap. 'Have a nice day at school, look forward to seeing you later,' she said in a sarcastic tone.

Nevaya picked up the money – she couldn't wait to get out of the car. She slammed the door shut, nearly taking it off its hinges. Tina wished she'd had that nip of brandy now.

'Kids,' she mumbled under her breath as she drove away.

———

Donny sat at his desk staring out of the window. His mind seemed to be all over the place this morning, he wasn't on the ball like usual. He looked rough too, stressed. Tina came into the office holding two cups of coffee and passed him one.

'There you go, you look like you need a caffeine fix. What's up with you this morning?'

Donny shook his head, back in the moment. 'Cheers, Tina, I was a million miles away then. Away with the fairies.'

'I know. Anyway, back to business. We have the new lad, Dan, starting today, can you meet and greet him? His mam is bringing him about half ten.'

Donny turned away, pretending to read through his diary. 'I've got to go and see Ged. But I'll sort it, find someone who can do it. What else have we got on today?'

Tina watched him closely from the corner of her eye as she replied as casually as she could.

'I said I'd take Amelia for some checks. She's confided in me – thinks she might have a STD and can't tell her parents. So, if it's alright with you I'll take her to the clinic.'

Donny ruffled through the paperwork on his desk. 'Bleeding hell, what is wrong with some of these kids. Have they never heard of condoms or what? Make a note for me to bring this up in the staff meeting. They clearly need to be doing more in the sex ed lessons. You'd think these kids would be on the ball with stuff like that but, on my life, if brains were dynamite they couldn't blow their bleeding noses.'

'Come on, boss. You know what it's like. They're not thinking straight half the time. These aren't normal teenage love affairs – most of them have only ever seen sex as a bargaining chip, or a power game. They've not exactly had many good examples around them growing up. That's how they end up where Amelia is. So, book me out this morning, yeah?'

'Yep, I'll manage. Just make sure while you're there that they have a good talk with her, give her enough condoms to keep her out of trouble. Otherwise next thing she'll be getting pregnant.'

Tina forced herself to smile. 'Leave it with me, I'll get it sorted. Right, I'll go meet and greet the students. You sort your head out and straighten your hair up. Honest, you look like you've been out on a bender.'

As Tina left the room Donny sat staring at his mobile, flicking through his messages with a grim expression on his face.

———

Ged was sat on the edge of his bed when Clare walked into his bedroom. 'How you feeling, love? I've rang school and told them you're home now and Mr Knight said he's coming to see you later.'

Ged went ballistic. 'What the fuck are you involving him for? You've got a right gob on you. As if I need the school on my back. You know Dad's getting out today and I just wanted to spend some time with him. His head's been done in, he's blaming himself for my attack, fuck knows why. He's allowed here to see me, isn't he, because if you say he's not stepping over our front door again then I'm going.'

'You're not going anywhere. The doctors have told you that you have to rest. Ged, you were stabbed, all those stitches. You could have died.'

He looked at her, challenging her. 'So, my dad is coming here, then?' Clare swallowed hard, she was backed into a corner. If she said no, then Ged would be out of the house to go and see his old man. Her hands were tied. She paced about the room twisting her fingers.

'He can come here, but Ged he's not getting his feet back

under the table. I'm telling you that now. I know him too well, he's a piss-taker. A free-loader.'

'I just want to see my dad. Stop dissing him and putting barriers there all the time. Just because he messed up a few times… He tried his best, Mam. He wanted to help us, you know, his family.'

Clare let out a sarcastic laugh. 'Stop talking out of your arse. The man was always up to no good. He promised me the world and told me time and time again that he was on the straight and narrow. Bullshit, it was all bullshit. I can't tell you how many times that man had me over.'

Ged hung his head; he'd heard this over and over. It was doing his head in. Maybe it was time to put his cards on the table and tell her how he felt.

'I don't care what he's done. He might have messed up, but come on, Mam, how many times have you messed up? My dad told me about when you left him and hooked up with his best mate.'

Clare's jaw dropped. What the fuck? How dare Kevin tell her son stuff like that. It was years ago. Ged seemed to be waiting for an explanation. She sat down on the bed beside him.

'Your father had no right telling you stuff like that. It was before you were born, Ged. Your dad was out all the time and I was left by myself when he was doing whatever he was doing. He said he was talking business, but come on, Ged, you can't believe a word that comes out of that man's mouth.'

'So, it's true?' he asked.

Clare was sweating now. She was quiet for a few seconds while she got her story together. 'Sam was a lovely man, and yes he was one of your dad's friends. I wouldn't class him as his best mate but, yes, they were mates. I'd been seeing your dad for a few months but we were on and off. Your dad never turned up when he said he was taking me out, and Ged,' she paused, 'I was sick of being sat all dressed up and the cheeky bleeder never turning up, never rang me or nothing he just left me high and dry. He always had an excuse, oh yes, something had always come up but, in the end, there is only so much a girl can take. So when Sam asked me to go out, I said yes. It wasn't like I was married or anything.' She stopped for a moment, looked awkward. 'In fact, I wasn't going to tell you anything yet, but while we are on the subject, you should probably know I've started seeing Sam again. He came into the club a few months ago and we got talking.'

Ged was silent for a moment then spoke more softly than before. 'My dad loves you and he always will. If he finds out about this, he will do you in. He'll go back to jail, Mam.'

'It's not my problem. I have a life to live too and I'm not being dictated to by you, or your bleeding father.'

'Slag.' Ged whispered under his breath but not so quietly that Clare didn't hear him. She asked him to repeat what he'd just said. He clamped his lips together and refused. They sat in silence for a few minutes, until Ged shook his head sadly. 'My dad said you broke his heart.'

'Oh, give me a bleeding break, Ged. It was over seventeen years ago so I don't know why he's still going on about it. He's after the sympathy vote, why on earth he's telling you this stuff anyway is beyond me. We're done, I can't change it can I?'

'Yes you can, Mam, let him show you how much he's changed. This Sam will never love you like my dad does. We're a family, we can make it work.' Ged was upset, he craved a proper family unit, truly believed that if his dad was back at home then all their problems would be over.

'Look. I've said he can come and see you but don't ask me to be part of it. I'll go in the front room and he can come in here.'

Ged didn't look at her. 'Whatever.'

Chapter Nineteen

Amelia stood nervously waiting for Tina in the school kitchen. She kept checking the clock on the wall as she fiddled with the ends of her hair. Rita was watching her.

'How you feeling this morning? Not feeling sick anymore?'

Amelia shook her head. 'No, I'm fine now. It must have been something I ate.'

Rita was alarmed. 'I hope you're not blaming my cooking, I do everything by the book in this place. It's bang on.'

Rita was beating eggs; she could see the girl trying not to gag and moved in closer. 'Get a smell of them eggs, they'll be ready soon if you fancy. Scrambled.'

Amelia covered her mouth as the colour drained from her cheeks; she looked like someone had poured a bag of flour over her head. Rita looked at her knowingly and walked away, calling behind her, 'Yep, just as I thought.' She carried on with her chores without another word.

Tina rushed in looking mithered and raised her eyes at Amelia. 'Are you ready to go?'

She nodded and reached over for her coat.

Rita turned to face Tina. 'So where are you off to?'

'Oh, just an appointment. We should be back by lunch-time so put a meal out for Amelia please.'

Rita studied them both. 'Are you sure she can stomach it, you know, with her problem?' She flicked her eyes at Amelia's stomach.

Tina tried to ignore her and started heading for the door, urging Amelia along with her. 'See you later, Rita.'

The minute they got outside, Tina turned to her student. 'What the hell have you told her?'

Amelia shrugged her shoulders. 'Nothing, I've never said a word. What are you even on about?'

Tina got into the car and waited for Amelia to fasten her seatbelt. She carried on talking as she started the engine. 'I've told you. If this is going to work you need to make sure that you don't say a word to anyone. If one single person finds out about this, then you're up shit creek. Right now I'm happy to help you and I will take the baby, but this will only work if it's kept between us and no one else. Do you hear me, our secret?'

'I never said a word, miss. She was just acting weird around me that's all. She's a mad one, Rita, everyone knows that, you're overreacting.'

Tina drove along the main road, keeping her eyes fixed on the traffic ahead. 'I don't even know how this is going to work, but when we sit down in a minute, we can go over a few things.'

'Like what?'

Tina swallowed hard – she knew what she was about to say would freak Amelia out. 'I'm going to rent a flat for you out of the area. You'll have to go missing.'

Amelia looked at her. 'What, not see any of my family, or my friends?'

'It might sound a bit scary at first, but you'll get used to it soon enough and it's not for ever. I'll bring you everything you need. It's the only way you'll be able to hide the pregnancy from everyone. I'm not talking miles away, just out of Moston.'

'Piss off, miss. There's no way I'm putting my family through that. Imagine my mam if I just disappear, it'll kill her. No, you need to rethink this. I'm not living in any fucking flat on my tod. I can't even cook or use a washing machine. Ask my mam, she'll tell you, I'm useless. Why can't I just tell them I'm giving you the baby?'

Tina wasn't going to let her fantasy go without a fight. 'Are you stupid or what? Do you think they just hand out babies to anyone who wants one?' She slammed the brakes on as she nearly drove into the back of the car in front of her. 'You can tell your parents you're pregnant then. You'll just have to deal with it yourself. I've offered you a lifeline, but, if that's what you want, I'll ring your dad when we get back to school and tell him you're having a baby and you don't know who the father is.' Tina hated hearing the venom behind her words, but couldn't stop it flowing.

Amelia covered her ears with her hands, reality was hitting home. 'No!' she screamed. 'You're not telling them anything.'

Tina pulled into a side street and parked up. She turned to face Amelia. 'Listen, this is not a fairy tale with a happy ending. You're having a baby. You're going to have to do what I say or go home and face the music. I'll tell you something too, the minute this comes out I bet social services will be all over your family as well. You'll be lucky to keep the baby even if you wanted to. It'll end up in the care system. Is that what you want?'

Amelia sobbed. 'I just want it to be over. Why can't I just get rid of it? You said you would help.'

'And I will help. But you're underage and I have a duty of care to tell your parents if you have an abortion. This way they never need to know. Can you see any other way of this working? If you've got any better ideas, then let's hear them.'

'If we do what you want … can't you come and stay with me? I don't want to be alone.'

'I have a family, Amelia. I can't just walk out on them.' She sat thinking for a few minutes before she carried on talking. 'I don't know. Maybe I could move in. If I'm being honest, things at home aren't great. Some time out might be good. And at least if I was there with you, I would know you are looking after yourself and the baby.' Tina felt a spark of excitement. Would leaving her husband be such a bad thing anyway? She was just a slave for them all and it'd show Chris this time, show him that she was sick of his shit and his unruly children. 'Leave it with me for now. Let me think things through.'

Frankie trudged into school. It looked like he had a black eye.

Donny was stood outside and watched him walk past without saying a word. He headed straight to his car. Ged had been involved in knife crime and Donny was heading round to his house to find out more. He'd catch up with Frankie later. When it rained it poured in this place.

Donny was so wrapped up in it all that he didn't notice the black car with tinted windows parked up near the school again.

Chapter Twenty

Clare was cleaning up; her anxiety was through the roof. Mr Knight would be here soon, and her husband was getting out of jail today. Her nerves couldn't take much more. It was one thing after another. Everyone could get to fuck, they were doing her head in. She just wanted to be alone, to curl up in a tight ball and be invisible.

Ged limped into the living room, using his hand on the door frame to steady himself. That was all Clare needed.

'What the bleeding hell are you doing out of bed? You know you need to rest. Get your arse back up to bed and don't be stupid.'

Ged ignored her as he stumbled towards the sofa. 'Nah, sack staying in bed all day. If the headteacher is coming to see me then he's not coming upstairs to my bedroom, he can see me down here. It's a shit-tip up there anyway, nobody is seeing my bedroom.'

Clare took his arm and helped him across the room. She couldn't face a fight. You had to pick your battles.

'Just sit down then. In fact, lie down I'll put a pillow under your head.'

Ged batted her away. 'Mam, stop faffing about will you? Just leave me alone, you're pecking my head and I've only been down here with you five minutes. And you wonder why I go out all the time.'

Clare sighed. 'The landline's been ringing all morning too. Nancy's been on about twenty times and Frankie rang too. Said he'd texted you.'

Ged ignored her and fumbled in his pocket for his mobile, which he'd left on silent. Missed calls, texts. He put it down again.

'So, what's the story with Nancy now, are you on or off with her? I'm not being funny but if you have no feelings for the girl then you should let her down gently. She seems kind of up and down at the minute, though that might be because of everything that went on. I'm grateful to her, I tell you, but it's down to you. Just be straight with her.'

'Why are you arsed, Mam? It's nothing to do with you so wind your neck in.'

'I'm only asking. She obviously cares about you so if you're binning her just be careful. She makes out she's a tough one but I can just tell that underneath she's fragile.'

'I've told you, back off. It's my life and I'll do whatever I'm doing. It's not like you can lecture me about relationships, is it? My dad only turned his back for a few seconds and you was on to someone else.'

'You cheeky little bastard, how dare you speak to me like that? Carry on, smart-arse and you'll see what I'm about. Who's been here all the time for you, not your fucking dad, so stop brown-nosing him. How did I know this would happen?'

Ged sat back and folded his arms in front of him. That was him told. His mother was still going on – he'd really pressed her buttons this time. 'I'll be telling him that too the minute I set eyes on him. Who the fuck is he to tell you stuff about me because we can all play at that game, can't we? Oh yes, I could tell you a few stories about him that he wouldn't be proud of.'

Clare raised her eyes to the ceiling. She was at breaking point and she was still having a go at Ged. 'I want respect in this house and if you're not willing to give it then you can get your bags packed and piss off with him too. He's only just getting out of jail and already he's upsetting the apple cart.'

Before Ged could say anything in reply, there was a knock at the door. They looked at each other. Clare straightened her hair and brushed at her cheeks. 'That'll be Mr Knight. I'll be telling him about your attitude too. Let's see if he can talk a bit of sense into you, because I know I can't.' She left the room and went into the hallway.

Ged sighed. He could hear talking, whispering. He strained to hear what was being said. Shit, they were coming into the room. He lay back.

'Here he is, the warrior.' Donny raised his hand in greeting. 'Glad to see you're alright. You had us all worried. You're very lucky to still be with us, lad.'

Clare followed behind and invited him to sit down. 'I'm banging the kettle on if you want a brew, Mr Knight?' Donny sat and tapped his hands on his knees. 'I'd love a coffee if you're making one.'

'Sugar?'

'No, I'm sweet enough,' he joked.

Ged pulled a face – was his headteacher hitting on his mother?

Donny waited for Clare to disappear into the kitchen and leant over towards Ged. 'So, fill me in, what really happened?'

'I just got jumped, sir. Unprovoked attack it was.'

'What, there was no arguing or anything? You can be straight with me, Ged. It doesn't make you a grass.'

'Nothing, I swear I never said a word to them, they just started kicking the shit out of me and one of them must have stabbed me up. I didn't even know I'd been stabbed at first.'

Donny looked concerned. He looked over towards the door and kept his voice low. 'So, you've been dealing, then?'

Ged's eyes were wide open. 'No, sir,' he stuttered. 'Who's been chatting shit about me because I'm not selling drugs, no way.'

Donny sat back and stroked his chin. 'I hear things, Ged, people talk. I heard you had drugs on you and that's why you got whacked in, is that right? County lines is serious business. It might seem like just something to do for your mates but there are nasty folk involved higher up, trust me on that. Have you heard anything about that kind of thing?'

Ged avoided eye contact. 'No sir, like I said. I got jumped for no reason. People need to stop gassing about me because if I find out who it is, I'll punch their fucking lights out.'

Donny nodded his head slowly. 'Calm down, keep your voice down. I have to ask you because I need to make sure you're going to be safe, Ged. We've all been worried about you lately. Your mam is out of her mind with it and you have to admit that you've changed recently.'

'I've not, I've just learnt not to take shit from people. I look after myself now and I don't let people take the piss out of me. What's wrong with that?'

Donny reached down into his bag and pulled out some paperwork. He understood this more than he was letting on; he'd been bullied, he'd been a victim. He knew how these things worked.

He started to read through his notes. 'You chill with Frankie a bit, don't you?'

Ged was alert now. 'Yes, why?'

Donny kept his eyes on the paperwork as he spoke.

'I think Frankie is up to something, he's come into school this morning and he looks like he's gone ten rounds in the ring, do you know anything about it?'

Ged sat up as best he could. 'No, I know nothing. Is he alright? Is he marked?'

'All I know is that whatever he's caught up in isn't doing him any good. Ged, if you know anything that might help him please let me know. I'll keep it between us two.' He looked at the teenager closely, watching his body language.

'I know nothing, so you're pissing in the wind, sir. Frankie is big enough to look after himself. If he's a marked man, then it must be someone who can have a fight because Frankie can hold his own.'

Clare walked back into the room holding two cups. She bent down to put them on the table. 'So, I hope he's talking to you nice, Mr Knight, because you should hear the abuse he's given me this morning. A right cheeky bleeder he is.' She blushed and shook her head. 'Sorry for swearing, but I'm at the end of my tether with him. His bell-end of a father is out of jail today and I'll tell you something for nothing; I can't promise to keep my mouth shut when he comes here.'

Ged was up in arms. This was his old man she was talking about, he was sick of it, sick to death of hearing her bad-mouth him all the time, even in front of Mr Knight now. 'She's only saying that because she's got a new man. Yeah, my dad's mate it is. She knows that when he finds out he'll be visiting Sam so that's why her arse is twitching. Payback time, isn't it, Mother?'

Clare gritted her teeth. 'Have you heard him? This is how he thinks he can talk to me now. I'll end up putting him in care, see how he likes that?'

Donny knew he had to intervene before it all blew up. 'OK, OK, let's just take a minute. It's a stressful time for both of you. Ged, you can't speak to your mother like that. You need to stop it, but Clare, you need to think about how you talk to your son too. You are the parent and you should lead by example. I'm here to help, but I didn't come round to watch you two rip each other to shreds with your words. Everyone needs to calm down. Ged, button it will you and just be quiet for a few minutes. You should be resting not kicking off.'

Ged was struggling to keep quiet. He had more to say for sure, but knew he had to pick his moments. Clare collapsed onto a chair, her head in her hands. Her hands were shaking, a lost look in her eyes. Donny reached over for his mug and sipped at his coffee. He'd done what he'd come for and he wasn't in the mood to be waiting around. Ged was still in one piece, he'd taken a statement, so in reality he'd ticked all the boxes to make sure his pupil was safe, what more could he do right now?

'Ged, I hope you get better soon, and we'll see you back in school as soon as you're well enough. You have your head screwed on and I know you know how important it is to make sure you sit your exams. You've still got a chance to make something of yourself if you make the right choices now. Please ring me if you need anything or if you need a talk.'

Clare slumped a little lower in her seat. Who was there for her? Who could she call for a chat? Bleeding nobody. Her new bloke, Sam, would run a mile if she let on what a shit-show her life really was. What fella would take all that on?

'Yeah, thanks,' Ged mumbled.

Donny packed away his paperwork and took a final mouthful of coffee. He stood up and straightened his trousers.

'Clare, keep me posted. Hopefully, Ged will be back in school next week if those stitches heal nicely.'

'Yeah, if I've not throttled him by then.'

Donny smiled and headed for the door. 'Bye, Ged,' he shouted behind him.

Donny waved as he walked down the path. He heard the sound of the front door shutting behind him and headed straight for his car. There was someone standing beside it, waiting.

'Nancy, what on earth are you doing here?'

The girl was scribbling something down and shoved it straight into her pocket when she heard him.

Donny edged closer. 'Were you taking my registration number down then?' he asked. Nancy ignored his question.

'Hello, sir. I'm on my way to see Ged, is he alright?'

'He's fine, Nancy, but shouldn't you be in school?'

'I'm not well, sir, bad period pains. My mam said I could stay off.'

'If you're not well then shouldn't you be at home in bed?'

Nancy walked past him and opened the garden gate.

'I can hang out with Ged. I've taken some painkillers so I should be alright. Anyway, I'm doing some research, so you could class that as schoolwork.'

Donny was never quite sure what to make of Nancy. He opened the car door and sighed. 'I'll ring your mother and double-check with her. And what kind of research are you doing?'

Nancy tapped the side of her nose. 'I'll let you know when I've finished it.'

'A mystery then' he said to himself under his breath and got into the car and flicked the engine over. He watched her standing at the door. What on earth was she up to?

Chapter Twenty-One

Tina was alone in the staff room, pacing up and down, her phone to her ear. 'Chris, I've given you chance after chance. I'm moving out so you'll just have to deal with it. Nevaya has no respect for me and Charlie is no better. And all you do is lie on the bleeding sofa all night long and I've had enough of it. I want more from life than listening to your kids argue and fight and diss me all the time.'

Chris had things to say too; she listened for a bit before jumping in again. 'I've made up my mind, Chris, I'm done. I'm moving out at the end of the week. Chance after chance you have had to make a difference but it's always the same and I can't take it anymore.'

The door creaked open slowly and Rita stuck her head into the room. Once she'd seen Tina deep in her call she backed away slowly before anyone noticed her. No point her disturbing her if she was busy, was there?

Donny was back at his desk replying to emails. There was a knock at the door and his face dropped as he spotted the new kid, Dan, stood there. He'd only been in the school five minutes – surely there couldn't be a problem already? He beckoned him in.

'Everything OK?'

Dan barged in and took a seat, slouched in the chair like he owned the place.

'What's going on, Dan? You can't just waltz in here like this.'

The boy stared at him. 'I think me and you need a little chat.'

Donny eyeballed the kid. If Charlie Big Spuds over here thought he was calling the shots, he had another think coming. He raised his voice.

'If there's something you need to discuss then you speak to your form tutor and then I take it from there if needed. We have rules in this school and they're there for a reason.'

Dan looked defiant. 'Oh, right. I just thought you would want us to keep this between ourselves. But, fair enough, if you want me to shout it from the rooftops that you're my father then so be it. I'll do just that then, *Dad*.'

Donny felt like he'd been slapped. He was choking, his windpipe was closing up, the colour drained from his face. He tried to take a deep breath. He had to be calm, think straight. He walked over to the window, loosened his tie and tried to look casual.

'Me, your dad, are you having a laugh or what?'

Dan didn't flinch. 'You remember my mum, Bethany, don't you? At least I bloody well hope you do.'

Donny started to sweat. The kid did bear a resemblance to him, he supposed. But could this really be his son? His flesh and blood? He tried to keep his cool.

'Yeah, that's right. She told me all about you, how you just packed up and cleared off with your family and left her up the duff, on her own to deal with it all herself. Not a very good daddy, eh?'

Donny had no choice but to brazen it out. He knew from Dan's age that the years matched up. But he didn't know this kid's birthday. Bethany could have got knocked up after he'd left for Manchester. And anyway, surely she'd have got in touch at the time. She must have just seen he was a head-teacher and figured he had the spare cash to pay maintenance. He'd have to shut this nonsense down immediately.

'Yes, thank you, Daniel. I did know your mother. But I didn't know she'd had a child.' He knew he should stay calm but he could feel panic getting the better of him. Before he knew it, more words spilled out. 'And as I remember, mate, I wasn't the only person hanging about with your mother at the time. There was a list as long as my arm, so how you can say I'm your dad is beyond me.'

Dan bolted from his seat and stormed over to where Donny was stood.

'Listen, you prick. You know full well you're my old man. Look at me, I'm your fucking double. So, don't be a smart arse trying to deny it. We'll do a test if you want. Don't see the bloody point though. You knew from the first second you seen me that I was your son. I could see it in your face that you knew, but if you're denying it then we'll have to do this the hard way. I wonder if your missus knows anything about your secret past? I might have to book my mum an appointment at that glitzy little salon of hers…'

Donny wasn't going to back down either, their faces were just inches apart. Normally he was the one to defuse a situation like this. But this was personal. And he knew his words about Bethany had added fuel to the fire.

'What do you know about my wife? You leave her out of this, you little fucker. Whatever your mother has told you is a lie. I'm happily married and I don't have any kids. She's got it wrong.'

Dan wriggled free and carried on. 'It's about time you started paying for your mistakes, isn't it? Did you think you could just sail off into the sunset and this would never come back to bite you on the arse? It's time to step up and pay your way.'

Donny spat his words right into the boy's face. 'So, that's what this is about, money. I thought as much. Come on, how much do you want?'

Dan walked slowly back to his seat and sat down. He seemed smaller somehow. 'I'm not sure what I want. I just know that you're my father and it's time you faced up to it. Do you know how it felt over the years growing up with no dad? My mam told me the truth from the start. She gave me photographs of you too. So let's make like I just want to be in your life. That's all I want – for now, anyway.'

Donny felt like he was in the middle of a nightmare. Apart from anything else, he knew that Susan would never accept that he'd had a child with another woman. It wasn't even the fact he had a kid. She'd never believe he didn't know anything about it – she'd think he'd hidden it. And though he'd never give Dan the satisfaction of admitting it, now he saw the fight in this kid, he was a chip off the old block. It should have been a proud moment – but there was no room for pride, or guilt or shame for that matter. All he felt was white-hot rage. No kid came into his manor and laid down the law. And certainly no little scrote was going to threaten Susan. This would break her heart, rip her in two. He had to make a stand.

'It's too late, Dan. Your mother and I went our separate ways long ago. I don't know anything about you. Never did. We have no bond, nothing.'

Dan couldn't look at him, the cockiness had left him, his voice was soft, choked.

'I've often imagined this moment, when we'd finally meet up and I'd tell you I was your son. I never, ever, thought it would be like this, that you'd just want to wash your hands of me.' And just like that, the shutters came down again and the hard look returned to his eyes. 'You're a dickhead, just like my mam has always told me. Well, Mr Fucking Knight, your world is going to fall apart just like mine has. You better tell your wife before I do.'

Donny was speechless.

Tina picked that exact moment to march into the office, though she didn't seem to clock what was going on; she was too deep in her own problems. Dan walked towards the door.

'Thanks, sir. I'll see you again soon.' And he was gone.

Donny sat down again, staring blankly at his computer screen, shaking his head. His heart was speeding like a runaway train and he felt sick. His world as he knew it would never be the same if Dan let the cat out of the bag. He had to think, he had to stop this lad from messing his life up, but how, how would he do this? Everything he'd worked for felt like a house of cards and this kid threatened to knock it all down.

It was lunchtime. Tina walked into the dining hall and scanned the place for Amelia. The racket was deafening; you couldn't hear yourself think in here today. Chelsea was the main culprit, as always, and you could hear her sounding off from the other side of the room. Frankie was sat on his own and Tina gestured to the deep bruise around his eye.

'What's happened to you, Frankie, where are those bruises from?'

He dropped his head low. She repeated her question. 'Frankie, are you alright?'

'Yeah, alright miss – just leave me alone. I'm fine.'

'Well, you don't look fine. After dinner come and see me, I want to talk to you.'

He completely ignored her, just carried on eating his food.

Rita was looking around the room to check she'd fed everyone. She caught Tina's eye and smirked. The teachers sat dotted about the room and ate their food too – there was no private space for staff to have lunch. That had always been one of Donny's things, everyone ate together in this school. She spotted Amelia, who looked like she was trying to be invisible. Tina sat at the end of the table, trying to catch her eye.

Melanie came over and sat down next to Tina with a deep sigh. 'Is it not the end of today yet? I've had a crap day so far and I can't wait to go home.'

Tina agreed. 'Tell me about it. The kids here kick off all day, and now I'm having the same at home. I need a break, I tell you.'

Amelia could hear the teachers' conversation and dropped her head low, unconsciously moving her hand to her stomach as she glanced over. Mel noticed, nudged Tina and whispered through her fingers.

'Ears everywhere.' She used her eyes to signal the kids all around, lowered her voice. 'But I'm so sorry to hear that. Are you alright?'

Tina nodded. 'Maybe we can have a proper chat after work? Do you fancy going for a drink later? A few glasses of wine are just what the doctor ordered. I'm sick of men, kids, bloody everything at the moment'

Mel bit into her salad sandwich. 'I need a few bottles never mind a few glasses. How have you stuck this place so long? It feels like two steps forward three steps back all day every day. I know these kids *need* our help – but it doesn't always feel like they *want* it. And as for men, I hear you. My ex still won't leave me alone…'

'From what you've said, he seems a right crank. There must be a way of him stopping him treating you like this.'

'I wish, Tina, he's a law unto himself. It's making me ill. I can't live like this anymore.'

Tina felt like the walls were closing in on her. The school

seemed to have more problems piling up every day. If it wasn't the students, it was the staff.

Donny was in a filthy mood too. He stormed into the room and shouted at them all to hurry up. It was a world away from his usual easy-going charm. Firm but fair was his normal style, but something was clearly eating away at him.

'Lessons start in ten minutes. If you've not finished your dinner, then it can go in the bin. You've had plenty of time to sit down and eat, so don't come crying to me if you're still hungry.' He looked at Frankie. 'Did you hear me? Don't just look at me like I'm an idiot, hurry up and finish your food.'

Frankie dropped his fork onto his plate and looked up. 'Don't you start on me again. I've finished my grub, save it for Chelsea and that lot over there, they've only just started eating.'

Chelsea heard him and stood up. 'This is the first thing that I've eaten all day so you can take a running jump if you think I'm rushing it down.'

Donny was in no mood for games today. 'You can take your food to my office then or you can make up the time missed from your lesson at the end of the day, simple.'

All eyes were on them both now. 'Listen, sir, stop taking your shit out on us. If you're in a mood then sort it out, we don't need you shouting and bawling all bleeding day. I can get that at home.'

Tina could see that Donny was about to lose the plot and she jumped up to intervene. 'Right, less of the backchat, just eat your food and get ready for lessons. Mr Knight, I'll sort this out, you go and have a break.'

Donny looked relieved. He needed a ciggie to calm himself down. After the shit had hit the fan with Dan he needed to sort his head out. If Susan got wind that he had a secret son she would pack her bags and leave him for sure. They'd discussed having a family when they first got together and agreed that they would try for kids, but not until they'd got where they wanted at work and were ready for it. Somehow that day had never come. He'd mentioned Bethany briefly years ago when they'd talked about exes and that but he never thought she'd be back in his life – let alone with a kid in tow. When he'd got caught out cheating before, the only thing that had made Susan stay was his word that he had no other skeletons in the closet.

Donny headed into the kitchen to have a go at Rita. 'Can you make sure that this lot are only served up until half past twelve. I don't care what they tell you, don't give them anything after that because they are taking the piss.'

Rita stood with her hands on her hips. She didn't get it. One minute he was making her come in early to do breakfast and saying never let a child go hungry and the next he was saying don't feed them. He needed to make his bleeding mind up.

'Donny, if a kid comes to me late, I feed them. They could have been late coming out of a lesson or something. I'm not to know, am I? And, if you remember, you've told me to make sure every child gets fed as it might be the only meal they eat all day.' There you go, right back at you.

Donny couldn't really argue with that. He felt like he was suffocating, needed some air. 'Just shout me in future before you feed them late then.'

He walked out through the car park and off school grounds and stood sucking hard on a cigarette. He had to sort this mess out, but how?

Donny scrolled through his emails on his phone until he found the one with Dan's new starter details. He couldn't put this off. He copied the number into his contacts and hit dial, his hands shaking slightly. The person on the other end picked up and Donny swallowed hard.

'Hello, Bethany, it's me, Donny. I need to talk to you.'

There was silence at her end. Donny forced himself to continue.

'Look, Dan barged into my office today and said that I'm his dad. That's bang out of order. Why are you letting this kid throw these kinds of accusations around? And as for you, if you're that sure he's mine, why are you dropping this bombshell on me now after all these years?'

Bethany had clearly been waiting for this call and had plenty to say. Donny was having none of it.

'You listen to me, Bethany. Do you think you can just walk into my life and destroy everything I've worked for? It's not happening. I'll destroy the pair of you if you don't back off. Two choices. Come and meet me tonight after school and we sort it out. Otherwise we can go down another road and, trust me, if we go there, you'll wish you never started this.'

Bethany was shouting down the phone now.

Donny hung up and stood looking up at the sky. What a mess, his life was coming apart at the seams. He needed someone to take away the sickness that he felt in the pit of his stomach. There was only one person who could fix him when he felt like this. He rang his wife.

'Hi babe, no, just wanted to hear your voice. I've got a meeting after work tonight and I'll be late but I just wanted to talk to you now.'

They chatted for a few minutes but he was choked up by the time he ended the call. He couldn't play the part of the tough guy like normal, but he didn't want her to hear he was upset. He needed to feel like he was the good man she thought she'd married. It really was like being trapped in a bad dream. Donny let out a growl and braced himself against the brick wall at his side. He had to man up. No one messed with him and got away with it. He'd sort this out, he'd make this problem go away. One way or another he'd put an end to this.

Chapter Twenty-Two

Clare opened the front door. Kevin was leaning against the wall. She hated this man with a passion. Her husband. Looking at him, stood there, like butter wouldn't melt in his mouth, she didn't feel even a flicker of warmth for him. Instead, anger bubbled inside her. How dare he smile at her after all the heartache he'd caused her? Clare studied him. He looked thin, frail. Was this really the man she'd loved with all her heart, the father of her child? He looked older, grey, haggard. Just hearing his voice sent shivers down her spine.

'Are you going to invite me in then or what?' He was still a cheeky fucker then, still full of himself.

Clare spoke through clenched teeth. 'Ged's in the front room.'

He brushed past her, not looking back. 'I know where it is, I don't need a guided tour.'

Clare slammed the front door shut and stood with her back against it for a few moments before she followed him, catching a whiff of cheap aftershave. He must have used half a bottle of the stuff. She could taste it in the back of her throat. She took a deep breath before going back into the living room. She wanted to keep a close eye on him. He was a thieving bastard, and leopards never change their spots.

Kevin had sat next to his son and they were sharing a moment. Ged was in his dad's arms, she could see he was emotional. Kevin's words sounded heartfelt but she knew him well enough not to believe him. He must have heard them in a film or read them in a book because they definitely didn't come from him.

'I'm here now, son. Nothing will ever hurt you again, I promise you. I won't let it.'

Clare rolled her eyes, she was immune to his bullshit. They were just words, and action spoke far louder than words in her book. But here he was, playing Father of the Year. *You can't pull the wool over my eyes, mate*, she thought. She could see right through his act.

Clare steadied herself, this had been a long time coming and she knew she had to keep her cool, play nice for her son's sake.

'Kevin, do you want a drink or anything?' See, she could be polite and calm when she wanted to.

Kevin lifted his head away from Ged and nodded. 'Can I have a coffee, nice and milky, you remember how I like it don't you?'

'No, I don't,' she snapped.

He chuckled. 'Two sugars and plenty of milk, babes.'

Oh my God, was he still calling her that? She hadn't been his babe for years so he could cut that shit out right now.

What a cheeky bastard, thinking he could just waltz back into her life and talk to her like they'd never been apart. Clare moved towards the kitchen as Kevin sat back in the chair still holding his son's hand – the hand he'd held to help him up when he'd fallen, the hand that held him tightly when he was afraid of the dark as a small boy, and the same hand that he'd shaken when he'd come to see him. Kevin's eyes were flooded with tears. His emotions were clearly sky-high and he was struggling to hold it together. Prison could do that to a man, Clare supposed, it could break them down and leave them bare. She turned away, glad to leave them to it.

'Son, if you want me to sort this out you have to be straight with me. I'm your old man and I love you more than all the world. But please don't insult my intelligence by telling me you got jumped. I don't want any lies, just the truth.' Kevin sounded like a man on a mission.

Ged couldn't look his father in the eye. 'Dad, turn it in, eh. I don't want you getting involved with anything. I can handle my own shit. You've just got out the nick and you need to keep your head down.'

Kevin wasn't interested in that argument. 'You're my boy and your troubles are my troubles. You can either tell me the score yourself or I'll investigate things my way. Trust me, I'll get to the bottom of it and when I do, heads will roll.'

Ged could see his dad was getting angry. 'Dad, just chill, will ya? We can have a talk later but for now, button it before my mam comes back in. That's all I need is her getting on my back.' Kevin nodded slowly. Bingo – he'd known all was not what it seemed.

Clare returned and plonked Kevin's coffee down on the small wooden table next to him. She'd put extra milk in it to cool it down so he could drink it as soon as possible and get gone out of her life. Every time she looked at him, she wanted to scratch his eyeballs out, tosser. He had led her a dog's life and she never ever wanted to go back to how he made her feel before he got sent down. The man had fucked with her mental health when he was in her life, she'd been on antidepressants, Valium, the lot. He had messed with her head and it had taken all her strength to get back on the level. Clare sat down on the chair opposite the two of them. All of a sudden, she felt cold, she was shivering. She reached behind her and grabbed her blue cardigan. Kevin stretched his arms above his head and yawned. 'It's good to be home, I've dreamt of being here with you two for years. I never thought it was going to end. I can tell you now that this sentence has broken my back. Doing time is a young man's game. I don't want to be one of those old geezers that have spent more time inside than out. That was the last stretch I'll be doing, let me tell you.'

'Dad, we're going to do whatever it takes to help you get back on your feet. I even spoke with my teacher to see if they can help. They know the system – all the help we can get. Who knows, you might be able to start your own gardening business like you said.'

Clare tutted and rolled her eyes. As if anyone in their right mind would let an ex-con like Kevin work in their home. He was a thieving git – and he wouldn't think twice about helping himself to anything he could lift. He clocked her expression.

'What are you laughing at? It will happen, I've been planning it for a long time. I can get all the stuff I need for cheap. You can laugh all you want but watch this space.'

Clare just couldn't help herself. Why should she sit there and have to listen to his lies any longer. 'Kevin, if I had a pound for every time you said you had a business idea, I would be a rich woman. Let me think. Oh yes, the window cleaning round that lasted two days, and don't forget the gutter cleaning business and the rest. You've got your head up your arse. You'll never work and hold down a proper job. You tried for years and you always messed up. Too lazy to do a proper day's work when you'd rather go on the rob. Do yourself a favour and stop chatting shit. I've heard enough to last me a bleeding lifetime.'

Ged hauled himself up to standing. His mother just couldn't keep her mouth shut, could she, she always wanted drama. Here was his dad fresh out of jail and she was kicking him when he was down. No support whatsoever.

'He will do it, Mam. Maybe if you had supported him his businesses might have taken off. Stop putting him down, give the man a chance.'

Clare wasn't going to listen to any more crap. 'A chance, are you having a laugh or what? I gave him years of my life and he just shat on me. He promised me the world and I was that young and naive that I believed him. I can't just sit here and let him do the same to you. He'll let you down, Ged. He always does. Everything he touches, he messes up. Take it from somebody who knows.'

Kevin sat there calmly and let her finish talking. This was a first, usually he would have been right back at her.

Maybe he has changed, Clare thought for a moment.

'Yep, she's right, Ged, I did let her down. But I've had a lot of time to think while I've been in jail. You realise when you are behind your door on your own each night who and what matters in your life. I've cried tears, I can tell you, so many regrets too. I messed up and I know that now. You two were all that mattered to me and I should have realised that back then.'

A tear started to roll down his cheek and Clare leant towards him a little to see if it was real. He was putting it on, surely. This man never cried, ever.

Ged reached over and took his dad's large hand in his own. 'Don't get upset, Dad. We can do this together, I'm here to help you.'

'Thanks, Son, but I can't depend on you to sort me out. I have to do that myself. Clare…' He paused and lifted his eyes up to look at her. 'I know you don't like me anymore and I can't say I blame you, but you have never left my thoughts, every minute of every day. All that I've thought about is you, us. I still love you.'

There was an awkward silence. This was not what Clare had expected.

Kevin kicked himself. Bleeding hell, what was he doing dropping the love bomb the minute he'd got out of the nick? He should have just played it by ear and seen how the land lay before he jumped in. Too much, too soon.

Ged was loving it though, smiling like his heart was melting. Maybe his parents could rekindle their love and they could be a happy family again. That's all he'd ever wanted, not loads of money or designer clothes, just his family together. Was it so much to ask?

But then there was this Sam bloke on the scene now with his mum – he needed to get out of the picture sharpish if these two were going to have a hope.

Clare stood firm, even though she could see what was going through her son's head. No. No way was Kevin playing the sympathy card to get back in her knickers. She had to shut him down.

'Whoa, Ged, let's get one thing straight. Me and your dad are over, done. He can have a relationship with you but as for me and him, don't even go there. That ship sailed a long time ago. I've moved on.'

Kevin tensed like someone had stabbed him deep in his heart. 'Fucking hell, Clare, kick a man while he is down, why don't you?'

'Well, I'm just making sure we are all singing from the same hymn sheet. I don't want to give you any false hope when there is none.' Clare was straight to the point, she owed him nothing. She stood up and grabbed her coat from the back of the chair. She couldn't fall for his smooth words again.

'I'm just going to the shop to get some fags. You two can have a chat while I'm gone. Oh and Kevin,' she turned to him before she left the room. 'I don't think it's a good idea that you come here all the time. When Ged is feeling better, he can come to your mam's house and see you there.'

'I'm not staying at my mam's, Clare. I'm on the sofa at our kid's for now.'

Clare was lost for words. Kevin had always gone back to his mother's house when he had nowhere to go – all the times she'd kicked him out for his lies and dodgy schemes. Why wasn't he staying there like he normally did?

'I'll sort something out with you later then, Kevin. Do you want anything from the shop, Ged?'

'Can I have a Twix, Mam, I'm just craving one.'

Kevin looked up at her with his puppy dog eyes. Bleeding hell, was she expected to get him something too? Less than twenty-four hours out of the nick and he was expecting her to wait on him hand and foot.

'Do you want anything?' she asked in an abrupt manner.

'Oh, yeah, ta. Can I have a Mars bar please, babe?'

He was at it again, calling her babe, making her skin crawl. She left the house ramming two fingers up behind her. He had more front than Blackpool and if she had her way he could ram his chocolate bar where the sun didn't shine, too.

Kevin waited until he heard the front door slam shut. No more beating around the bush. It was time for the truth, and he didn't waste any time in getting it. 'So,' he paused and looked at his boy. 'Let's have it then, no lies, just fill me in. The truth.'

Ged was white-faced. His dad would go ape when he knew what his son had been up to. There was no way of sugar-coating it.

'Dad, before you start, I was doing this for us. I wanted to help my mam out and try and get you a few quid for when you got out of jail.'

Kevin nodded his head, waiting for the rest of the story. Ged carried on. 'I think I was set up. I was doing a few drop-offs for my mate Frankie, the one I told you about, and when I told him this was the last one he wasn't happy. And then I was jumped in Blackpool when—'

He never got to finish. 'Fucking Blackpool? What kind of drop-offs were you doing? Don't think I don't know how these things work just because I've been off the streets for a bit. You mean to tell me you was up and down the country supplying drugs? Are you fucking right in the head? If you would have got caught you would have had a four-year stretch, you daft cunt.'

Ged fidgeted. 'Frankie told me that I'll have to work the debt off and pay back what was lost.'

'So how much are you in the hole for? Are we talking weed here or what?'

Ged dropped his head in shame. 'No Dad, heroin, crack, cocaine.'

Kevin's mouth swung open and he swallowed great gulps of air trying to get his breathing together. He rammed his finger into the side of his son's head. 'What fucking planet are you on? Fucking dealing smack, you daft muppet.'

Ged was getting riled too now. 'Yeah, I know, but come on where did you expect us to get money from? You've been in jail for years so you can't talk. I done what I done to survive, to keep our heads above water. So, don't fucking judge me when you know shit about what we've been going through. We had bills to pay, food to buy. I couldn't see you sending any money to us so shut the fuck up.'

Kevin was livid. 'You could have spoken to me. Told me how bad things really were. I could have sorted something out, got a borrow or something. You're a kid, a fucking stupid bastard kid who could have gone to jail.'

Kevin stood up and walked towards the back door. They both needed to calm down. What was the point in shouting and screaming now it had already happened? 'I'm going to get a bit of fresh air. Ged, you've shocked me, knocked me for six. I'm gutted, heartbroken in fact. How could you have been so stupid? I'm no saint but I thought you were too smart to repeat my mistakes.'

Ged closed his eyes; he'd let his old man down and he knew it. 'Dad, I'll fix this. I'll just sell weed to work off the debt.'

'Over my fucking dead body you will. Give me a few minutes to get my head around this and we will sort it out. No lad of mine will be getting done over, trust me.'

Kevin stormed into the garden leaving Ged with his head in his hands.

———

Clare sat chewing on her Snickers and played with the wrapper in her hand. She flicked her eyes one way then another. Had she missed something here or what? Since she'd got back from the shop Kevin was deathly quiet and Ged was barely saying a word.

'Are none of you eating your chocolate, after I've gone and got it for you?'

Kevin pushed the bar to the end of the arm of the sofa. 'Lost my appetite, babes, shove it in the fridge.'

Ged reached for the remote for the TV and didn't say a word. You could cut the atmosphere with a knife.

'So, when are you two meeting again? I'm not rushing you, Kev, but I need to get ready for work soon.' Had she just called him Kev? Old habits die hard, eh?

Ged turned to face his mother and knew before he asked that she wasn't going to like what he had to say. 'If you're at work, why can't he stay with me for a bit? I mean, you don't get in until after midnight?' The little shit, why the hell was he telling him that? Kevin turned to face her.

'I'll be gone before you come home, and it will be good that we can spend some quality time together.'

'No, Kev, I don't want you here when I'm not. I've said he can come and meet you where you're staying once he's well enough.'

Kevin shook his head. 'I've told you I'm sleeping on a sofa at my brother's.'

She was backed into a corner. If she said no, then she'd be the bad guy yet again. She shrugged. 'Just be gone before I get home then. Ged, do you want me to make you something to eat before I go?'

Kevin jumped in before he could answer. 'I'll get us a kebab later if that's alright. Is the Doner Hut still going or what? Eh, Clare, do you remember when we had it nearly every night? It was mint.'

She nodded and for the first time she broke a smile. 'Do I remember? Of course I do. I banged on about three stone because of them kebabs. It's took me ages to get that weight off.'

Kevin was quick off the marks. 'You'll always be perfect to me, babes, whatever size you are.'

Nancy had been texting Ged all day. She wanted to come over and chill with him, but he kept blanking her. She had texted him to say she had some news to tell him, big news. But he hadn't replied. He had his dad now.

Kevin sat with his feet up. Clare had gone to work, and it was time to relax. It felt like he had never been away. He'd told Ged that everything was just like he remembered it, and in fairness it was.

They sat eating their kebabs when there was a loud knock on the door. Kevin tensed. Being in jail made a man jumpy. Ged sighed.

'That will be Nancy, I told her yesterday I was chilling with you, but she's still come over, the cheeky cow.'

'Bring her in and don't be tight. It'd be nice to meet her. Check you out with a bird and all that, go on, Son.'

Ged heard her knocking again and got up slowly to go and answer the door. As he walked into the hallway, he could see Nancy's face squashed up against the glass trying to see inside. He yanked the front door open.

'I thought I told you I was busy tonight. My dad's here and I'm spending some time with him.'

'Yeah I know, but I needed to speak to you. Can I come in or what? I don't want to discuss it here. People might hear us.'

Ged had no other option. He closed the door behind her and followed her inside.

Kevin was all smiles as soon as he saw Nancy. 'Oh, so you're the girl in my boy's life. Hiya, I'm Kevin, his dad.'

Nancy, as usual, was not shy in coming forward and went straight to where he was sat and flung her arms around him. Kevin was taken aback.

'You've got a little beauty here, son. Lovely, aren't you?'

Nancy grinned as she sat down. 'I keep telling him I'm a keeper, but I don't think he's so sure, lets his mates dictate to him who he can see and who he can't.'

Ged could have throttled her, was she right in the head telling his father their private business? He sat on the edge of the sofa, impatient to know what she had to say now she was here. 'So, go on then, what do you know?'

Nancy was alarmed, did Ged not realise his dad was listening to them? She looked worried.

'It's alright, Nancy, my dad knows everything.'

'Phew, I thought you'd lost the plot then.'

'My lad has no secrets from me, love. You fight one of us, you fight us both.'

Nancy smiled, remembering she'd told Ged the same thing. 'I went back up to Blackpool the other night—'

Before she could carry on, Ged interrupted. 'What the fuck are you going back up there for? You could have got nicked.'

'If you let me finish, I'll tell you. Stop talking.' Her eyes were dancing with excitement and she couldn't keep still. 'I'd had an argument with my mam and you know what I'm like; I just go on a mad one and go all over the show.'

Kevin was intrigued, there was more to this girl than met the eye.

'I was sat at the train station in my usual spot when I saw Frankie out the corner of my eye. He didn't see me, so I hid while I was watching. I don't know why but I thought I would follow him. I wasn't doing anything else, was I?'

Ged was caught up in the story, his eyes wide open as he urged her to continue.

'He'd got off the train from Blackpool, so I followed him. He never seen me; he was walking along on his phone all the time. I could hear him talking from where I was. He was chatting to somebody called Wes.'

Ged punched his fist into the sofa sending a cloud of dust flying into the air. 'That's Wes from down this end. He's a prick, I don't like him he's always got something to say for himself. Apparently he was grafting in the same area as me.'

Nancy raised her voice. 'Shut up, will you, I've not got to the best part yet. I kept listening and what he said next made me want to puke. He's a rat, a snake just like I told you. I heard him say well done for sorting Ged out. He called you a muppet, just sat laughing with Wes telling him how you had to pay the money back. Ged, he set you up just because you told him you wanted out. I knew he was a wrong 'un. He was never your friend, he just used you and then had you over. You don't owe him anything. He's got the gear he got those kids to take off you and he's got you down to work off the debt at the same time.'

Ged was white as a sheet. He had to get some air.

Kevin waited til Ged had gone outside, then started to interrogate Nancy. 'So, tell me more about where I can find this Wes and Frankie. I heard a bit about Frankie when our Ged come to see me in jail and he sounded like an alright lad.'

Nancy shook her head. 'Honest, he would cause trouble in an empty room. He knows how to charm people, sure. But it's all front. He's never liked me, and it was him who told

Ged to get rid of me. I told Ged he wasn't to be trusted but he never listened to me. He thought the sun shone out of his arse.' Nancy gave Kevin a bit more information before Ged came back into the room.

'Are you alright?' Kevin asked him.

'Yeah, I think it's these antibiotics knocking me for six.'

Nancy was as proud as punch of her detective work but now she held her head to one side looking puzzled. 'There's something that's still bothering me though. When I followed Frankie, he met some guy in a car. He was in there for ages and I heard lots of shouting. I sneaked up as close as I could and it looked like Frankie was getting a right doing down. I could hear him yelling. Whoever it was fucked him up good and proper because he was clutching his face when he got out the car.'

'Fucking good,' Kevin snapped. 'See, it's a dog-eat-dog world when there are drugs involved. There is no loyalty, everyone has each other over, trust me I've sat with so many lads in the nick who have told me stories about their so-called mates who'd set them up to earn a few quid.'

Ged still couldn't believe it. Frankie was his friend, they were brothers-in-arms, how could he do that to him? He had nearly died. But then who had decked Frankie? He'd never clocked who Frankie's supplier was – he was too new to the scene to know the chat about who really ran the show. Lost in his thoughts, he didn't notice that Kevin had gone quiet, off in a world of his own. But Nancy could see what he was thinking. Blood was thicker than water – and a father's urge to protect his son was stirring.

Chapter Twenty-Three

Donny sat waiting for Susan to come home from work. He was restless, a bag of nerves. He couldn't do this anymore. He'd come out of work early so he could prepare to drop this bombshell on his wife. There were no words to soften the blow, he knew she would go ape. But then who would take something like this lying down? Any woman who was told her husband had a child he'd never thought to mention would act the same way. The shit was going to hit the fan for sure.

After his conversation with Bethany, it was clear that his wife would find out his dirty secret no matter what. His ex wanted money. She wanted Donny to step up as a father and look after his child. But why now? He didn't even know the kid. He was a stranger to him. Bethany was adamant that he should take a DNA test if he kept trying to suggest Dan wasn't his son. The bitch had told him that he was going to have to pay in more than just cold, hard cash, too. She'd been clear that she'd make sure his wife knew about it too; he had no choice other than to come clean.

Donny checked the clock on the wall for the hundredth time; Susan would be here any minute. He was sweating, smoking like a chimney even though he knew she'd go off on that too. Might as well be hung for a sheep as a lamb. But, what if she left him on the spot – bin-bagged him right there and then – what would he do? His mind was racing, he couldn't think straight.

A key in the door. He froze.

'Donny,' she shouted from the hallway.

'In here, love,' he replied, doing his best to keep his voice level.

Susan hung up her coat and walked into the room; she could tell just by looking at her husband that something was wrong, terribly wrong.

She dropped her car keys gently onto the table.

'Donny? What's up? You look a mess. Oh my God what's going on?' There was a pause. 'Please tell me it's not the gambling. I thought you were on a lucky streak – enough left over for some treat money. I still remember the time you were down after a bet and those guys came knocking. But you told me you always settled what you lost now and all that shit was over. This is why I keep telling you to pack it in.'

Donny swallowed hard and wiped his forehead with the back of his hand. 'Susan, love. Just come and sit down, please, just sit down.'

Susan was looking at him intently as she took a seat next to him on the sofa. He reached over for her hand and squeezed it tightly. She could feel how sweaty his palms were. What the fuck was going on?

'Babe, I need to talk to you about something. It's from my past and I hope you will understand how much of a shock it's been for me.'

Now it was his wife's turn to swallow hard. Susan clutched at her chest. 'You're scaring me, Donny, just tell me for crying out loud.'

Donny knew he just had to get the words out. There was no other way to do this. 'When I was younger, before you, long before you, I was seeing some girl called Bethany. It was just a kid thing, we were only together a few months.'

Susan was holding her breath and he could already see her body was trembling. Donny forced himself to continue.

'I don't know how to say this, only I have to tell you. She's been in touch. Told me her son, Dan, is mine. And what's more, he's just joined Second Chance.' He dropped his head and cringed, waiting for her response.

Nothing, not a word.

Susan stood up and walked out of the room. Donny rushed after her into the hallway and put his hand on her shoulder to try and turn her round to face him. She grudgingly looked at him before she spoke.

'Take your fucking hands off me. If you so much as come near me again, I'll do something that I will regret.'

He panicked. 'Babe, this is not my fault, I'm in as much shock as you are. I was a kid myself. I certainly didn't want a baby with some random slapper. She was a right slag, everyone was banging her, honest, she was anybody's. I know it hasn't happened but I've only ever wanted children with you, the woman I love. Susan, we have to talk about this, you can't do this when I'm trying to do the right thing by telling you the truth.'

'Fuck off!' she screamed in his face. 'I'm leaving. You make me sick. I can't be with you anymore. You're a liar, a filthy fucking deceitful bastard. And this is the last straw. How can I be with you now knowing you have a kid to someone else? Did you never think to mention this to me when we met? You're a rat, a dirty no-good fucking rat.'

Donny was desperate. 'I told you I had no idea until now. I've asked for a DNA test. And it's like I said, Bethany was a slag, everyone was flinging one up her, the kid could be anyone's. It's a fucking lottery who his dad is.'

Susan pressed her face up close, her anger radiating from every pore. 'So go and get a DNA test because I'll tell you something for nothing. I won't be with you until you do. And you can stop fucking calling her a slag and all that – it takes two to tango, Donny. I can't believe this. I thought you were going to tell me you'd lost a monkey or something, but this, Donny, this has pure killed me. I feel sick, I can't even look at you. Move out of my way while I get my stuff together. I'm out of here.'

Donny wasn't too proud to beg. 'Please, baby. I love you more than life itself, please don't walk out on me. We can get through this together, me and you, remember, the dream team.'

She looked over at him and spat in his direction. 'Fuck you, Donny Knight.'

Donny sat on the sofa watching the fire burn. It didn't seem to calm him like it usually did. He wanted the world to burn – like the wreckage of his life. He typed out a text to Bethany.

> I want a fucking DNA ASAP. I'll pay for it if
> needs be. You and your son are not ruining
> my life.

He hit Send and turned round to see Susan stood near the door with a suitcase at her feet. Tears, lots of tears.

He choked up at the sight of her, couldn't get his words out properly. 'I'll sort this, Susan. I bet the kid isn't mine, you have to believe me.'

Not a word. Susan just looked at him coldly before she turned and walked out of the house. The walls shook as she slammed the door behind her. Donny screamed out like a wounded animal. This was his perfect life, how dare anyone come along and try to spoil it? He sat for a few minutes before wiping his eyes and picking up his car keys. He needed out of here, he needed to sort this mess out as soon as possible. Heads were going to roll, he'd make sure of it.

Donny marched into the boozer and headed straight to the bar. He needed a stiff drink, something to take the edge off his nerves. He called over to the barmaid, 'Double brandy,' before slouching against the bar as if his legs were going to collapse. As he paid for his drink, he heard someone calling his name and twisted round quickly. For crying out loud, this was all he needed.

'Donny, come and join us, I'll budge up, you can sit here.' Mel was sat with Tina. How could he tell his work colleagues to piss off, he wanted to be alone? He sighed and walked slowly over to join them.

'Bloody hell, Donny, you look like I feel,' Tina chuckled. 'Did you get everything sorted out today?'

'Yeah, all sorted. Anyway, what are you two doing in here on a school night?' He tried to sound his usual confident self but he could hear how hollow his words seemed.

Tina sighed. 'Domestic. I might as well tell you, I'm leaving Chris.' Donny was shocked. Bleeding hell, it was all going on here, wasn't it? Mel wasn't going to be left out of the conversation. 'And I have an ex that, won't take no for an answer. But, aye, you knew that, didn't you?' Tina followed Mel's eyes to Donny, clearly surprised that these two had been having conversations about their private lives.

Donny ignored Melanie and took a large swig of his drink. 'Are you alright, Tina? That's a big thing to do. Chris is a good guy, are you sure you're doing the right thing?'

Tina sat forward in her seat; it was clear she'd already had a few beers down her neck. 'Donny, you don't know the half of it. I have his kids disrespecting me all day and all he does is lie on the sofa and tell me to ignore them. His ex is back on the scene and they all think the sun shines out of her arse. I've had enough. I gave him chance after chance to sort it out and he's done fuck all.'

Mel was keen to add her two penn'orth. 'Girl power. Men, they just don't get it. I feel sorry for her, Donny, some of the things she's been telling me about, stuff would make your toes curl.'

Tina folded her arms, her head held high. 'I don't need him anymore. I've got my job, and I've got…' She trailed off, looking awkward. 'I mean, I've looked at my life over these last few months and do you know what?' She was starting to get upset and Mel leant over and patted her arm before she continued. 'I don't need him. All he does is take, take, take. As long as everything is alright in his life and his tea is on the table and his washing is done, he's not bothered about me. He's seen me on my knees with everything that's gone on and still he carries on like nothing has happened. Selfish bastard he is.'

Donny was regretting that he'd come and sat with the pair of them. He really didn't need this – he had enough of his own shit to deal with. He necked the rest of his drink and looked at them both. 'Ladies, I'm so sorry but I have to go. I only popped in for a quick one. I hope you get sorted out. I'll see you in work tomorrow and we can have a coffee and a catch-up.'

Mel was clearly not pleased. 'I thought you might have stayed with us, Donny. We are damsels in distress.' She fluttered her eyelashes coquettishly, but Donny had already stood up to leave.

'Sorry, like I said, I only called in for a swift one. See you tomorrow.' He was out of there. Life was complicated enough right now without taking on anyone else's troubles.

Donny stood outside the pub and breathed in a mouthful of cold air. It was windy tonight and it had started to rain, pissing down. He jogged towards his car, the raindrops pelting against his skin. Suddenly he stopped dead, his mouth gaping. *What. The. Fuck?* His misery was quickly replaced by surging fury. Every window in his car had been smashed in. He'd only been in there twenty minutes.

Donny quickly scanned the area looking for the culprits, but nobody was about. He put his coat around his hand and started to knock the rest of the glass out of the shattered windows, fuming and muttering under his breath. Suddenly a voice from behind him made him jump.

'Oi.'

Donny turned his head slowly. The voice had come from a tall man who was built like a brick shithouse, he could see that much, but against the glare of the only street lamp his face was nothing more than a silhouette.

'Are you talking to me, mate?' he asked, trying to keep the fear out of his voice. Not much rattled Donny normally – he could handle himself – but he prided himself in never getting into a tight spot unless he knew his opponent. Out here, alone, in the dark with a stranger with a grudge, this wasn't good.

The man's growl was deep. 'Yes I am talking to you. And I'm telling you now, keep your fucking hands off Melanie. She's mine and always will be.'

Donny dropped his coat on the floor and faced the man fully. But it was dark, and he couldn't see much more. Still, knowing this was to do with Mel's shit rather than his own problems, gave him his confidence back.

'So you're the bully, are you? The one who won't leave her alone?'

The man shook his head. 'She's a liar. Did she tell you she

was in bed with me on Saturday night? No, I bet she didn't, did she?'

Donny was really not in the mood. 'It's none of my fucking business who she spends her time with outside of work. Now unless you've got something useful to say, you can see I've got my hands full sorting out this shit. Did you see who smashed my windows?'

The man nodded. 'Kids, three of them. They were on pedal bikes. I was sat in my car over there and seen it all.'

'Little bastards.'

The stranger carried on talking. 'Mr Knight, I've heard a lot about you recently and a word of advice, stick to sorting out fights with kids and whatever else those toerags at your school get up to. I'm telling, you nice and friendly like, to step away from shit that doesn't concern you otherwise you won't know what's hit you.'

Donny looked the bloke up and down, weighing him up. He was big but he reckoned he'd knock this chancer right out if he wanted a straightener. He bit down on his bottom lip as he thought about what he wanted to do; should he nut the guy or walk away?

'Mate, you're the one talking shit. I'm married. I've never been interested in Mel like that, she's a great girl but we're just workmates.'

'I've seen you dropping her off and she's been saying things about you too. Donny this, Donny that, a proper superhero you are aren't you?'

'As I've just said, I'm happily married so you're barking up the wrong tree if you think we are an item because we're not and we never will be.'

The guy wasn't listening, just started to walk away laughing out loud. 'You still don't recognise me do you, Donny Knight? I knew our paths would cross again one day. I'll see you soon. Give my regards to Susan, by the way.'

What the hell? Donny stood in the rain trying to make sense of what had just happened.

He cleared the glass off the driver's seat and sat with his head resting on the steering wheel. He just wanted everything to go back to normal. He wanted his wife back home where she belonged and to be curled up on the sofa with her. He looked at his phone; nothing from Susan. He tried calling her but the phone just rang and rang, no answer. He'd text her instead. He had to tell her again how much he loved her, adored her and how sorry he was that this had come back to haunt him. He read over the message a few times before he sent it. He had to find a way of convincing her it was all just a mistake and he could put this nightmare behind him.

Donny was just about to turn the key in the ignition when he noticed a car creeping past him. Why was it going so slowly? He squinted into the darkness but he couldn't see who was driving. Things were going from bad to worse.

Chapter Twenty-Four

Tina rushed up the stairs with Chris screaming behind her. 'Why are you leaving like this? We can sort things out. I'll have a word with the kids and things will change. Don't leave me, Tina. I love you.'

She headed into the bedroom and opened her wardrobe. 'No, Chris. It's time to start thinking about what I want in life. For years I've been a fucking skivvy for this family and it's only now I can see it. Working all hours at school then coming home and doing it all over again. You've sat on your arse and let me run about after your bleeding kids. All I ever wanted was my own child and you didn't give a flying toss.'

He was behind her now, trying to turn her to face him. 'I wanted the same as you, love. It's not my fault you couldn't have a baby. I wanted the same as you, I love you more than anything.'

'Change the fucking record, Chris. You wanted someone to look after you and your kids. Their mother has been back in their lives for ten minutes and it's like she's the fucking chosen one. Where is my thanks for all I have done for them?'

'I've backed you all the way, Tina. Nevaya has been told, Charlie has too. The kids love you. It must be hard for them seeing Wendy again after all these years. She is their mother.'

Tina was throwing clothes onto the bed. She froze and looked him in the eyes. 'And I'm not a mother. That's just it. I want a baby, I need a baby, something that is mine. My own flesh and blood.'

Chris sat down heavily on the bed and dropped his head into his hands. 'I can't make that happen, Tina. I wish I could, but what can I do? I'm not a miracle worker.'

'We could have adopted, go on, why have you never suggested that? We could have used a surrogate. There were options, Chris. Options we could have explored, but no, it's always the bleeding same, as long as you're alright and your tea is on the table everyone else can take a running jump.'

Tears were streaming down the side of his face now. He was broken. 'Baby, don't do this to us. I get things have been shite for you lately, but we can get through this together. Leaving me won't change things or make things any better. What, are you going to live with your parents for the rest of your life?'

Tina shook her head and started to fold her clothes into neat piles. 'I'm renting somewhere. If I'm leaving here, then I need somewhere of my own.'

The colour drained from Chris' face. 'You've been planning this, haven't you? Have you met somebody else? Oh my

God, you have, haven't you? Wow, this makes so much sense now. All the texting … who is it?'

Tina's shoulders dropped. 'Don't be daft, there's nobody else.'

'So who is it you're texting all the time then? Don't think that I've not clocked you on your phone in the middle of the night. Go on, tell me who it is. If you're cheating at least have the balls to admit it.'

'I'm not texting anyone. I just go on my phone when I can't sleep. Stop making things up. The reason I'm leaving is because I can't stand my life here anymore. I want peace, Chris, not dramas all the time. Nevaya and Charlie won't even care I've gone. After a few days, I doubt you will either.'

Chris stood up and dragged his fingers through his hair. 'No, this isn't making any sense. I know you inside out, Tina. This is not you. Something is going on and I want to know what.'

Tina shrugged him off and bent down to grab a suitcase from under the bed. She opened it up without thinking.

Silence. Chris looked down at the piles of tiny baby clothes. He reached down and slowly picked up a small cardigan. His eyes found Tina's. 'What … what are these?'

What could she say?

Chris pulled the suitcase over towards him and rifled through the contents. What the fuck? He was sweating now. 'Tina, what the hell is going on? How long have these been here? Why would you be buying stuff when you don't have a baby?'

Tina yanked the case away from him. 'Get your hands off them. I will have a baby soon, you'll see. I'm not a headcase,

Chris, so don't look at me like I'm losing the plot or something.'

'Tina, please sit down. We need to talk about this. This is serious. You're buying baby clothes when we don't even have a baby. This is not right, you need help. First thing tomorrow, I'm calling the doctor's. You need to tell them about these.' He held a pair of tiny knitted bootees in his hand.

Tina let out a shriek of anguish and fell to her knees. She broke down, smashing her fist against the floor, screaming. 'All I want is a fucking baby. I cry every night, Chris, my heart is broken into a million pieces and do you even know how hard it is for me to get up every morning and face another day, because let me tell you, it's hard, so bleeding hard. It's killing me. I've been drinking again too. Every day, necking the brandy, see you didn't even know about that either, did you? That shows how much notice you take of me, doesn't it?'

Chris crossed the room and took her in his arms. 'Tina, Tina, shhh. We'll look into adoption if that's what you want. I will do anything to make you happy. But this,' he pointed at the suitcase, 'it has to stop. We can get through this together, we can work it out but only if you let me in. We can get you help with the drinking too. First we get you well again, then we'll talk about kids.'

Tina was sobbing her heart out, wet strands of hair stuck to the side of her face. It felt like forever until she was able to stop long enough to speak. She looked up at her husband. 'I can get us a baby, Chris. I really can.'

He wiped her tears away with the side of his hand and

kissed the end of her nose. 'We'll sort it, together we will sort it.'

Tina reached for his hands and squeezed them before she brought them to her mouth and kissed them. 'I mean it, Chris. I can get us a baby. There are other ways than the usual ones. But did you really mean what you said? Do you really love me? Do you want to raise a child with me? Because so help me God, if you're just stringing me along, I'm out of your life for good.'

He didn't even have to think about his answer. 'I love you with all my heart, always have, and I always will. But what do you mean, you can get a baby?'

'I've … I've …' She paused. He held her tightly and kissed the top of her head.

'What is it, Tina? Get it out, get it all out.'

She closed her eyes tightly and her whole body was clenched as she spoke. 'A student needs help at school and I'm helping her. She's only young and she could never look after a baby, she has her whole life ahead of her and here's us wanting a baby and, well, I've told her I will take it.'

Chris was stunned into silence, trying to digest what she'd just said. 'I … Tina … I don't understand, what are you saying here? You're going to have to spell it out for me.'

'Amelia is a student at the school, and she is pregnant. She doesn't want the baby and her family would kick her out if she told them, so I've said if she has the baby, I will bring it up as my own and it will want for nothing. It makes sense, doesn't it, Chris?'

He let go of her and held her at arm's length. Was she off her rocker? She seemed to have lost it big time.

'It doesn't work like that, Tina. You can't just take a young girl's baby. Are you for real or what? This is fucked up, Tina, I mean really fucked up.'

Tina was defiant. 'I can do this and I am. I've rented a flat and Amelia is there now. Nobody knows she's there and a few months is not that long to be missing from home. Teenagers get lost on the streets every day. At least this way she's safe and the baby is wanted. She can go back when she's had the baby, and nobody will be any the wiser. I've gone over and over this a million times in my head. It can all work out, please help me.' She was crying again now. 'You said you loved me and would do anything for me. Amelia can ring home and tell her parents she's alright, it's not like she is going missing off the face of the earth.'

'Tina, can you hear yourself? This is not right. This kid needs proper guidance, she doesn't need hiding away as part of some mad scheme you've come up with. You could lose your job, everything you've worked hard for. Are you ready to put your neck on the line for this? Think about it, it's not right. You need medical help. If you want to adopt then we can go through the proper procedure. I promise. But you can't just take the law into your own hands and take the girl's baby, no matter how desperate she is. How were you going to explain that you suddenly had a kid?'

Tina flew at him. 'Why did I ever think that you would understand? I should have kept my mouth shut and carried on without you. I'm giving you the chance to make us happy and all you can do is put a spanner in the works. If I tell people we've been waiting to adopt, who's going to know any different? You owe me, Chris, you owe me for the years

I've been a mother to your children, for every night I've spent crying alone, you owe me.'

Chris was silent. He looked at the pile of baby clothes and shook his head. He dropped the knitted shoes he'd been holding, small and unworn.

———

Amelia sat watching the TV, she was bored. She flicked through the channels and sighed. Somebody was at the door, a key sliding into the lock. She'd not seen anyone all day.

Tina walked in holding a bag of food. 'Sorry I'm late. I've had a situation to deal with.'

Amelia snatched the takeaway bag from her hands. 'I am starving. All I've had all day is toast.'

Tina held the door open behind her, startling Amelia. 'What the...? Who's he?'

Tina smiled. 'It's OK, Amelia. This is my husband. I've told him everything and he's here to help.'

Amelia was apprehensive. She kept her eyes on the stranger as she started to unpack her food.

Tina gestured to Chris to sit down. 'Amelia, this is Chris.'

Amelia said nothing in reply, just nodded her head slightly. 'Hi, you alright?' he asked her.

'I will be when I've had something to eat. All day I've been craving this. Tina, I need chocolate too. I've eaten the last packet of biscuits. I was in a feeding frenzy and nothing was touching the sides.'

'I've brought you some shopping. It's in the car, I'll get it in a minute.'

As Amelia ate, she broke off every so often to wipe the side of her mouth with her sleeve. 'Has anything been said in school about me being missing?'

Tina coughed to clear her throat. 'The police have been in. They've interviewed all the students too.'

'I'll have to bell my mam soon; she will be screwing about me. Her nerves will be shattered. She's a worrier my mam is.'

Tina flicked her hair back over her shoulders. 'Yes, you're right. I need to get you a cheap phone, something we can get rid of so it can't be traced.'

'Can I not have my own phone back? I've not been on WhatsApp or Snapchat since I came here.'

Tina rolled her eyes. Her tone was firm. 'What have we spoken about? No social media and no phone. The police would find you in five minutes flat. We have to stick to the plan. Chris, go and get the shopping and you can bring the bag with the clothes in it too. I want to show Amelia just how well looked after this baby will be.'

Chris did what she asked but it was clear that he was unsettled.

Tina waited until he'd gone and sat down next to Amelia. 'Let's have a little feel of your tummy. I can't wait until we can feel the baby moving about.' She dropped her head to Amelia's stomach and started to speak to it. 'Mummy can't wait to meet you. You're going to be so loved.'

Amelia looked uncomfortable, but didn't stop her and soon Chris was back with the bags. Tina started to pull out small items. Little cardigans, hats, bootees.

'Look, Amelia, look at the size of this, imagine the baby in this.' She was in a world of her own again.

'Tina, love, put them away.' Chris looked awkward. But his wife held the cardigan to her nose, breathing in the softness of the wool.

Amelia looked over and raised her eyebrows. The young girl clearly thought the woman was a couple of butties short of a picnic. She changed the channel and tucked her feet up under herself. Whatever happened from here, they were all up to their necks in it. Amelia rested her hand on her stomach. Sometimes, however much you want to go back, the only way through something is to face the unknown.

Chapter Twenty-Five

G ed was going back to school today and his stress levels were through the roof; his head was all over the place. Kevin was taking him, had told him that he wanted to have a quick word with the teachers to make sure he was alright, but Ged had refused point blank. No way did he want his old man coming into school and showing him up. He reckoned his dad was up to something too. He was cagey, shifty – and Ged knew no one got through a stretch in prison without getting good at keeping secrets.

Nancy stood waiting near the gates and smiled when she saw Ged. She was persistent, he'd give her that. He needed to make up his mind one way or another what he was doing with her. She was a nice girl, a bit messed up in the head but who was perfect? Everyone had their scars – only some were more visible than others.

Kevin patted his son on the shoulder. 'Ring me if you need me. Any shit in here and I'll fly over. I'll be here before you know it.' He patted his pocket and winked at his son. 'Dad's here now.'

'Dad, just go to the job centre and sort your benefits out. I'm a big boy now and don't need you or anyone else fighting my battles.'

Kevin kept his voice low. 'I'm not saying you do but this lot you're messing around with, well, you've seen what they can do. Trust me, I'm a long time in the game, son.'

Ged sighed and walked over to Nancy. Once his dad had gone, he wanted to have a quick ciggie before he went into school. He'd binned the weed and he hadn't been stoned since everything had gone on. His head felt clearer and he seemed to have more energy. No more mood swings.

'Morning, hope you're ready for this lot in here,' Nancy was her usual ebullient self.

'Am I fuck. I can't be arsed, to tell you the truth. I just want to go back to bed, I'm knackered.'

Nancy walked with him as he headed towards the brick wall at the side of the school. 'If you want we could just do a bunk and spend the day together. We can get the train some-where if you like?'

Ged popped a fag into the corner of his mouth and sparked it up. 'I'm not in the mood, Nancy, maybe some other time. I've got a lot of stuff going on in my head that needs sorting out. I need to face this lot in school at some time – and I'm here now.'

Nancy moved in closer to him and kept her voice low. 'So, what's the script with Frankie, are you going to confront him or play it by ear? He's still going to want his money back, isn't he?'

Ged growled back at her. 'He's getting fuck all from me. That's one thing my dad and I agree on. And I have to tell him that too. Frankie needs to know I don't owe him a penny. Who would do something like that to a mate? I could be fucking dead. It's bang out of order. But I need to find out who decked Frankie. If he's a marked man in a turf war, I don't want the fight coming to me. I'm not making a habit of getting stabbed.'

Nancy loved a drama. She hated Frankie with a passion and couldn't have been more delighted that he was no longer stuck to Ged's side. She rubbed her hands together against the cold. 'You getting shanked is old news in this place. You've missed loads of drama in school. Chelsea has been caught sleeping with some girl's boyfriend. The girl came to school looking for her. On my life, Chelsea shit her knickers, she wasn't mouthy when she was thought she was going to get her head kicked in, let me tell you. She was sat in the head's office bawling her eyes out. Fucking mard arse, that one. She's a dirtbag and everyone knows that. Oh,' she was on a roll now, 'guess who's gone missing?'

Ged sucked hard on his cig and blew out a cloud of smoke. 'Who?'

'Amelia, she's been gone a few days now. We've all been interviewed by the staff. The dibble are involved too. A few of the kids are saying she's ran off with an older man, she was always talking to older guys online, that's public knowledge. So, it wouldn't surprise me.'

Ged shook his head. 'She seemed alright, her. She never said much but a few of the lads said she puts it about. I thought they were chatting shit, but Liam showed me a video of her getting shagged at some party. Nasty it was.'

Nancy reached over and took the cigarette out of his mouth to have a blast before they went into school. 'You shouldn't watch that shit. Fucking jealous is what most of the lads in this school are. Spreading that kind of rubbish just coz they're not getting any. Anyway, if you go by that rule, you'd be calling most of us girls slags. And the boys are worse – dick pics, hassling girls for porno selfies, fucking upskirts – and then they call a girl a slag as revenge for getting turned down. Sodding pathetic, the lot of them. I think I'm the only one who doesn't have a new bloke every week. I've only ever slept with you. You was my first.' She was looking at him with puppy dog eyes. Mesmerised. 'You know I only have eyes for you, don't you, Ged?'

Fuck. It was too early for this. Ged stomped on his fag butt and started to head into the building. Out of the corner of his eye he spotted Frankie walking towards the school. His heart was racing, his mouth dry.

'Yo, Ged,' he heard from behind him.

The adrenaline kicked in and his body started to shake.

'Carry on walking,' Nancy whispered. 'Ignore the scumbag.'

Ged couldn't do it. 'Nancy, I'll see you later. Go inside, I'll be fine, I don't want you involved in any of this.'

It was easy to see she was uncertain, but she knew not to cause a scene.

Frankie trudged towards Ged. He still had yellow bruises on the side of his face. 'I didn't know you was coming back into school, a few of the lads said you wasn't coming back. I knew they were chatting shit.'

Ged took a deep breath. 'Maybe, if you would have belled me and spoke to me, instead of texting me giving it all that about the money you say I owe you, you would have known.'

Clearly, this wasn't what Frankie was expecting. 'What's with the fucking attitude? I texted you about the money because it's your debt. You lost the parcel and the money, so it's up to you to pay it back. You know the rules, I don't make them. So, don't have a go at me. And, sort your fucking attitude out, gobshite.'

'Still, I was stabbed up and all you cared about was the fucking money. Some mate you are. What happened to you having my back, brothers-in-arms?'

Frankie's nostrils flared. He stepped closer. 'So, when are you sorting out the cash? The big boys are not going to wait all day. If it wasn't for me, they would have come through your front door and kicked the fuck out of you. Who do you think did this to me?' He gestured at his swollen eye.

Ged shrugged his shoulders. 'Who are they? Tell me who they are and I will go and see them myself. I'm not scared you know. I don't need anyone to fight my battles.'

Frankie was losing it now, bouncing about and waving his arms. 'You listen straight, I brought you into this game when you had fuck all and I helped you earn some decent wedge. As I recall, your old man was in the chokey and your mam was working all hours to keep her head above water, so I done you a fucking favour.'

Ged looked around to make sure no one was listening. 'Word on the street, Frankie, is that I was set up. Set up by one of your other boys, what do you know about that?'

Frankie looked like someone had slapped him. 'Who's telling you that? Because it's pure bullshit.'

'Well, I hope it is because I'll get to the bottom of it and when I do people will get hurt if I've been had over. I know people too, you know? Plenty of people will do anything for a few quid or a bag of brown.'

Frankie had heard enough. He bit down hard on his bottom lip and started to walk into the school. 'Pay the money back, simple as. I've already had my collar felt about it and I'm not taking another beating because you got had over. You need to get selling again, otherwise face the consequences.' Frankie looked about, dipped his head and carried on walking.

Ged hurried behind him. 'I'm not doing shit. Give me the names of who I owe the debt to, and I'll sort it out myself. I don't need you being the middleman. You're fucking shady.'

Frankie stopped dead in his tracks then ran at Ged pushing him up against the wall his hands round his neck. 'Muppet, I'll do more than stab you up if you carry on. Who the fuck do you think you are, talking to me like I'm a fucking nobody? If you want beef with me then carry on. Your old man is out of jail now, isn't he?'

Ged didn't like the look in Frankie's eyes. He wrestled free. 'Leave my dad out of it. He's keeping his nose clean so don't be involving him in anything. It's fuck all to do with him. You wouldn't like me bringing your parents into it, would you?'

Frankie was spoiling for a scrap, but he spotted Donny was walking down the corridor. He spat in Ged's face and scurried off. 'Sort it, prick. Trust me, the big man knows who you are, he knows you're the weak link in the chain and he's not a patient man. He's got a lot to lose if this operation goes tits up. He's watching you.'

Ged knew Frankie meant every word he'd said.

'Morning, Ged, nice to see you back.' Donny looked rough and not his usual pristine self. He still had his wits about him though. 'Did I just see you talking to Frankie? Is everything alright, looked like you were having words with him.'

Ged couldn't wait to get away. 'No sir, nothing I can't handle.'

Ged heard the confidence in his voice hiding how he really felt. Despite the act, he knew a storm was brewing.

Outside, deliberately off the premises, Donny rammed a fag into his mouth with shaking hands. He paced up and down; he was going to wear a hole in the tarmac at this rate. He typed out a text as he smoked before looking up in time to spot Dan walking towards him. There was nowhere to hide.

'Morning, Daddy dearest,' Dan chuckled. The kid was as full of himself as ever and he knew how to press all the buttons.

Donny looked at him. 'I am not your father, so the sooner your mother gets the DNA test done we can put this to bed.'

'Nah, you're my old man alright – and soon everyone will know it.'

Donny inhaled deeply; this was getting out of hand. 'Listen, you cocky prick. I've told your mam to get a test as soon as. Back in the day she was anybody's, so stands to reason that anyone could be your dad.'

Dan froze. 'Don't you ever disrespect my mam. She's looked after me for years without a penny from you, so keep it shut, you daft prick.'

Donny was well aware that he needed to get away from the situation; his temper was boiling and he was ready to punch this kid's lights out. But his job was at stake. His live-lihood. He walked away before he did something he'd regret. This had to be sorted out. He'd always thought of himself as a lucky guy. But everyone's luck ran out in the end.

Chapter Twenty-Six

Donny sat staring into space. The DNA test results were back; today was D-day. Two weeks without his wife in his bed by his side had felt like a lifetime.

Susan had agreed to meet him, though she'd made it clear that if the test proved he was Dan's father then their marriage was well and truly over. He could get to fuck, she'd said. There was no way she was playing mummy to his bastard child.

Donny had chewed his nails to the quick, the skin around them red and sore. The sooner this mess was over, the better. He wanted his life back, his wife back where she belonged. He'd barely seen her since this all started – she'd made sure to work early and late shifts at the salon, staying out for dinner with the girls so she wouldn't have to spend an evening at home with him. She stayed at Sadie's, or he'd kipped on the sofa. And when they did cross paths, there were rules; no touching, no kissing, no nothing. He missed the closeness they'd had. Susan was a tough cookie when she wanted to be. She was distant now, frosty and suspicious at all times. But then even before this she'd been acting strange, he reminded himself. He shook his head. Maybe it had been broken long before all this. Like a plate with a crack running all the way through it – just waiting for the moment that would finally break it beyond repair.

Donny had agreed that they would all meet in a park near the school. Get it all settled once and for all. A huge tree hung over the bench where he sat now, leaves fluttering in the breeze. It was a beautiful tree, romantic even. He let himself dream that one day soon he would bring his wife here again and they could have a picnic together, just the two of them. He spotted a figure walking down the hill towards him. His jaw tensed.

They'd arranged that Bethany would bring the letter here for him to open. That way he would be the first to receive the news and he could be sure no one had meddled with the envelope. Bethany was full of herself, as ever. She looked rough – hair scraped back in a ponytail, baggy tracksuit bottoms and battered trainers. She was the opposite of Susan, he thought. No class here, just a sly bird who lived her life on handouts and kept her eye out for any other way of making easy money on the side.

'Where's your wife? I thought she was going to be here too?'

'She's on her way.'

Donny could see the envelope in her hand and just wanted to get it over with. Panic fluttered in his chest. Maybe he could pay her off, give her some cash to rip the envelope up unopened, make her promise that he'd never have to see her or Dan again.

The moment seemed to last forever.

Bethany sat down next to him on the bench and pulled out a cigarette packet out of her pocket. She offered one to Donny, but he refused. He wanted nothing from her, only the truth. He could smell stale tobacco on her clothing; she stank of it. He didn't take his eyes off the letter.

Bethany sparked up and sucked hard on the cigarette. 'I don't know why you've even wasted your money on a test. Dan is your son, why you don't believe me I'll never know.'

'Fuck off, let's not pretend you weren't a shag-bag before you were with me. Who's to say you weren't sleeping with someone else? There were plenty of rumours you know.'

'You cheeky fucker, how dare you speak to me like that?' She thrust the letter into Donny's hands. 'Go on. Open it and we can put this to bed, you fucking arsehole.' Bethany smirked and pointed to a woman approaching. 'Is this the missus? A proper fancy piece, isn't she?'

Donny held his breath as he saw his Susan marching towards them. He'd have to watch her like a hawk; he reckoned she would scratch Bethany's eyeballs out given the chance. She wasn't a fighter but when her cage was rattled, she could give anyone a run for their money.

Susan looked tired. Her hair was in a plait and she was dressed casually in jeans and a pale blue T-shirt. Dressed for a fight? Donny's heart melted when he looked at her. He knew now how stupid he'd been to risk what he had with her. Messing around, keeping secrets, he'd kept her in the dark so many times. He realised he'd needed her to adore him, to believe the bullshit he'd fed her. He loved her with all his heart, but perhaps he'd broken hers one too many times.

Susan shot a disdainful look at Bethany and sighed. 'So, do we know if he's your kid or what, Donny?' She was blunt and straight to the point, she clearly didn't care how she came across.

Bethany interrupted. 'The kid has a name. He's called Dan, for your information.'

'Means nothing to me, love. Just tell me if he's your kid, Donny, and then I'll be off.'

They both looked at him. He had to open the envelope. Slowly, his index finger slid under the flap and he reached into the envelope and pulled out the letter. Susan was shuffling her feet, her breath getting louder and louder.

Donny unfolded the paper and started to read. His eyes fell, and for once he was speechless.

Bethany took this as her cue. 'I told you you was his father, you prick. Now you can man up and start providing for him.'

Susan's legs buckled and she started to hyperventilate, gripping the side of the bench for support.

'No,' she sobbed. 'No, this is not happening.'

But Donny looked over at Bethany and jumped to his feet, shoving the letter in her face, ramming it under her nose.

'I fucking knew it, you dirty scrubber, the kid isn't mine. Read this. You life-wrecking bitch, get back under the rock you crawled from and take your bastard son with you.'

Donny rushed to his wife's side and wrapped his arms around her. 'Baby, it's negative. I'm so sorry you have had to go through this. I love you so, so much. The kid is fuck all to do with me.'

Bethany was up in arms, reading the letter over and over. 'It must be wrong; they must have messed the test up. It can't be right. You're Dan's dad.'

Susan pushed her husband out of the way and ran at Bethany. This was her war now, nobody messed with her life and got away with it. She gripped her by the throat. 'He's just told you that he's not the fucking father so leave us alone. If I so much as hear you've tried to contact my husband again, I'll rip every hair out of your bastard head.'

Bethany fell to her knees. She screamed after them as she watched Susan and Donny walk off into the distance. 'He's your son, Donny. He's your fucking son.'

But no one was listening. She stayed where she was, crying her eyes out until a noise from behind her made her stop and turn round. Somebody was there. She tried to get a better look. Nothing. Whoever it was had done a runner.

Donny held his wife's hand tightly. 'Will you come home now, babe? I just want to put this mess behind us.'

Susan took a deep breath and stopped walking. She turned to face her husband and narrowed her eyes. 'You always come up smelling of roses, don't you, Donny Knight. I'd just like to know what else you are hiding.'

Donny pulled her closer and squeezed her tight. 'It was years ago, babes, long before we met. I never in a million years ever thought she had had a kid, let alone me being his dad. I love you, babes, me and you always. Please just let's get back to normal, I can't stand you not being with me.'

Susan was still looking at him like he was a shite on the bottom of her shoe. 'Things change, Donny, I don't know if I can ever trust you again. I feel like you're a born liar,' she said.

'Susan, for fuck's sake. Please don't make me beg, I said I'm sorry, just let's get back to normal and let me make it up to you. I can make this right, please let me try.'

She looked at him, pursed her lips. 'I'm not moving out, Donny, because after all I made that house, not you. Just don't expect too much from me.'

All Donny cared about was that his wife would be back in his bed, he would feel safe again, right now nothing else mattered. After a few days she'd calm down and everything would be back to normal. He'd buy her a gift, a flash handbag, yes, he smiled at the thought. Donny felt his usual bravado coming back. His missus loved him again and life would be back to normal in no time. And this time, he'd be careful – he'd come too close to losing it all.

Chapter Twenty-Seven

Kevin sat on Eastford square and sucked slowly on his cigarette, tapping his foot. He felt like a cowboy hidden away in the darkness. He looked around. This was a waiting game but he knew that if he played his cards right, it would all work out. Good things come to those who wait and all that. The streetlights left pools of muted yellow light on the pavements. Kevin could hear shouting in the distance, and watched as a few youths started to gather, on the lookout for trouble. He didn't know these kids but he recognised the type. He'd been one himself. He bet local residents complained, asked the council to move on the gangs and the trouble their bitter rivalries brought. But some things never changed, and after dark he knew the residents were effectively prisoners in their own homes.

No one challenged these kids. They held no respect for anybody. They had nothing except what they'd fought for – and they'd fight to keep it.

Kevin watched intently as he clocked a young lad in the distance serving up drugs to a man sat in a car. He knew the script well regarding dealing, no surprise given he had dabbled in drugs for years. He sat cracking his knuckles, until ... bingo. He froze. That's what he was waiting for. As soon as he spotted the lad starting to walk away from the car he jumped to his feet.

It was showtime. His voice was cocky as his pace quickened. 'Oi, can I have a quick word, mate?'

The youth turned his head, didn't know who the man was talking to. He was apprehensive. 'Are you talking to me?'

Kevin jogged over to him and led him to a dark corner where no one would see them. He had to play his part well if his plan was going to work out how he wanted.

'Got any weed, mate? Ged said I would get some here. A bit of cheese or haze would be mint?'

The teenager nodded and reached inside his pocket. 'Yeah, I can give you anything you want, brown, white, you name it I can get it.'

Kevin took a deep breath before grabbing the boy by his neck and slamming him up against the wall. The kid looked terrified.

'Who the fuck are you dealing for? Tell me now or I'll kick ten tons of shit out of you. Fucking spill, don't waste my time because trust me, I'll snap your fucking jaw.'

The boy was struggling to break free, but Kevin had him in a killer grip. 'I'll strangle you, mate, honest to God, if you don't tell me who the main man is, I'll end you. Start talking, prick.'

But the kid couldn't speak if he'd wanted to. All that came out were choking noises, the kid's eyes were bulging in their sockets, his windpipe closing up, his lips now tinged with blue. He was whacking the side of his arm, trying to nod his head, he was ready to talk. Kevin finally released the grip enough to let him speak. The lad was gasping for breath, he fell to his knees, sucking in large mouthfuls of air. Kevin stood over him, ready to act if he needed to. He booted him in his stomach as a reminder that this was no game; this was serious shit. The kid's voice was shaking as he cowered, waiting for the next blow.

'I get it from Frankie, he sorts it all out. I don't know where he gets it from. Honest, that's all I know. Please leave me alone. I'm just trying to earn a few quid that's all.'

Kevin picked him up and threw him into the corner. He knelt down to his level and gripped him by the ears. 'Don't lie to me, tell me what you fucking know.'

The kid was desperate now, still trying to get his breath. He had to give him something if he wanted to survive. He kept his voice low. If anyone heard him grassing his life would not be worth living. Snitches got stitches.

'Frankie is the only one I know. Please, I don't know any others. I've only been doing it a few months. He meets the big man and gets it off him. I just pay my money to Frankie, we all do. Honest, I swear down on my mam's life, no crosses counted.'

Kevin could tell he was telling the truth. He was shaking like a scared animal, cowering with his hands held up high trying to protect himself. He'd pissed himself too.

'Where can I find Frankie?'

'He's at the park. I just spoke to him about ten minutes ago. You are the second person who's been looking for him tonight. Another guy was on the square about an hour ago looking for him too.'

Kevin patted the kid down and made him empty his pockets. There were a few bags of weed and around seventy pounds in cash. He pocketed it and smiled. 'I'll be taking this and when I get my hands on Frankie, I'll be taking his shit too. I don't know who you fucking young 'uns think you are, running shit around here. It's time you all learnt a lesson. This is my patch now.'

The boy pulled his legs up to his chest and dropped his head low. He sat there shaking. For the first time he understood that this world was a very dangerous one indeed.

Frankie perched on a wall in the park, kicking his legs against the cold bricks. He was scranning a piece of chicken and looked around as he filled his face. It was quiet tonight, not a lot happening. Frankie paused mid-bite as he suddenly heard rustling, branches crunching behind him. He turned to look. Nothing. He waited a few more seconds then carried on eating his food.

He was getting paranoid lately; smoking weed was seriously affecting his mental health. *Dickhead*, he thought to himself, he should have stuck to selling the stuff, not sampling the goods. As he shook his head a large hand reached over and gripped him from behind.

'Francis Owen, I'm arresting you for supplying class A drugs, you don't have to say anything but anything you do say may be recorded and used in evidence against you.'

Frankie spat a mouthful of food at the copper as the cuffs were slammed around his wrists. They were tight, the cold metal cutting into his skin.

He was slammed to the floor, the side of his head pushed into the wet grass, then dragged back up onto his feet and marched to an unmarked car not far from where they stood. Once he was in the back the officer climbed in and sat next to him. A plain clothes officer. Frankie swallowed, this was not what he needed in his life. But he was caught, bang to rights.

The copper studied Frankie. 'I'm going to be straight with you. How long I keep you here will depend on you and what you tell me. We can do this the easy way or the hard way. Let's see how sensible you are.'

Frankie was white, trembling. He knew the minute he was searched he'd be done for possession and the rest of it. Fuck, fuck, fuck. There was no hiding it. He had large amounts of cash on him and bags of weed ready to sell. This would be pure time in the big house, two or three years at least. He was old enough to go down properly – he couldn't get away with young offenders or a slap on the wrist.

The officer nodded his head slowly. 'We've been watching you for a long time, Frankie. But we're not interested in you. We want the big man, the one you deal for. I've seen you meet him a few times and I know who he is. Question is, are you willing to help us send this prick down? Or am I taking you down to the nick and throwing the book at you? It's your call. Tell me what I need to know, and you'll be out of here and we can forget anything has ever happened.'

Frankie squirmed; he was no grass. 'Nah, fuck off, I'm no snitch. You've got fuck all on me. What, a few bags of weed that I'm carrying and some money. I can account for the money if I have to. You know the dance. So, fuck off out of my face.'

The officer shook his head. The kid had balls.

'All right, let me tell you a bit more and then we can have a little chat. Do I need to go into your visits to Blackpool, the parcels you take and the money you bring back? I reckon you'll be looking at a five stretch for sure. We've watched you for months, you're the ringleader of all these young kids running drugs up and down. And,' he paused, 'we can prove it. So, my friend, we've got you by the short and fucking curlies.'

Frankie's eyes opened wider. This was a different ball-game now. Fuck that, he didn't want to go to jail for years. But, on the other hand, would he be a Judas? He sat thinking, scratching the end of his chin, anxious. He stared out at the night sky and ran his tongue over his teeth. He'd always demanded loyalty from his lads, and he'd always thought he'd be the same, but then nobody would know what he'd done, would they? Who knew he was talking to the dibble anyway? He had to look after number one. There was no way he was getting slammed if he didn't have to. He had to think about this but his head was all over the place. The guy could be setting him up, leading him down the garden path and stitching him up like a kipper. He had to play for time. 'Have you got a cig?'

The man reached into his jacket pocket and pulled out a full deck of Benson & Hedges Gold. He flicked his lighter and lit two, passing one to Frankie.

'So, tell me again how this works because I'm saying fuck

all until I know the script. You pricks are well known for not sticking to your word.'

The copper nodded his head slowly. 'It works well for both of us. Let's say I have an old score to settle with the big guy and I want payback. I've waited a very long time for this cunt and all I need now is a little more information. I'm not really arsed about the foot soldiers, I just want the top man.'

Frankie sucked on his fag, thinking. The big boss had left him bruised because of what had happened to Ged. Said he'd picked the wrong kid – and that getting one of his foot soldiers stabbed would get the coppers looking at their little operation. He'd smashed his face into the dashboard of his flash car to ram the point home. That hadn't exactly left Frankie in the mood to do him any favours. And, if he was being honest, he was sick to death of working for peanuts. The main man was getting the real cash, Frankie was getting pennies and he was the one taking all the risks. It wasn't fair, was it? Frankie sighed.

'I'm keeping the money I have on me and the weed though. If I tell you what you want to know, how do I know you're not going to come for me again when this is all over? You pigs are bent as fuck.'

The officer blew the smoke through the side of his mouth. 'Listen, you can do well working for me, kid. I'll look after you. This can be our little secret; you scratch my back and I'll scratch yours. I'll look after you, like I said.'

Frankie was thinking out loud now. If he was going to squeal he had to get everything he could. 'The big man's been good to me though, he helped me out when I needed someone.'

The officer let out a laboured breath. 'You mean he helped himself to a young kid to do his dirty work for him. Who's the one with all the cash here, you or him? Where's your top gaff, your nice car?'

Frankie still wasn't sure, grassing was against everything he believed in. But going to jail, no way, he couldn't hack being banged up for years. He loved his freedom too much. There was an awkward silence before Frankie cleared his throat. 'Right, I'll tell you what you need to know.'

The copper nodded. 'I want you to set up a meeting. You'll need to hand over money or pick up more drugs. I need to catch him in the act.'

'Fucking hell, that's on top, he'll know something is not right if I'm not arrested too, won't he?'

'No, I'll time it so you're out of the picture. Like I said, I'm only after that cunt, not you.'

Frankie fidgeted nervously. 'I've got to drop some money off tomorrow night. I meet him at the bottom of Fernclough Road, near the Spice Cabin, in the car park.'

The officer rubbed his hands together. 'Right, that's sorted. Let's go through all the finer details and then you can be on your way. You've done the right thing, pal. This fucker has taken advantage of you for a long time and it's about time he got what was coming to him.'

Frankie stared out of the window as he leant his head against the glass. He was a grass. Eventually he let himself out of the car. As he walked away he looked smaller, younger.

He didn't see Kevin Grey hiding in the shadows, listening, smiling. He didn't stand a chance, as for the second time that night, a hand grabbed him from behind. But Kevin Grey wasn't like the police – he had no deal to offer Frankie. This was rough justice, pure and simple. Frankie didn't even have time to shout before the first punch hit him.

Chapter Twenty-Eight

Amelia sat staring out of the window. The beige curtains were kept closed but she could still see through the small gap in the middle. She was bored, she hated being locked up in this place, no friends, no contact with the outside world. It was crap. She moved quickly as she heard a key in the lock, throwing herself down on the sofa and staring at the TV trying to steady her breathing. Tina hurried into the room with yet another load of bags.

'I've spent a bomb on baby gear. This child is going to want for nothing. Just let me nip for a wee and I'll be with you.' Tina dropped the bags near the sofa before leaving the room. Amelia heard the toilet door close and dipped her hand into the black leather handbag on the table, rummaging through the contents. She pulled out a mobile phone and fumbled as she switched it to silent before ramming it down the front of her bra. Noises from the other room. She was back in her spot on the sofa before Tina returned.

'I'll cook you something nice for tea. You must be sick of eating fast food. And the baby needs a healthy diet, stuff like vegetables and fish.'

Amelia wasn't keen. 'Don't be feeding me any rabbit food. I don't eat all that shit. So, don't try and change me. In fact, while you're here I need to get a few things off my chest. I can't stay in here every fucking day looking at four walls. It's not going to work. I'm going stir-crazy sat in here every day. I need fresh air and to see people.'

Tina tried to dismiss the flutter of panic in her gut. She put her arm round Amelia's shoulders. 'Bloody hell, you're in a bit of a state, aren't you? You're the one didn't want your parents to find out you were pregnant. Imagine if someone sees you outside, then all of this will have been for nothing. We made a deal with each other and you need to stick to your part of the bargain.'

Amelia shrugged Tina's arm away. 'It's not you who has to sit here every day, is it? I can't do it. I've not even got a phone to speak to my friends.'

Tina snapped. No more nicey-nicey. 'You can't bleeding talk to your friends, you idiot. Not unless you want your parents to know that you have been pulling your knickers down for every Tom, Dick and Harry. I've put a lot of work into this plan and there is no way you're going to mess it up. You stay in here like we discussed. I'm having this baby no matter what and I'm not going to let you mess it up for me just because you're bored.'

Amelia had never seen this side of her teacher before. She gave as good as she got. 'Well, fuck it, I'm not arsed!' she yelled back. 'I'll go home and tell my parents that I'm having a baby. And I bet it won't be as bad as you make out. You've brainwashed me, you have. I should have just got rid of the kid like I wanted and I'd have been back to normal by now, nobody would have known anything about the baby and I could have got on with my life. But there's no going back now. I'm over three months' gone thanks to believing your bullshit.' She shook her head in frustration. 'It's you who's messed this up, just because you want a fucking baby. Have your own baby and leave mine the fuck alone. I'm getting out of here, you're a fucking nutter.'

The colour drained from Tina's face. Her hands were shaking. This couldn't be happening; her perfect plan was falling apart. She had to make Amelia see sense, stop her from leaving. She took her arm. 'You're just having a bad day. It's your hormones playing up. Sit down and I'll make you something to eat.' She tried to get Amelia to sit back down on the sofa, but the girl struggled and broke free.

'Get off me!' she screamed. 'I'm not staying here and I'm not eating any more of that shit food you keep trying to ram down my neck. I'm going, I'll face whatever I have to but I'm not staying here anymore. It's alright for you – nothing has changed and you get what you want at the end of it. What about me? What do I get apart from being a prisoner? My mam and dad are probably stressed out to death worrying where I am, and all you care about is a daft fucking baby.'

A red flush rose up Tina's neck as she gritted her teeth together. The little cow was not ruining her dream, not now they'd come this far. She tried again but this time she made it clear who was boss. 'Amelia, you're tired. Have a sleep and stop being daft. We've talked about this time and time again. This is the only way it will work.'

'What, the only way it will work for you. What about me, eh? What about what I want? I want to be normal again and see my family and friends. I thought I could do this, but I can't, I'm sorry. I'm going home to face the music.' Amelia had started to walk towards the living room door when her head was pulled back and she was dragged to the floor. Tina stood over her ready to strike. Her face was red and her eyes blazed with anger.

'You are going nowhere. We made a deal. Don't mess with me, because I'll ruin you. Just calm down and stop playing silly beggars. I've put my neck on the line for you and I'm having this baby. I could lose everything because of you, so think again before you open your mouth. Trust me, it won't end well.'

Amelia lay stunned; this wasn't what she signed up for. Where was the kind, caring teacher who'd been there for her and told her everything was going to be alright?' Tina backed off and watched as Amelia climbed to her feet. Something fell as she stood up and Tina swooped to pick it up before the girl could get to it. It was her iPhone. Amelia's eyes opened wide as Tina put two and two together.

'Don't move.' Tina checked the call log and messages before turning back to Amelia who was trembling and held her hands up to protect herself.

'I never used it, honest. I just wanted to go on Snapchat and my Insta and check what was going on with everyone. I'm sorry. I was desperate.'

Tina was rattled by the near miss. This was bad. She

hadn't planned for anything like this, she'd thought it would all be plain sailing once she'd got the flat set up for Amelia. She'd even thought she'd be grateful. How stupid she'd been.

She sank into the nearest chair and dropped her head into her hands. She needed to think. As a teacher, Tina was used to being the one in control but it hit her now that Amelia – young, broke and pregnant as she was – was actually the one with the power. She was going to have to tread carefully.

Minutes passed. Amelia didn't dare move a muscle after what had happened before. When Tina finally lifted her head the look in her eyes chilled the teenager to the bone.

'You're having this baby just like we planned. I'm going to look after you until it's been born. But, for now, you're not going anywhere. Not a chance.'

Amelia sat with her legs drawn up to her chest, rocking to and fro. How had it all got so out of hand? She wanted her mother, she just wanted to be at home with her family.

It was nearly midnight when Tina left; she wanted to be sure that Amelia had come back round to her way of thinking. The girl was sleeping now. Tina stood at the bedroom door and watched her sprawled across the bed. She closed the door gently and crept down the hallway, then stood with her back against the cold wall, banging her head against it slowly, rhythmically. What the hell had she got herself into? She needed a plan, a new plan to make sure the girl stayed put.

She closed the front door behind her. Then quickly turned the key in the lock and then she was gone.

Amelia was too scared to move. It was the middle of the night but a noise had woken her. It sounded like somebody was at the front door knocking. Her body froze, though her heart was racing like a speeding train. She tried to steady herself then slowly she crept into the hallway and checked the door. It was locked. It was always locked. Tina made sure that nobody could get in – or out.

A silhouette suddenly appeared behind the glass. Amelia sank to the floor and sat with her legs pulled up to her chest. Who on earth could it be at this time? Nobody knew she was there. She heard the flap of the letterbox being lifted up with the slightest of movements and saw a pair of beady eyes searching through the darkness. She dropped out of sight as quietly as she could, her heart pounding. Had they seen her? Who the hell was it? She lay in terrified silence. The knocking had stopped and she could hear footsteps. She crawled to the window to see a large figure trudging away.

Amelia covered her mouth with her hand to try and quieten her breathing. Her whole body was shaking. Slowly she got to her feet and went back to bed, cowering under the covers. This was bad. Someone knew she was there. She was meant to be safe in the flat but her refuge had become her prison.

Chapter Twenty-Nine

Donny stood outside the school having his usual smoke before the kids arrived and started banging on about 'one rule for them …'. Tony the postman was heading his way; his pace quickened when he spotted the headteacher.

'Morning, guvnor,' he grinned.

Donny nodded his head and smiled as he stretched his arms above his head and yawned. 'You're early this morning, pal, you're not usually around at this time.'

'Yeah I got an early start, mate. Got a few things to do later.' Tony's voice dropped to a whisper. 'Did you bring my little treat along? I could do with it. I'm proper on my arse and need to pay a few bills.'

Donny checked that no one else was around before dipping his hand in his jacket pocket and pulling out a brown envelope which he passed surreptitiously to Tony. 'I can't thank you enough, mate, for sorting my little problem out. I never thought we would pull it off if I'm being honest.'

Tony nodded. 'It wasn't easy, I don't mind telling you. I had to wait for the letter to arrive in Dispatch and get to it without anybody seeing. It was tricky. Had to shove it down the front of my keks till I could get it here for you to sort out. But aye, hats off to you, Donny. A smart idea that was. You don't need the stress of a kid in your life, do you? You've rescued enough kids in this place – you've done your bit, I reckon. Like I said, Donny, I'll never breathe a word, my lips are sealed. It could have fucked your life right up let me tell you. If it was my wife she would have left my sorry arse and I would never have seen her again for dust.'

Donny sighed. 'You saved my life, honest mate, if the real letter had landed on Bethany's door it would have caused World War Three. Susan would have taken me to the fucking cleaners and left me with nothing.'

Tony rubbed his hands together and stuffed the envelope into his trouser pocket. 'It's behind you now. And I was glad I could help,' he patted his pocket. 'And the cash will help me out a lot. I've got bills coming out of my arse. I can't seem to get straight.'

Donny patted the top of Tony's shoulder as he turned to go. 'Nice one, mate. Top lad.'

Rita appeared at the door and shouted over to Donny, 'I'm putting the kettle on. Do you want a coffee?'

'Yes please, I'm coming now so you can bang me some toast on too.'

'Cheeky bleeder,' she shouted back.

'She's in early, isn't she?' Tony remarked.

Donny scratched his head. 'I know, every morning recently she's opened up. I'm not moaning about it though;

she's doing me a favour. I get an extra ten minutes in the feather. And, if she's happy doing it then who am I to question her?'

Tony started to walk off. 'Keep smiling, mate, see you tomorrow.'

'Yep, see you tomorrow,' Donny replied as he headed back inside through the car park.

As Tony walked slowly along the road he noticed that a car seemed to be following him. He picked up speed and crossed the road. What was that all about?

Donny leant against the canteen counter and looked at Rita as he slurped the hot coffee. 'Rita, is everything alright at home? I mean, you're here every morning at the crack of dawn, opening up. I never used to see you until five minutes before your shift started.'

She turned to face him. 'Yes, everything's good. I just like to help out where I can. Plus, it gives me extra time to prepare the food and do the students' breakfast.'

Donny reached over and took a piece of toast from the plate before she placed it on the table. The butter was melting across the hot surface. He didn't normally have breakfast but hey, rules were made to be broken.

'Never mind me, Donny, I should be the one asking you the same question. Your head's been all over the place for weeks. You notice everything when you're in this job. It's you, you should be worried about.'

Donny stuffed the rest of the slice in his mouth and spoke

with his mouth full. 'Don't you worry your pretty little head about me, Rita. I'm fine. I just had a bit of stuff going on at home, nothing I can't handle. It's sorted now anyway. Normal service has been resumed.'

'Good to hear it.'

The door swung open and a windswept Tina marched in.

'Morning. Bleeding hell, how early do you two get up? I thought I was going to get some peace and quiet by coming in early.'

Rita jumped in to answer. 'I'm always in before Donny now. I just open up and flick the heating on, every little helps, doesn't it, Don?'

'It sure does, and look at the treatment I get too, coffee and toast. I don't even get that at home. I'm not complaining, no way.'

Tina pulled a face. 'Favouritism, that is. She doesn't give me coffee and toast.'

'Oi, I always ask you if you're hungry and you always say no. I treat everyone the same in this place. I hate the lot of you.'

Tina chuckled. 'Only joking. Do you want me to make you some toast?'

'Right, I better move myself and get ready for the students.' Donny wiped the butter off his fingers. 'I've got Ged's dad coming in to have a word today, and I'm not looking forward to that. The guy's just got out of jail and no doubt he wants to play the concerned parent card when it comes to his son's education.' He rubbed his eyes. 'Oh yes, and Tina, we've got the police in again to see if there is any update on Amelia. It's baffling. There's been no sight nor sound of her.'

Tina stood twisting her hair. 'Do I have to deal with the police? I've already told them no one here has a clue where she's gone. Can't I sort Ged's father out and you speak with them instead of me?'

Donny shrugged. 'I don't see why not, good luck with Ged's dad though, he'll be on the warpath.'

'I'm sure I can handle him, Donny, I'm a hard case when I need to be.'

Donny just raised his eyebrows and left, humming 'Eye of the Tiger' as he went.

Rita stood leaning against the massive fridge and looked at Tina. 'It's a mystery where that poor girl has gone, isn't it? Somebody must know where she is. I mean, how can a kid disappear from the face of the earth just like that and nobody has a clue where she's gone. It just doesn't sit right with me. It's very peculiar.'

Tina nodded and changed the subject quickly. 'I know. Anyway, I'll go and check all the rooms to make sure that they've been cleaned. Last week there were two classrooms that hadn't been touched. Honest, the bins were stinking in there. Apple cores and empty crisp packets ... hanging it was. We need to keep an eye on those cleaners.'

Rita carried on preparing breakfast, but her eyes followed Tina as she left the room.

Tina walked into the rec room and did a double-take. Why were the sofas pushed together? And who had left a bag on the floor? She approached it cautiously and picked it up.

Slowly, she started to pull out the items inside it. Hairbrush, soap, deodorant, toothpaste, knickers … What the hell?

'Rita!' she shouted through the open door. 'Come here and have a look at this lot.'

The cook's face was scarlet as Tina held the knickers out in front of her. They were passion killers, baggy and discoloured. 'Do you know who owns this lot? Is someone planning a trip? I tell you what, nothing surprises me in this place anymore.'

Rita edged closer. 'Give them here. I'll bang it in the lost property. Leave it to me.'

Tina passed the bag over and turned to carry on with her tour of the classrooms.

Rita checked her watch. Still time before the kids turned up. She quickly followed Tina into one of the rooms and pushed the door shut behind her.

Tina looked up. 'Did you want something else, Rita?'

The cook nodded. 'I'm just a bit concerned about the whereabouts of Amelia.'

But there was an unusual tone to Rita's voice. A coldness.

Tina sat on the edge of one of the desks and ran her hand through her hair. 'We all are, Rita. She'll turn up no doubt, they always do. She's probably met some boy and is holed up somewhere with him.'

Rita wasn't moving; she stood firm, blocking the door. Tina was starting to get nervous.

'Can I get past you, Rita, I have to get some other checks done before the students arrive.'

'I followed you,' Rita hissed.

Tina looked rattled. 'Followed me where exactly?'

Rita bent forward and ran her tongue around her lips. 'To the flat where you've got the girl locked up. I'm not bleeding daft. I worked it out ages ago when Amelia was in the toilets spewing her guts up. It isn't rocket science, is it? Give me some bleeding credit, love, I wasn't born yesterday.'

Tina's jaw dropped; she was lost for words. She was going to have to bluff her way out of this one. 'I don't have a clue what you're going on about, Rita, so please move out of my way and let me get on with what I have to do.'

'No,' she snapped. 'I'll tell you what I know shall I, so we can cut the crap.' She took a deep breath and continued. 'Amelia is tubbed. And,' she paused, 'let's think who we know who can't have children … erm, let me think.' She narrowed her eyes and stepped closer to Tina. 'You, is that correct?'

Tina forced herself to stand tall and shrugged the comment off. 'Don't be silly, Rita, have you heard yourself? Now, move out of my way and stop talking shit.'

Rita clenched her tobacco-stained teeth together and small balls of spittle sprayed from her mouth as she spoke. 'Listen, I can make this easy for you or I can speak to the police the moment they step through that door and tell them where she is. I will you know, because I know you've got her. You want that baby she's carrying, don't you?'

Tina couldn't breathe. Rita stood waiting with her hands on her hips. 'I want money, nothing major, just a couple of grand to help me sort out my finances. It will be our secret, easy really, isn't it?'

Tina started pacing as Rita continued. 'I've been evicted from my house. I've been staying here at the school. Why do you think I've been opening up every day?'

Tina looked out of the window and tears ran down her face. The game was up. 'All I've ever wanted is a baby. Amelia could never look after a kid and she had nowhere else to turn. I'm giving her her life back.'

Rita raised her voice. 'But it's not that simple, is it? It's illegal for starters, Miss Fancy Pants. You can't just take a baby when you feel like it. Imagine the police when I tell them what you've done. You'll lose it all, you'll be banged up in the nick for years. Think of the story in the papers – *Teacher Turns Into Baby Stealer*. You're sick, you know that? Amelia's parents are worried out of their brains and here's you walking around the place without a care in the world. And you're a cheeky cow if you ask me. I've seen the way you look at me as if I'm dirt, but in fact, it's you who is the worthless one, isn't it? You're just a desperate woman doing whatever you want to get your own way and unless you make it worth my while, I won't stand by and let it happen. No fucking way.'

Tina eyeballed Rita. She had to up her game and stand up to her. 'Don't you dare speak to me like that. I'm a decent woman who works hard every day to have the life I do. It's not my fault that you've lost your home, is it? Maybe stop buying all those bleeding scratchcards and sort your life out.'

'Correct, it's not your fault. But you can help me get it back. I want four grand. It's quite a good price considering, but I'm not greedy. I won't keeping coming back to the well. I just want to get my life back on track.'

Tina knew she had her in a corner. But she needed time to think. Chris would go ballistic if he found out there was someone else who knew about what she'd done. Let alone knowing she'd caved in to a blackmailer. He'd make her come clean before the shit hit the fan. This was turning into a nightmare.

'I'll meet you later after work to talk about this. I have things to do now, so please, just get out of my way.'

Rita stepped to one side and opened the door to let Tina go past. 'Remember, four grand and your secret is safe with me. No funny business or I'll be straight to the dibble and tell them everything that I know. I will, go on, test me.'

Tina stormed out without a word.

Rita smiled and rubbed her hands together. Today was going to be a good day after all.

Donny sat at his desk staring blankly at his computer, the way he always seemed to when he had something lying heavy on his mind. He was in no mood for work today. He looked out of the window, his eyes following a black and white magpie that was jumping about in the car park. He saluted it and mumbled something under his breath. He'd always been superstitious, and he blamed his mother for bringing him up that way. Don't walk under a ladder, don't put new shoes on a table, don't smash a mirror otherwise you get seven years bad luck, the list was endless. He spotted Frankie coming across the car park. Was he limping?

Donny got up and walked over to the window to take a closer look. Yes, definitely limping. His black eye from the other day had barely healed and now he looked like he'd been in the ring.

'Frankie, come straight up here and see me,' Donny shouted from the top window

The student kept his head down and carried on walking. Frankie had changed. Maybe it was the weed. He never sat and joked around with his classmates anymore, just kept himself to himself. Donny stayed by the window. He saw Ged's dad sat in his car parked up across the road from the school. He was a shady one for sure, dodgy. Donny checked the clock and then hurried down the stairs to try and catch Frankie before he went into the rec room. He got there just in time.

'Oi, Frankie, wait up. What's up with your leg? I saw you limping. Have you fallen or something?'

Frankie's cap was pulled down low and he made no eye contact whatsoever. 'Like you care. I fell off my bike last night. I'm just a bit bruised that's all.'

'You and me need to have one of our little talks. My office. Lunchtime.'

Donny was about to add something when Tina came rushing up. 'Can I use the office for my next meeting? I was going to use the side office, but it's already booked out.'

Donny replied to Tina as he watched Frankie slink off. He looked edgier than usual. 'Yes, crack on. I've just seen Ged's dad parked up outside, so he'll be here in a minute. Try to have him in and out pronto. I don't trust him in this school. Thieving fucker.'

Tina rolled her eyes and looked round to check none of the students had heard the headteacher. Sometimes he forgot where he was. Donny slung his jacket over his shoulder. 'I'm going to have a quick cig before the police come about Amelia. They'll be here for a while and I will be gasping if I don't get one now. I believe they want to speak to a few of the students again.'

Tina swallowed hard but remained silent, not trusting herself to utter a word.

Kevin sat down and faced Tina. He seemed confident, not afraid to open his mouth. He was unshaven and you could smell stale tobacco smoke on his clothing. He leant forward and clapped his hands over his knees. 'Right, I'll get to the point, shall I? I want my lad out of here and back in main-stream school. This place is fucked up, he's not like these kids in here, he's got a brain, he's clever. I think he went off the rails a bit when I got put in prison but I'm home now and I'll sort him out.'

Tina twisted her pen in her hands. 'Ged is doing fine here. And getting him back in mainstream school is something that doesn't just happen overnight. We'll have to wait until his grades are better and he's more settled. I'm not sure if you're aware, Mr Grey, of the incidents he's been involved in. He's trashed a classroom and assaulted another student. This is not the kind of behaviour that will get him back into his old school.'

Kevin dismissed her last comment and shrugged his shoulders. 'Nah, don't give me any of that bullshit. The kids in this school are messed up in their heads. Ged's not like that, he's got a good head on him and I don't want him mixing with these delinquents anymore. I've heard about some of the stuff that goes on in this school and it's not right. Drugs, girls who'll open their legs for anybody. Nah, I want my boy out of here.'

Tina sat up and looked at Kevin thoughtfully. Was he for real? Talk about the pot calling the kettle black. 'I beg your pardon, Mr Grey, but this school has got a great Ofsted report. We change students' lives here, so whatever you have heard isn't right. We work hard to help every child that comes here. In all schools you have the same problems if you care to do your research.'

Kevin stepped up a level. 'Fuck research. I know what I can see. Ged won't be coming back here. He'll get a job or something if he can't go back to normal school. He needs to make something of himself. I have few mates in the building trade who can hook him up with something. That's all he needs.'

Tina opened her eyes wide. 'I take it you work then?' Kevin looked awkward and Tina smirked. 'Is that the trade you're in?'

'Erm, no. I'm just sorting myself out and then I'll find work. Anyway, it's not about me, it's about my boy.'

'Ged needs to finish his exams. He needs good grades to get a decent job. If he stays here he's got the best chance of sitting those exams and getting the kind of grades that will give him options in the future.'

Kevin slammed his hand on the table causing the pieces of paper to go flying. 'Are you on the same planet as me, love, or what? You're not getting it, are you. I'm not asking you, I'm telling you. Ged is not coming back to this shithole of a school. I'll find him work and sort him out. If he needs to take exams then I'll bring him back for them, but apart from that over my dead body is he stepping foot through this door again. It's simple as.' He was going for gold.

Tina took a few seconds to digest what he had said. 'All I can say is that if you pull him out of education then you can expect to be fined and taken to court. You and your wife have a legal obligation to your son to make sure he goes to school. But, if that's what you want to do then so be it. I have told you what the consequences are and if you want to end up in court then it's up to you. Personally, I think going back to court and mixing with the justice system after you've just come out of jail won't look too good for you, but, if you think you know the law better than me then my hands are tied.'

Kevin laughed and got to his feet. 'Do you really think the justice system bothers me? I've done more time in jail, love, than you've had hot dinners. I'll do what I have to to protect my son. Second Chance, my arse. It's like a young offenders' school this is and not somewhere I want my lad to come.'

Tina had heard enough and couldn't wait to see the back of him. As Kevin made his way to the door she stood up and walked slowly behind him.

'Goodbye then,' Kevin muttered.

Tina didn't waste her breath replying, just stood watching him walk down the corridor towards the exit. 'Fucking tosser,' she muttered to herself. 'And he has the cheek to call this school a waste of a space; he needs to look closer at himself that one does.'

Chapter Thirty

Tina stood waiting, stressed. The rain was pounding the pavements and dark grey clouds hung low from the sky like a dull blanket of despair. Rita should have been here ten minutes ago. Where the hell was she? Tina checked her watch again. She pulled her phone out of her pocket and was just about to make a call when she spotted the large figure trudging towards her. She backed into the shadows of the night and waited anxiously. The park was quiet tonight and there wasn't a soul about. An eerie silence broken only by the sound of footsteps. She stepped out from the darkness. Rita smiled expectantly, standing with one hand on her hip. Her hood was pulled over her head, and a woolly scarf that had seen better days was wound round her neck so that only her eyes were clearly visible.

'Bleeding hell, it's chucking it down. I don't know why we had to meet here, we could have just met near school, instead of me getting piss-wet through. Anyway, just give me the money and I'll be off.'

Tina's eyes seemed different, vacant. She stepped closer to Rita. 'Why are you such a nasty bitch? Amelia is in trouble and all you are thinking about is filling your pockets. How on earth do you sleep at night?'

Rita backed off. 'I don't sleep because I have no home. I lie awake every night wondering where my next meal is coming from. I've not got the cushy desk job, nice house and husband to run back to like you. I've had to work my arse off all my life and still I've got nothing, I've lost it all. Do you know how it feels to have nothing?'

'Like I said, if you spend all your money on scratchcards and God knows what else ... Everyone knows you're a gambler. You need to get some help. Every penny you have you spend on them daft bleeding cards that you'll never win on. You need to get help, not just money for more.'

Rita was taken back. 'Sometimes I win. And who are you to dictate morals to me when you've taken a kid and locked her away. I'd rather be a gambler than a bleeding criminal. You've got a screw loose love, honest, you're a lunatic.'

Tina shoved her hand in her coat pocket and fumbled about.

Rita stood waiting, growing impatient. 'Just give me the money, will you, and I'll be off. Honest, all I want is the cash and nobody will ever know about this. Call it our little secret. You'll have helped me out so to speak so I'll help you by keeping my gob shut.'

Tina took a deep breath to steady her nerves but didn't move.

'Just give me the money, I'm not waiting about. I'm getting soaking wet stood here.'

Tina still said nothing. It was as if she was in a trance.

Rita shook her head and turned to walk away. She had to call her bluff. 'Fuck it then, I'll go to the police. I can't be arsed with mind games. Why would you have me traipsing all the way here when you had no intention of giving me the cash. You're out of order.'

Tina's hand stayed in her pocket and kept a tight hold of the knife she'd stashed in there. Could she use it? She marched after her blackmailer. She dragged at her coat and turned Rita to face her.

'You're evil you know. Rotten to the core you are. You're not getting a penny from me. I can't just pull four grand out of the air just like that. It will take time, you idiot. Who has thousands of quid just lying around in their bank account?'

Rita stood with the rain pelting at her face. 'I need the money. Come on, how long will it take for you to get it sorted? I'm a fair woman. Just give me something to tide me over. But the clock's ticking. I won't wait for ever.'

The fight had left Tina. She pulled her hand from her pocket, empty, and sank to her knees looking up at the sky. She stared at the ground, despairing.

'I can't give you what you want. I'm up to my eyeballs in debt just like you are. I've borrowed just to get the flat set up. Please don't tell anyone. I'll find a way to see you right, but I can't find four grand. Not now and no time soon.'

Rita looked down at Tina and shook her head, spat at her before she started to walk away. She was humming something.

'Hush little baby, don't you cry ...'

It flipped a switch somewhere deep inside Tina. She pulled herself to her feet and stumbled after her. There was no way anyone was stopping her having this baby, not now she'd come this close. She gripped the knife again, not knowing what she was going to do it with it. Hurt Rita? Threaten her?

But before she could decide, Rita turned round. Even in the gloom she could see the blade. She shoved Tina and the knife fell to the ground. Tina scrabbled madly in the grass looking for where it had fell.

'Dozy cow. Did you think I've not had a knife waved at me before? I wouldn't even peel my spuds with that. Now get out of here – and drop the tough bitch act. You're a fucking liability. You're a second-rate teacher at a crap school, helping kids because you can't have your own – and you never will.' She almost screamed the last words.

Tina couldn't find the knife but as Rita's words hit home, she grabbed at a branch that was lying by the side of the path. Without thinking she lifted it above Rita's head and smashed it into her skull. The attack from behind was so fast that Rita didn't have a clue what had hit her. She dropped to the floor like a lead weight. Tina stood over her, pummelling the wood into her victim over and over until she stopped moving.

It was only then that she seemed to come to her senses. She stepped back, shaking. What had she done? And even more pressingly, what was she going to do now? She had to move her. But how? She grabbed Rita's ankles – she knew it would take all her strength, but desperation powered her on. Looking all around in case anyone else was out, she kept dragging her until she was out of sight and into the bushes. It was a struggle, the dead weight taking every ounce of her strength to move.

'Look what you made me do, you stupid woman. You should have kept your nose out of my business and none of this would have happened. Look, look what you have made me do.' Tina finally collapsed down next to Rita's limp body and rocked backwards and forwards, lost in her own world. 'Mummy's going to sing you a lullaby,' she sang under her breath.

———

By the time Tina got to the flat she was exhausted and soaking wet, strands of hair plastered to the sides of her cheeks. Her eyes were red and vacant. Amelia didn't know what to say when she opened the door to her. 'Are you alright, Tina. You're scaring me. Look at you, you're shaking. What's wrong?'

Tina stood in the doorway, not rushing in like usual. 'It's all gone pear-shaped. I just wanted a baby. I didn't want all this. Look at me now. I don't recognise myself anymore. I'm lost. What can I do now I've gone too far?'

Amelia grabbed Tina's hand, her eyes wide open as she noticed the smears of blood. 'What's happened? You're covered in blood. Look, it's on your legs too. Tell me what's happened. I'm scared.'

Tina tried to wipe her legs. Then she smiled absently, stroking Amelia's tummy with her cold, damp hand. 'It's fine, don't you worry, everything is fine. I just knocked a dog down on the road. It was dead when I got to it. I'm in shock, I think. I need to wash my hands.'

Tina scurried from the hall, still double-locking the door behind her on autopilot, and into the kitchen where she wet the white dishcloth and scrubbed at her body until her skin was raw. Her phone started ringing. She took a deep breath and answered the call.

'Hiya, Chris, yeah I'm good. Are you coming over here? I'm thinking we could stay here tonight. Amelia needs a bit of company, she's down in the dumps.' Tina listened to her husband for a few seconds and her expression changed as her voice got louder, impatient.

'Oh, just do whatever it is you're doing. I'll stay here. I thought you loved me. I thought family came first. It doesn't seem like it anymore. Just fuck off, Chris.'

She stood in silence, her hands still in the cold water, now pink with the blood. She didn't know how long she'd been standing here until a text alert brought her back to her senses. Tina tried to make sense of what she was reading.

> I'm still here bitch. Rot in jail, you had your chance.

She felt a tightness in her chest, her vision closing in, she could feel a full-blown panic attack starting. The phone fell from her hands and landed on the floor as she started mumbling over and over. 'No, no, no, no, no.'

There was knock at the front door. Amelia had no idea what to do. No one but Tina had been round here since the time she'd seen the shadowed figure.

'Let them take me!' Tina yelled through to Amelia. 'I don't care anymore. I can't take it, I just can't take it,' she sobbed.

A voice came through the letterbox. 'Tina, it's me, Chris, open up.' Amelia rummaged in Tina's bag for the keys and ran to the door. She unlocked it with shaking hands, panicking.

'Is she here?'

'Yeah, she's in there but she's just been sat there for the last half hour talking to herself and I swear she's hyperventilating. She's not moved, Chris, I think she needs to go to the doctor's. I had an uncle who done something like this and he got put in the bloody nut house.'

'Just lock the door, will you, and shut up.' He waited for her to go back into the living room and followed closely behind.

Chris took one glance at Tina; he could see straight away that something wasn't right. He rushed to her side and held her hands.

'Babes, I'm here now. Are you alright? What's happened, why are you like this?'

Tears started to stream down Tina's cheeks like someone had left the tap on. She turned to face him. 'Chris, you're my world and I love you with all my heart. I'm just mixed up in all this and I can't get back out.' She cradled her head in her hands, rocking, humming – a nursery rhyme that was barely a whisper. 'It's got to stop; I can't do this anymore. It has to stop. I want it all to go away.'

Amelia stood over them. 'What's happening? She's scaring me.'

Tina reached over and touched the side of her leg. 'Go, love, go home. I'm not keeping you here anymore. Go home to your family.'

Amelia backed towards the door, unsure whether it was a trap. She spoke in a small voice. 'What, you don't want the baby no more? I can go? If you let me go I promise I won't say a word. I'll just say I scarpered to get my head around being knocked up. Tell my dad I was that scared I did a bunk. If I'm lucky they'll be so glad I'm home that they won't kick me straight out again on my arse. But is that it? The baby's mine now?'

Tina screamed at the top of her voice to make her point. The walls shook. 'Go home, get gone. Go and see your parents. Please leave me alone.'

The teenager looked behind her at the keys hanging in the lock. She hesitated for a few seconds, then darted to the door. Her hands were shaking as she turned the key. She was free, she could go home and see her family. She ran and ran, never once looking back.

Chris came to his senses first; he looked at the open door and panicked. He was involved in this too now and the police would be coming looking as soon as Amelia got home. He couldn't believe she'd keep her word and keep her lip buttoned. He rushed out to look for her, looking first one way then the other, then sprinting down the street.

Chris looked shattered as he walked back to the flat. The girl was quick, there was no sight nor sound of her. It was with a heavy heart that he walked back in through the front door.

'Tina!' he called. There was no reply. He shouted her name again, louder this time as he put his head round the living room door – it was empty. 'Tina, where are you, love? Amelia has gone, we better get our story straight before the boys in blue come knocking. Fucking hell, the shit's really going to hit the fan as soon as she breathes a word about where she's been.'

He checked the bedrooms, the bathroom. Nothing. Only the kitchen left. He tried the door. It was wedged shut. Using his shoulder, Chris battered the door and forced his way inside. He'd only been gone twenty minutes. What the hell had she done? He stood over his wife, panicking. Small white tablets were scattered about the floor, an empty pill bottle held in her hand.

'Tina, Tina, love, it's me, Chris. Wake up, what have you done?' As he shook her an empty bottle of tablets rolled onto the floor. Beside it lay a bottle of brandy. Nothing left. 'Tina, wake up. God, God. Come on, love, wake up. Please, open your eyes, don't leave me, don't you dare leave me.' His hands were trembling as he fumbled in his pocket and pulled out his phone, they were properly shaking as he dialled the emergency services. 'Hello, hello? Send an ambulance quick, it's my wife, she's taken tablets, please hurry up, she's not moving, please, please hurry up.' He sobbed his heart out as he gave the details to the voice on the other end of the phone.

He stayed on the floor, cradling his wife's inert body, kissing the top of her head. 'Everything's going to be alright, baby, just hang on in there, please. Tina, stay with me, stay with me.' Tina didn't move. Chris lay there on the lino floor and sobbed.

Chapter Thirty-One

Kevin sat across the room from Clare studying every inch of her. He was turned on, he wanted her back, she was the love of his life. She just needed to remember that. All the bad shit between them was gone for him and his heart melted as he looked at her. She was his woman and he was going to try every trick in the book to win her heart back. He looked cleaner than he'd done in a long time. New trainers, new tracksuit, a fresh trim. He smelt half decent too. Ged watched his dad from the corner of his eye, it was clear what he was up to. He turned back to the TV. Best to pretend that he hadn't clocked him. His old man had a game plan and it amused him to see him in action.

'I'm thinking you can have a break from cooking tonight, Clare, and I'll take us all out for a curry if you fancy it?'

Clare looked at her ex and shook her head. She let out a laboured sigh – how many times did she have to knock the guy back?

'Why would I even want to be seen in public with you? I've told you enough times, we're done. I'm no longer that girl who sits about and waits for you. I'm immune to your charm and bullshit now.'

'Come on, love, it's a curry, not a fucking honeymoon in Mexico.'

'Save your breath.'

Ged covered his mouth with his sleeve and tried not to laugh. His mum could give as good as she got.

Clare sat leafing through her magazine and trying to ignore Kevin, but he wasn't giving up that easily. They didn't call him Mr Smooth for nothing. It was Clare's night off, her one night off, and all she wanted was a bit of peace and quiet. Feet up, chick flick, a few glasses of wine.

'What if I get us a takeaway, then? We can bang a film on and have a family night just like we used to. We can cuddle up on the sofa if you're feeling adventurous, just saying.'

That was enough for Clare. 'Family nights usually consisted of me sat here waiting for you for hours on end, while you were out with your mates or up to some dodgy deal. Are you forgetting that, Kevin?'

'Fuck's sake, Clare, can you not let sleeping dogs lie? That was years ago and, like I said, I've changed. Look at me, how can you resist this beautiful face?' He delved into his pocket and pulled out a wad of cash.

'Here, take this and get us all a proper feed. There's enough for a takeaway with plenty left for you to treat your-self. But straighten your face. I just want a curry with my family – is that too much to ask for?'

Her eyes were open wide now. It was a good count, at least a couple of hundred quid. What she could do with that. She shook her head – what was she even thinking?

'Oh, I knew it wouldn't be long before you started grafting again. Ged, ask him where he's got his money from and see what he tells you because he never tells me the truth.'

Ged looked over at Kevin. 'Did you get that job then, Dad?'

Kevin stuck his chest out like a champion pigeon. 'I did, son. Only a few days a week, but it's a start isn't it?'

Clare was taken aback. Shocked. She looked from Kevin to Ged and back to Kevin again. 'What, you're working now?'

'I told you, Clare, this is the new me. Jail has broken my back this time and there is no way in this world that I'm going back there again. I'm on the straight and narrow now.'

'Well, fuck a duck. I never thought I'd see the day. If you're buying then I will have a curry. I'll have a bottle of wine too if you're flush.'

Kevin rubbed his hands together and kicked off his trainers. He was back in the good books. 'You can have two bottles if you want. You know that second one always makes you horny.'

Ged covered his ears. 'Wow, Dad, get a room or something. I don't want to know stuff like that. Too much information.'

Clare cracked a smile. 'Better just get me the one then. The last thing I want is to land in bed with you. Been there and done that and got the bloody T-shirt.'

'I'll get two just in case you change your mind,' he winked at her.

Ged tutted and squirmed.

Kevin stood up and grabbed his phone from the table. 'I'll ring for it and go and pick it up. I need to get some fags and that from the shop too. Clare, do you need any?'

Bloody hell, this was a turn up for the books. The man never usually had a pot to piss in.

'Twenty Lambert silver, please.'

Ged wasn't missing out on a treat if his dad was buying. 'Will you get me some chocolate, surprise me with something. Nothing with raisins in though.'

'Right. OK, write me a list of the stuff you need from the shop. Maybe a bit of bacon for a butty in the morning?'

He was trying it on again but Clare couldn't help but smile. The wall she'd built around her heart seemed to be caving in. Old habits die hard and all that. She'd given Sam the push; didn't need the aggro from Ged after everything that had happened. Better to be on her own for a bit. It wasn't like it had been serious anyway, if she was being honest. A booty call. No strings. A curry with Kev for old time's sake wouldn't do any harm – would it?

Kevin rushed across Eastford Square, his head held high. This was his patch now and he'd fuck anyone up who dared to step on his turf. He spotted Frankie across the way and jerked his head at him. 'Oi, word,' he beckoned with his finger to a quiet corner. Frankie's head was bowed. He was bricking it. Kevin grabbed him by the ear and pulled his face up, squeezing his cheeks.

'The bruises are clearing up. It was what you deserved,

though. Nobody has my boy over. You're lucky I didn't finish you off, you little ferret.'

Frankie edged back. The guy was a nutter. He wasn't a full deck. He'd already leathered him, and he wasn't taking any chances on rubbing him up the wrong way again.

'So, is it sorted then?' Kevin had a hungry look in his eyes. 'We'll be sitting pretty soon enough. Fucking result that, thanks to you, we get the police to do our dirty work. Once you've delivered Mr Big to them, they won't give a shit about who's running this patch. I'll get one of my mates to set up a supply line and we'll be laughing. All you have to do is play your part. You sure he suspects nothing? Are you still on for the drop?'

'Yes, I'm going there soon.'

'Make sure you do. Once this prick is out of the picture, we can box it off together. Like I said, Frankie, this stays between me and you. Hand over the cash and make sure them muppets of yours are doing what they should be instead of fucking standing about talking. There's a new sheriff in town and I won't have any pricks taking the piss. I'm the man now.'

Kevin went to slap Frankie on the shoulder and the kid flinched.

Kevin laughed. 'Jumpy, ain't you?'

'You said we could start again with a blank sheet.' All of Frankie's tough guy act had faded when faced with a man who'd been there, seen it and done it.

'And, we can. Just go and meet the man and let's get him out of the picture for good. This is my patch now, do you hear me, mine?'

Frankie nodded his head, wanted to keep him onside. 'Yeah, I've told the lads that they need to be on the ball too. Any fuck-ups and they pay, they know the script.'

Kevin kept his voice low. 'If my boy finds out about any of this, I'll put you in a body bag. This is a cushy little number here and if you use your head you can earn a right few quid too. Under new management, tell them.'

Frankie flinched as Kevin clapped his hand on his shoulder. 'Give us the cash then. I'll collect the rest of it tomorrow, just keep it safe and don't let any of it go walkabouts. If the count's low, you're responsible for it, no excuses.'

Kevin enjoyed the look of fear in Frankie's eyes. A leopard never changes its spots and Kevin knew where there was fear, there was opportunity for a man like him.

Chapter Thirty-Two

Frankie was stressed, didn't know if he was coming or going. His black jacket was zipped up tightly and his Nike cap pulled down low over his eyes. He checked his phone. It was nearly showtime. He was in this deep now – no way out. He had to see it through. He was a double-agent. A triple-agent if he counted Kevin Grey, too. He lifted his head as he spotted a silver car pull up in the layby. The headlights dipped then switched off; a sign that the guy was nearly ready for him. There wasn't much traffic about and it was quiet, eerie. Frankie lit up and sat on the wall facing the bus stop waiting for his phone to ring. He watched the cars driving by in the distance and wished this nightmare was over. Maybe after all this had been sorted, he would get on his toes and go somewhere new, a place where nobody knew him. The world would be his oyster. The money he'd already earned would set him up for a few months. He could stay in a hotel, maybe even rent a caravan. In this game you could never predict what was around the corner and you always had to be prepared for the worst. Frankie had always been wise with his money so far, stashed it away for a rainy day. And now he had to admit, it was proper pissing down. It was time to move on; nobody would miss him anyway. His mobile started to ring and his heart sank. He tried to stay calm, deep breaths, long, deep breaths.

Frankie jumped down from the wall and flicked his cigarette butt to the roadside. He approached the car with caution before opening the passenger door and climbing inside and trying to brazen it out.

'You're late. You should have been here at ten o'clock. I thought you wasn't coming. Five minutes late you are, don't make me wait again.'

The man kept his head down. His black beanie hat was pulled down low.

'Have you got the money?'

'Yeah, count it if you want. It's all there, every penny.' Frankie handed it over like it was burning him.

The man took the bundle of notes and rammed it into the glove box. He pulled out a packet of white powder and threw it over to Frankie.

'Get that lot bagged up as soon as and get it over to Blackpool.' Frankie held the drugs in his hands. They were shaking. He tried to steady them. The guy was talking to him but nothing he was saying was going in. It was like someone had turned the volume down in his ears. A mobile started ringing and he answered it, started talking. What was Frankie meant to do now? A few minutes passed. Frankie tapped him on the arm to get his attention. There was no way he was sitting about waiting for him to finish the call.

'I'm gone. I'll go and sort this and get it shipped out.'

The man nodded his head, turned away and carried on with his conversation. Frankie hoped that was the last conversation he'd have to have with him.

Frankie slipped out of the car quickly and motored towards the fields nearby. He was sweating and his hands were clammy. His work here was done, and he wasn't hanging around to get his collar felt too.

It all happened so fast. The car was swarmed within seconds. Sirens, blue lights flashing, shouting, screaming. The driver's door was flung open and the man was dragged out and pinned to the floor face down while two officers searched the car. He was going ballistic, shouting and screaming, but no one was listening. Watching over it all, the plain clothes officer stood tall with a wide smirk on his face, looking down at his captive.

He kicked him sharply in the side. 'Well, well, well. It doesn't look like you're having a good night, does it, Donny Knight?'

Chapter Thirty-Three

Donny lifted his head as best he could, but still couldn't see who was talking to him. But he recognised the voice.

The copper dragged him up and held him over the bonnet with his face down while his colleagues slammed the silver cuffs around his wrists.

'I've been watching you for months. Playing the good guy, Donny Knight, headteacher, saint and saver of lost souls. While all the time you're lining your pocket. And it doesn't stop there, does it? Bit of a reputation as a ladies' man, I gather. Despite that lovely wife of yours thinking the sun shines out of your backside. I've told you to steer clear of my ex-girlfriend already. You like Melanie, don't you, you bent fucker?'

Donny couldn't take in what the fuck was happening here. But he realised where he knew the voice from. It was the guy from the night when his car windows got done. He'd forgotten Melanie had said her ex was a copper, and a mental one at that.

After everything that had happened, was this what was going to bring him down, he thought, a drink with a woman he didn't even do anything with? He'd been so bloody careful to always keep out of the attention of the law. Hiding in plain sight, he called it. But now, one woman with a jealous copper for an ex and he was on the brink of losing everything.

'I never fucking touched her, go on, ring her and ask her. You've got the wrong guy.'

His captor laughed, slammed his face down into the metal of the car. 'You still haven't worked it out, have you? Go on, turn round and look at me properly and see if you can work it out then.' The officer's eyes were dancing. He couldn't wait for Donny to put two and two together.

Donny's heart was racing, He had to do anything he could to try and talk his way out of this. He stopped struggling and tried to stay calm.

He turned slowly and looked at the copper blankly. 'So what, we met the night some toerag glassed my car. You can stop fucking about playing games and tell me who you are.'

The officer moved his face close to Donny's so that he could feel his breath, hot against his cold skin.

'Little Trevor Beats has done OK for himself, hasn't he, Donny?'

Donny's heart thudded. Trevor Beats. The bully from his schooldays who'd made his life a misery.

'You? You always were a fucking nutter, mate. Sack that, get my solicitor on the blower, this is a stitch up. You lot have set me up, fucking pigs.'

Beats read him his rights and pushed Donny back against the car, making sure he could hear him as he pulled his head back by his hair and looked directly into his eyes. 'I've been watching you for a long time. I know about the Blackpool team, about the kids you have dealing for you. I know everything. You are going to jail for a long, long, stretch Donny Knight. So it looks like I have the last laugh after all doesn't it?'

Donny was struggling now, yelling at the top of his voice. Another officer came over and showed Beats the pile of notes and the package of drugs that he'd found in the car. Beats nodded. As the officer went back to the search, Beats checked that no one could hear him before addressing Donny again.

'You're going to lose everything – just like I did, you wanker. You left me with no friends, no honour, nothing. You took it all from me and I promised that one day you would know exactly how that feels. It's been a long time coming but revenge is sweet, Donny Knight, and it tastes good.' He licked his lips.

Donny was flailing as he tried to kick out. 'You were a bully, a dirty prick who picked on vulnerable kids. You got what was coming to you. You made my life a misery for years, but it wasn't just mine, was it? Lots of kids. But I was the one who stood up to you – where is the crime in that, you twisted fuck?'

Trevor laughed. 'Vulnerable kids? You mean like the ones you have travelling up and down the country selling drugs? And you a headteacher – the media are going to love this. You're going to pay, sunshine.'

Donny was still trying to fight back, but he didn't stand a chance. He was surrounded now. Eventually he slid back down against the patrol car and sat slumped on the ground.

He heard the clip clip of high heels on the pavement. Beats gestured to the other officers to leave him for a minute.

Susan. His heart leapt when he saw her. But why was she here? A cold trickle of fear ran down his spine.

She smiled and bent her head down so Donny would get a proper look at her before she whispered into his ear. 'Hi, babes, doesn't look like you're having a good night, does it? Did you think you could get one over on me, you and your fancy piece? Trevor has told me all about Melanie so don't waste your breath. You're a dirty no-good bastard and I wouldn't piss on you if you were on fire. You don't even know how to tell the truth. You told me your money came from gambling, you lying, cheating cunt. And all this time you've been giving me fucking dirty money to put through the salon. Drugs and kids, Donny – it's the lowest of the low. I knew you did things your own way – but I always thought your heart was in the right place. We get results, that's what you always said about Second Chance. But you didn't care, did you? Not about me and certainly not about those kids.'

She turned to face Beats. 'I want the money he had and the keys to the car, as we agreed.' She smiled. 'We work well together, Trevor. And looks like I'm single again now.' She held out her hand as Trevor dropped the car keys into it.

Trevor chuckled. 'You're right. Looks like you are.' He shook his head slowly. 'What a day, I've caught Donny Knight red-handed and watched him get his heart stamped on. That's what you call a great day at the office.'

Donny was screaming now. 'Susan, how can you do this to me, to us? Please, Suze, don't believe a word he's said. He's a fucking psycho. He always was. I'm not lying this time, please help me. The money was for us. To give you the life you deserve. And the kids? I gave them a chance to earn more money in a month than most of them would in a year in dead-end jobs. I didn't plan it all – but once I saw what life was really like for these kids, I realised if I didn't do it, they'd soon end up working for much more dangerous men than me. I paid them, I gave them structure, responsibility – and told them never to sample the goods. It sounds bad, I know, but you loved the life it gave us …'

His wife looked at him. She leant in and looked deep into his eyes, smiling.

'Rot in jail,' she hissed as she spat in his face and walked away.

Beats whistled for the other coppers to come back over and within seconds Donny was launched into the back of the police van as he nodded at his colleagues. 'Cheers, lads, I owe you big time. If you ever need help, I'll have your back. The money's gone to his missus so keep that off the record but the drugs will be used as evidence. Enough evidence to lock that cunt up for a very long time. Great job, lads, great result.'

The team had done well tonight. With the video footage Beats already had of Donny collecting drugs and talking to other dealers, he was fucked.

Banging, kicking, screaming from inside the police van. 'You fucking wankers, you pricks, get me the fuck out of here. Get my solicitor. This is a stitch up. You've set me up. Get me out of here! Trevor, you twisted bastard, you'll pay for this, trust me, as long as I've got a breath left in my body, you'll pay for this so watch your back.'

Chapter Thirty-Four

Donny Knight sat in the dock at Manchester Crown court cracking his knuckles. He was thin, unshaven, dark circles under his eyes. He glanced over to the public gallery where he could see the reporters – eager, pens poised, waiting for the gory details. He could imagine the headlines, 'Headteacher turned drugs mastermind, his students running county lines …'

Donny's solicitor had told him straight that he was going to get a custodial sentence today, no matter what. And not a short one either. If he was lucky, he would get a seven stretch. *If* he was lucky. They were likely to throw the book at him, make an example of him, a statement to the public that no matter who you are, you cannot dodge the law.

Donny dropped his head into his hands as he watched the prosecution team talking. They kept looking over at him and shaking their heads, judging him, looks of disgust.

When he'd seen all the evidence they held against him, he knew there was nothing he could do to deny it – he threw his hand in and pleaded guilty at the earliest opportunity. He claimed he had lost a load gambling, had to sell drugs to clear his debts. The coppers had laughed back in his face. Did he think they were born yesterday? He knew exactly what he was doing and now he was going to pay the price. He'd lived like a king for years, never wanted for anything, had the best of everything. But now he was going to face the music.

The news that their headteacher was a drug dealer devastated his pupils. If they couldn't trust someone like him, who could they trust? He'd abused his role and let every one of the kids down. He'd picked off the ones who might be useful to him and groomed them as drug runners – in that way he was no different from the criminals they had been warned about on the streets. They'd seen Donny as a responsible adult – often the only one in their lives – who banged on every day about the choices they made and how they would affect them in the future, yet here he was licking shot. What a hypocrite. The shockwaves reverberated around the school.

Tina Davies, former deputy head, had been found dead. 'Accidental overdose' was the official line but darker rumours circulated the school. In fact the only person who'd seemed to have had any luck recently was the old cook, Rita. She wrote a postcard to tell them how she'd come into some money, and buggered off to a villa in Turkey. Said she needed the sunshine to recover from surgery for something.

After Donny's arrest half the kids in the school had requested counselling. It was the last straw, too much for some of them to take in. They had a deputy head who'd died and a drug baron for a headteacher. Small wonder they needed someone to talk to.

Some pupils never made it back in. Amelia was occasionally spotted outside the school gates, but she'd never crossed the threshold since she'd reappeared. Pretty soon she'd be pushing a buggy by the looks of things.

Frankie had been nowhere to be seen since Donny had been banged up. Word on the street was that he'd been seen getting on a train to Blackpool.

Nancy Parker had given a statement to the police too. She was on the ball that one, worked out that Donny was a wrong 'un when she clocked his car in Blackpool when she was off on one of her jaunts. Noted down his registration and everything and checked it when she was back. She told everyone about it too; she was the detective here, not the police. Female intuition she called it, but in another life she'd have made a pretty good copper, she said to her boyfriend, Ged.

But we don't get another life, is what Ged had told her. This life was all they had, and you had to play the cards you'd been dealt. That was why he'd not gone back to Second Chance. Nancy didn't ask where his cash came from, and now his dad was back on the scene Ged was happier – if sometimes a bit elusive. Kids like them, Nancy knew, had to make their own luck even if that meant breaking a few rules.

Justice Wilson walked into the courtroom and everyone stood up. He looked a right sour-faced fucker – Donny gulped. As the judge sat down, he peered over his gold-rimmed glasses at the courtroom, poured himself a glass of water and opened the file in front of him. It seemed to be happening in slow-motion, prolonging Donny's agony. The noise in the courtroom subsided; you could have heard a pin drop. The reporters sat on the edge of their seats, keen to get the story ready for the evening news. Donny was asked to stand up and confirm his details. He swallowed hard, you could hardly hear him speak. Two heavy-set security guards stood close to the dock. If Donny was going to kick off, they'd be on him in seconds. They'd already manhandled him into the courtroom. He'd called them every name under the sun.

Donny sat back down and leant forward in his seat. He knew his life would never be the same again. He'd spend his life banged up, always having to look over his shoulder. The days that lay ahead were dark and depressing. He'd be an old geezer by the time he got out. If he got out.

The judge opened with a summary of the case. It seemed to Donny that he was relishing it, going on about how this man had been alleged to have preyed on young teenage boys to run his empire. The prosecuting barrister laid it on even thicker, talked about the evils of drugs, how they wrecked homes and stole children from parents. And there in the front row sat Susan, savouring the scene of her husband in the dock. Donny looked at her and clenched his teeth together. This was what betrayal tasted like. Some might say it was a taste of his own medicine but for Donny, it was just confirmation of what he'd always known inside: you're on your own in this life. If you don't look out for yourself, as sure as shit, no one else will.

Susan was flanked by her brothers and they all glared down at Donny. He'd got off lightly in their eyes, he was a very lucky man.

Donny's defence barrister tried to be positive as he summed up, but there was no way he could sugar-coat what his client had done. He told the court about the good things Donny had done with his life, the difference he'd made to so many children with their education, but the truth was there for everyone to see. Donny was a drug dealer and any good work he'd done in the community meant nothing anymore because of what he was being sentenced for today.

When he'd finished his summary, the barrister sat down and reached for a cold glass of water.

The judge was ready for sentencing now and asked Donny to stand up. Not so easy; Donny's legs buckled and for a few seconds he could barely feel them. His mouth was dry and his heart was pounding. He closed his eyes for a few seconds, and whispered under his breath. Maybe he was asking the Lord above for forgiveness and to be spared from a long time behind bars. But not even God almighty could help Donny now.

The judge cleared his throat and looked over his glasses. His body language made it clear that justice would be served here today. The public interest in the case had – inevitably – been huge and the media were hungry for more. He wanted to make a point. He had zero tolerance for crimes of this nature and anyone who ever came before him should know that. He was stern as he addressed the accused. 'Donny

Knight, you abused your position as a headteacher at the school where you worked. You have preyed on young vulnerable children to build your empire and put their lives at risk for your own gain. You are a weak man whose greed for designer labels and expensive cars has destroyed any sense of right and wrong. My sentence is a message to others so that they understand that crime does not pay, no matter who you are. You have hidden behind a cloak for long enough and I owe it to the public and the parents of the children entrusted into your care to put you behind bars ...' He took a long, deep breath. 'Donny Knight, I sentence you to ten years imprisonment.' There was a buzz of voices in the public gallery as reporters scribbled down their notes. 'Take him down.'

Donny was in shock. Ten years! Ten fucking long years! The colour drained from his skin and he started to shake. He pressed his hand against the glass inside the dock – as he was pulled away his fingerprints remained for a moment, before slowly fading.

As he was led from the room he delivered a chilling message at the top of his voice. 'You'll pay, you bastards, every one of you will pay. Susan, watch your back because one day I'll be there right behind you.'

Susan raised her eyes. He didn't scare her anymore. She picked up her handbag and left the courtroom with her two brothers close to her side.

John kept his voice low. 'Once we find out which jail he lands in we'll make sure he gets a visit or two. We know enough people to make sure he gets eyes on him always, even behind bars.'

Dave chuckled and nodded. 'He'll never have a full night's sleep again.'

As the three of them made their way out of the building, Susan spotted Detective Constable Beats. She quickly made her way over to him. 'I reckon we can celebrate tonight,' she whispered. 'Crack open a bottle and then who knows?' She raised her eyebrows. 'We're the dream team now, Trevor, me and you.'

He smiled back. 'We sure are, baby, me and you.'

The journey from the cells to his new home felt like forever. Donny arrived at the prison now ready to come out of the sweat box. The van had eight compartments inside it, each with its own door. He could hear someone kicking, screaming at the top of their voice. He swallowed hard and sighed as he heard voices in the compartment next to him.

'Get me out of here, you dirty pigs, before I boom the fucking door off its hinges.'

It would be him next. The hairs on the back of his neck stood on end and he was filled with a dull sense of dread. The sound of keys jangling. The door opened slowly, and he could see the face of the screw for the first time.

'Welcome to Strangeways, the place that makes dreams come true,' the guard joked.

A voice behind him made him turn round.

'Right, Charlie, let's get this lot booked in. I'm not in the mood for any drama today so best to let them know that. Any fucking about and I'll personally drag them down the block myself.'

'Message understood.'

The screw faced Donny. 'You hear that? The boss is in a right mood today and he won't stand for any messing about. You've been warned.'

As Donny was escorted from the van he squinted in the bright yellow sunlight. As he was lined up with five other new inmates, Donny twisted his head slightly to look at them. The prisoner who'd been making all the noise was being led out now – a mental case for sure. He had long black hair that looked like you could fry an egg on it, his skin looked dirty and grey and his eyes were hollow. The man next to Donny muttered to him. 'They better not put that fucking junkie near me. He looks like he's riddled with God knows what, the dirty bastard.'

Donny agreed. 'He better not come near me either, fucking hell, I can smell him from here.'

The man introduced himself. 'John Stanley, mate,' he nodded his head.

Donny could barely get his name out in reply. 'Donny Knight.'

John stared at Donny, weighing him up. He moved in closer. 'What you in for, pal?'

'Dealing,' he said. The man shrugged, water off a duck's back. Maybe Donny would fit in here after all. A little glimmer of an idea was lit inside Donny. Prison was a system, a rat race like any other. He'd played the game to become a headteacher. Now the game had changed but if he was smart, he could still make it work to his advantage.

Slowly, the men were marched into the prison. The junkie was still kicking off, and the screw dragged him away from the other newbies.

John sighed. 'This jail is fucking full of spice-heads. I hope I get shipped out as soon as possible. I can't be arsed with jawing these fuckers all the time. I swear, the last time I was in here I caught one in my pad going through my stuff. No fucking shame. They'd have your eyes out and come back for the sockets the thieving pricks.'

Donny looked at him. 'So, you've been in here before then?'

'Yes, pal. It's like home from home, this place to me. I'm in and out all the time. You'd think I'd learn, wouldn't you?'

'How long you in for this time then?' Donny asked.

'Not a big one this time. I just got three years shoved up my arse. I swam the channel really; I was looking at a five stretch. It's a shit and shave sentence.'

After they'd sorted out the various formalities, it was time to go to the wing. Donny shuddered as he walked through the prison. Men were shouting and screaming, banging things.

The screw stopped and unlocked a door with a long brass key. As it opened, Donny could see his cell for the first time. He couldn't handle it, it was a small confined space, he was scared of being closed in. He put his hand against the cold wall and looked at the screw, panicking. 'I can't go in there. I need something bigger. I'm claustrophobic.'

The guard looked at his colleague and sniggered. 'Oi, Ryan. Mr Fucking Golden Balls here wants a bigger apartment with an en suite. Can he be booked into the VIP lounge?'

Ryan doubled over laughing, his shoulders were shaking. He loved the banter in this place. 'I can check the waiting list if you want?'

The screw used the flat of his hand to push Donny through the door. 'Do yourself a favour, mate, and get your head down. This is a jail, not the bleeding Hilton. Nobody likes being locked up. I've never met a prisoner who did, so, join the bloody club, mate.'

Donny watched the door slam shut. He pummelled the back of the door. 'Let me out, please, I can't do this. Can you hear me, let me out?'

But his words fell on deaf ears, one more angry guy in a jail full of them. You live by the sword, you die by it.

Donny sank to the floor. Shit just got real. Welcome to the pen, Donny Knight.

Epilogue

The new headteacher at Second Chance was strict, authoritarian. It was his way or the highway. The students piled off the minibus and started to make their way into school. There was no laughter today, no shouting and screaming, no banter. Dan was the last student off the bus. As he walked slowly across the car park, a voice called to him from outside the gates. He was confused, did the man want him? He pointed at himself. 'Me?'

'Yes, you. Can I talk to you for a minute?'

'What's up?' Dan was puzzled. He hadn't been at Second Chance long enough to know many people, but this guy was familiar.

Tony the postman looked uncomfortable and didn't say anything immediately. What Donny had done had shocked him to the core, pained him. He'd lost his brother to drugs a few years back and he hated everything to do with the scene. So maybe this was his payback.

Dan was getting impatient and started to walk back towards the school. Tony called him back.

'Hold on, I need to get something off my chest.' He dug inside his coat pocket and pulled out a white envelope. 'Don't ask me how I got this, but I think you should know the truth.'

Danny held the letter in his hand as Tony walked away. Slowly, he opened the envelope. His eyes scanned the headed paper and his jaw dropped. This was a game-changer.

He punched his fist into the air and grinned.

'So, Daddy. I think you need me now, don't you?'